FRONTIER HIGHLANDER
VOW OF LOVE

BOOK FOUR

AMERICAN WILDERNESS SERIES ROMANCE

DOROTHY WILEY

Frontier Highlander Vow of Love

Dorothy Wiley

ISBN: 1511522224

ISBN-13: 978-1511522229

Cover design by Erin Dameron-Hill

Frontier Highlander Vow of Love is a fictional novel inspired by history, rather than a precise account of history. Except for historically prominent personages, the characters are fictional and names, places, and incidents either are the product of the author's imagination or are used fictitiously. Any resemblance to actual persons, living or dead, businesses, companies, events, or locales is entirely coincidental. Each book in the series can be read independently.

For the sake of understanding, the author used language for her characters for the modern reader rather than strictly reflecting the far more formal speech and writing patterns of the 18th century.

Other Titles by Dorothy Wiley

WILDERNESS TRAIL OF LOVE

NEW FRONTIER OF LOVE

WHISPERING HILLS OF LOVE

Dedication

To my dear mother-in-law

Roberta Virginia Moore

Happy Mother's Day 2015

"...down where the Naver runs clear;
And the land a brave race had for centuries owned
Is now trod by the sheep and the deer.
The halls, where our ancestors first saw the light,
Now blackened in ruins they lie.
And the moss-covered cairns are all that remain
Of the once pleasant homes of MacKay."
—by Elizabeth MacKay
Bridge of Allan 1889

Prologue

Strathnaver, Scotland, Summer 1792, 'The Year of the Sheep'

The Strathnaver Valley is a rich green fold in Scotland's earth, a narrow twisting glen through which the dark blue waters of the River Naver run south to north, from the loch of its name to the Atlantic. Nearby, along the most northerly rugged coast of Scotland, waves pound spectacular high cliffs, ancient sea caves, and sandy beaches with the enthusiasm of a passionate lover.

Artis MacKay's clan, by name or allegiance, lived there, on the estate of the Countess of Sutherland. Artis' simple but well-loved home stood with two dozen others, near the southeastern shore of Loch Naver, in a crofters' village named Achadh an Eas. Nearby a noisy cascade flows from hills where Norsemen once buried their dead after ferocious battles with the Picts.

When Artis stood near the loch and gazed behind her the mountain took the shape of a sleeping woman, her head turned away from Strathnaver. Artis wondered if the sleeping woman was dreaming about her future, as she often did. Since she turned fifteen, she seemed to spend even more time daydreaming. Sometimes she would ponder her future for hours—wondering about the man she would love someday. The man she would marry. Where was he? What did he look like? He would have to be handsome, that much was certain. Would he be kind like her father had been? Would they share their dreams and aspirations? And, would their home be here? She certainly hoped so. She loved her birthplace.

The people of Achadh, including Artis, considered their home a grand paradise. The landscape, an extraordinary blend of texture and color, both intense and subtle, provided a source of solace and inspiration. Their thatched roof dwellings and abundant peat to burn kept them warm and cozy. The pastures surrounding them stretched for miles—as far as any of them could see or care to walk—where flocks of sheep and goats, and herds of cattle and horses, also lived contentedly. The river supplied fresh fish. The villagers turned cow's milk into butter and cheese. Farmers tilled small plots of land that yielded potatoes and grains. And hunters found abundant fowl and other game in the hills and windswept moors.

And if they wanted to hear the Gospel, they would assemble on the Sabbath morning beside the flowing waters of the Mallart as the river swept past them a few yards to the east. Artis was always keen to learn more about heaven.

But this morning, she heard only the sounds of hell.

At the clamor of galloping horses and shouting men thundering into the center of their village, Artis peered out her window. To her dismay, she saw Patrick Steller, the Sutherland Estate factor, on his grey stallion. At least a dozen armed men, all bearing fiery torches despite the bright sunshine, followed Steller.

She abhorred the unscrupulous man and the way he swaggered about. She'd rebuffed his advances for a year, ever since her father died. She had no interest in the self-important braggart, and never would.

The last time she saw him, she made her contempt for him clear. He'd threatened to make her pay for her disdain. What would he do to her?

"Tenants of Achadh, go where you like," Steller yelled from the center of the village, "provided you do not stay on Sutherland land!"

The estate manager's voice sounded as brutal as his words.

Artis couldn't believe this was actually happening. She'd heard the rumors of Highland clearances and the inhumanity inflicted on many tenants by their Lairds. Some were evicted, in the most inhumane and cruel ways imaginable, to turn the land over to profitable sheep farming. The tenant farmers had no choice but to leave the land they had rented and worked for generations and be cast into the wilderness of the moors and bogs along the coast.

The MacKays were a strong and hearty people, but their preacher had told them that thousands of Highland Scots, driven from their homes, were dying from starvation and disease. Others were seeking to immigrate to the American colonies. But many would not survive the passage across the Atlantic.

Could a clearance really happen here? Could the Countess be that cruel? Her mind refused to accept it.

She looked to her mother for answers. Mary MacKay's venerable countenance bore the impress of fifty-seven winters and her still beautiful green eyes flashed with her well-known stubbornness. But her mum offered no answers.

"I'll not leave my home!" Mary swore. "But ye will my daughter." Her mother hauled a traveling bag from beneath her own bed and tossed in onto Artis' bed. "Pack yer bag, quickly now!"

"No, I'll not leave ye," Artis disputed.

"Och! Ye'll do as I say. Now grab yer clothes and cloak. And take yer Bible. I fear ye will need it."

Artis gathered her things, her fear building. She could hear the other villagers struggling to save the most valuable of their possessions, the frightened cries of women and children, the bellowing of the terror stricken cattle, and the yapping of shepherds' dogs amid the smoke and fires.

She quickly stuck her tresses in her silver hair clasp and donned her tartan shawl for warmth. Her mother grabbed her bag and carried it toward the door. As Artis followed her, she strapped on her grandfather's old dirk, and hid the dagger's leather scabbard beneath her long shawl.

"I have a few coins I've saved over the years. Hopefully it will be enough and ye will na have to indenture yerself as so many others have," her mother told her while retrieving the coins from their hiding place. Her mum tied the money into a handkerchief, and knotted it tightly. "Put this between your bosoms!"

"Mum, no! You may need your funds."

Her mother shoved the knotted cloth well down into Artis' stays just as one of Steller's snarling men barged through their plank door.

"Out! Now!" the big man bellowed.

"How dare you drive us from our cottage! My family has called this home for centuries. This land is rightfully ours," Artis shouted. Her eyes burned with indignation and the tears she struggled not to release.

With an air of authority, Steller strutted in behind his man. "Yer animals who deserve nothin'. Sheep are more valuable now." Condescension twisted his thin mouth.

"Ye're a savage," Artis yelled. "What kind of man would place the value of sheep over men? Only a savage would put the needs of sheep above his fellow Scot."

"Aye, ye have it right daughter. The man's a savage of the devil's own tribe," Mary spat.

"Sometimes savagery is necessary for the greater good," Steller declared, his jaw thrust forward. A smile that did indeed look demonic spread across his merciless face.

"Yer home is already set afire. Ye need to get out now," Steller's man warned.

Artis could smell the smoke now and with each rapid breath, her alarm grew.

Steller turned his dark eyes toward her mother. "The flames are making rapid progress, Widow," he snarled. His eyes glistened with the ire of evil.

When she glanced up, Artis' heart thundered within her chest. She could see flames begin to encircle her home. The fire crackled and

4

crunched like a hungry beast as it seized the ancient timber that supported the roof of turf and then devoured it. She could feel the heat of the beast's breath on her face. Between her breasts, sweat popped out, dampening the cloth that held her mum's coin.

But she would not leave without her mother. "Mum, we must go," she pleaded. "Please."

"Nay, darlin'," she said. "Remember this, I love ye and always will."

Was her mum saying goodbye? Panic spurted through Artis. What if her mother refused to leave?

"Take the girl," Steller told his man, his voice grim. "I'll take care of this one." He shot Artis a bitter smile. A muscle quivered angrily at his jaw.

He wasn't going to bring her mother out at all. Her rage almost choked her. "You bastard!" she yelled. "Leave her alone! It's me ye should punish, na her."

He turned his hate-filled eyes back to her Mum. What was he going to do?

"Please, I beg you, do na hurt her," Artis entreated Steller.

Desperate, Artis turned to the big man who gripped her arm. "I'll go willingly. Please, carry my mother out of here! I beg ye."

Steller peered at his man and shook his head no. "She'll walk out, or she does na leave."

"I'll na leave me home till God takes me out of it," Mary swore, her flinty eyes squinting at Steller. "And ye'll never marry my daughter. She will na lower herself to marry a loathsome bog scum like ye."

"I'm tempted to haul ye outside right now, pull up yer skirts and take ye, because I can. And then take yer daughter's virginity, because I want to," Steller threatened.

Her mum drew her hand back and slapped Steller hard.

Stunned, Steller's eyes widened and his face turned crimson. "Bitch."

With her hands fisted and firmly planted at her sides, Mary spat in Steller's smug face.

Steller yanked out his dirk and lunged toward her mum.

"Nay!" Artis cried. She tried to stop Steller, but the man who held her jerked her toward the door.

She stared back in horror.

Steller vindictively ran the blade across her mother's slender neck. Blood followed the path of the knife's edge.

Artis screamed. "Nay! God no! Nay!"

As her mum's body crumpled, so did Artis, her shock crippling her.

"Ye do na want to die here lass," Steller's man said. "Get up, we must hurry."

"Damn her, the old witch. She should have listened. Let her burn!" Steller snarled and stormed out.

Steller's man grabbed Artis, his strong fingers pressed painfully into her wrist. With an iron grip, he yanked her toward the door but she struggled against him.

With an immense snapping and hissing sound, a portion of the roof collapsed onto the alcove that served as her snug bedroom her entire life. Bright orange cinders flew everywhere and swirls of smoke and ash filled the air.

With her free hand, she reached out, straining towards her mother's body, wanting to touch her kind face one last time. Deep sobs racked her chest. Unfathomable sorrow seized her heart. "Mum…"

The man grabbed her bag—his one small act of kindness—and then drug her through the door. Towing her by her arm through the dirt, he deposited her and her bag well away from the blazing house.

Mounted on his stallion now, Steller glared down at her. "Do na bother to hide. I'll be back for ye." His voice felt as cold and lashing as a winter gale.

Unable to control her fury, she pushed herself up. Her breath came raggedly, but she spit out, "If ye come back for me, I swear I'll find a way to kill ye."

"I warned ye before and ye did na listen. If ye reject me further, next time, tis ye that will die." Briskly whipping and twisting his horse around, he rode off to join his men.

She lifted her eyes and wept in horror at the sight of her burning home—her dear mother's funeral pyre. The spectacle of the roaring flames seared her heart, and forced her to squeeze her eyes shut and sink to her knees.

The others, old and young, lingering nearby, also wept, their whimpering cries mingling together in a pitiful chorus.

In shock, they all joined Artis on the ground, planting themselves amid the few belongings and furniture they had managed to drag out of their homes. A few coughed as the awful smoke and heat scorched their throats.

On the other side of the township, Steller's men lit a stack of peat, used for fuel, taking away their only means of warmth along with their homes. Then, the few trees around their homes were set alight, no doubt to stop rebuilding. Delivering even more cruelty, they set fire to their crops.

Amid the chaos, they heard faint cries coming from one of the burning homes—the home of Donald MacKay, nearly 100 years of age and bed-ridden. No one had thought to save her uncle. Steller's men had left him to the cruelty of the flames!

Artis started to raise up to run toward her uncle's home, but the other women held her back. Several of the village men were already rushing to Donald's home. They rescued him and carried the poor suffering man toward the others.

Artis scrambled on her knees over to her aged great-uncle. She placed her hands upon his chest. "Uncle Donald," she cried through her sobs.

Smudges of soot covered his timeworn face and wrinkled arms. His aging blue eyes looked up at her as he unpinned his silver brooch and handed it to her. "Go to the colonies my dear lass," he whispered, his voice faint and hoarse. "Yer destiny is na longer here."

"But this is my home," she said, taking the precious symbol of clan MacKay from his trembling hand.

He reached up with the shaky tip of his index finger and tapped her chest, right above her heart. "Nay, dear one, yer home is in here. When I see God, I will ask Him to send ye a brawny man to love ye and give ye another family, so ye can find happiness."

"Happiness?"

"Aye, happi…" The thin milky skin of his lids slid down.

"Uncle," Artis whimpered, "do na leave me. My mum is gone. I'll be all alone if ye leave too."

But Artis could almost see the soft wind carry Donald's soul away, to join his brother's daughter, and her beloved mother, Mary MacKay, in another world entirely.

Artis laid her head upon his chest and wept until the others lifted her up and offered her comfort for her losses. But she found no solace in their words as both raw grief and visceral anger consumed her.

After one last act of cruelty, using a whip on a village man trying to stop the flames from consuming his family's home, Steller and his minions departed. Every village dog, including her own, barking and growling at the heels of the departing horses, followed the wicked men for a while.

In but a few minutes, through tear moistened eyes and mute wretchedness, Artis could see the smoke of yet another MacKay clan village burning, reducing to ashes the homes of others along the Strath.

As Steller set further settlements afire that day, a heavy dark shroud of smoke and sadness soon enveloped the whole countryside, and even reached far out across the sea.

Chapter 1

Near Cumberland Falls, Kentucky, Early Fall 1799

I'm glad we're finally gettin' this house finished for ye," Bear MacKee told his adopted brother Sam. "I even have splinters on me arse."

"I'm glad too—I won't have to listen to your imaginative complaints anymore!" Sam said. "Now, if you would be kind enough to pick up that mantel and get it placed where Catherine wants it."

"Aye, I'll be sure to put it exactly where yer lovely wife wants it placed. If not, she'll na doubt make me do it again."

Bear heard Sam laughing as he trudged toward the new home they were putting the finishing touches on. The six-foot plank was a good four inches thick and for most men carrying the heavy mantel would be a job for two. But his shoulders and arms did not seem to mind the weight. He'd always been a strong man, but all the lifting and hauling he'd done helping Sam build the house and barn had made him even more so.

Bear made his way to the home's spacious parlor and carefully laid the beautiful piece of wood atop its supports.

"A little to the right, Bear," Catherine instructed. "No back an inch or so to the left. No, no, back a few hairs toward the right."

Bear turned his face toward Catherine. "A wee bit more?"

"No, that's perfect. It looks splendid!"

He heard happiness in Catherine's voice. She married Sam two years ago and, with each day that passed, their marriage reflected their contentment and shared joy even more.

Watching them lately made him wonder about his own future. Was it time he found a bride for himself? But here in the middle of frontier Kentucky the only female he was likely to meet was one of Sam's mares or a cow with four tits.

He would have to leave Sam, Catherine, and Little John. He understood that. He also dreaded it. He'd always been close to Sam—they'd grown up together and were more alike than any of his other four adopted brothers. Actually, only three now. Little John's father, John, had been brutally killed by buffalo hunters. He and Sam had seen John's murder avenged, but the loss was still raw to them all.

After John's death, Sam adopted the lad and when he proposed to Catherine, made her understand that she would also be accepting Little John. Catherine readily agreed and the three seemed to quickly become a happy family. Watching the boy's love for Catherine and Sam grow made Bear even more convinced that someday he wanted to start a family of his own.

"It's taken us more than a year, but I do believe we have finally finished Bear!" Catherine said.

"Aye, it's a fine home. One ye will enjoy for many years to come."

Catherine sat down in her rocker and let out a deep sigh. Bear could see that being with child continued to take a toll on her energy.

"Are ye well?" he asked, concerned.

"Oh, indeed. It's perfectly normal for women with child to become tired."

Sam hurried in with his arms full of firewood. "I thought we would christen the new fireplace mantel with a roaring fire. What say you my

10

beautiful bride?"

"What a marvelous idea!" Catherine answered. "These fall mornings are getting cooler and my toes are cold."

"Your toes are always cold," Sam said. He exchanged a smile with her then bent to his task of building the hearth fire. When Sam finished, he stood to admire the mantel. "That's fine workmanship, Bear. It looks just right."

"It was a pleasure to make it for the two of ye."

"You and Sam—and Mister McGuffin, until he left to go live with William and Kelly—all worked so hard building this house," Catherine said. "And, of course the housewright and craftsmen, too."

"Aye, McGuffin seemed beyond eager to get back. When he found out he was to be a grandfather, he danced and skipped around here with his saw and hammer in his hands for weeks," Bear said.

"But all your efforts were well worth it. I love my new home. It's as grand as my English estate."

Bear and Sam, looked at each other. Both knew that was an exaggeration. Catherine was a wealthy woman, raised in Boston, from a noble English family. Her grandfather left his English estate, and a mansion called Brympton, to her. Sam had never seen it and neither had he but, from her descriptions, he could well imagine its grandeur.

Sam deserved to be proud of what they'd built here. It was a fine, sturdy, and spacious two-story home, among the nicest built in frontier Kentucky. Bear saw a few grander homes, as they passed through Virginia and Tennessee, but none finer in Kentucky.

They also constructed pens for horses and a large barn with ten stalls—five on each side. The stable would allow Sam to stall his prize stallions and best mares during the winter. The rest would take shelter in a sizeable shed.

"It may not compare to Brympton, but I promise you, we will love living here with Little John and our other children," Sam said, looking at Catherine with adoring eyes.

Bear did not miss the spark that passed between the two. He longed for someone that would make him feel that way. It was definitely time for him to leave. "Sam, Catherine, I've decided somethin'."

Sam glanced up, his rugged face registering the seriousness in Bear's tone.

"I need to leave for a while. It's time I found me a lass of me own," Bear said. He could feel his cheeks flushing, but he stood a little straighter, certain this was what he needed to do.

"Bear!" Catherine said. "I had no idea you were thinking of leaving."

"For some time now, I've been givin' it considerable thought. I can see how much happiness ye've brought Sam, and the joy Little John has given ye both. I'd like a chance at the same."

Sam reached over and patted Bear on the back. "We wish you God's speed and help in sending the right woman to your path."

Bear chuckled. "I'd rather He sent her into me arms!"

"Indeed," Sam agreed.

"When do you plan to leave Bear?" Catherine asked.

"Tomorrow," Bear answered, "that is unless Sam has anythin' else he needs help with."

"Bear, you've been more than generous with your time. We could find projects to work on together for the rest of our lives, and then some," Sam said. "At some point, a person needs to stop thinking about work and start thinking about happiness. I believe your time for that way of thinking has come."

"I agree," Catherine said. "You deserve all the happiness in the world, Bear. You've been the best brother a man could possibly be for both of us."

"You've risked your life fighting for us. You've worked day and night helping us. And you are not only my brother, you're a loyal friend," Sam said. "It won't be the same around here without you."

"Without him?" Little John barged into the room, carrying several rocks in his dirty hands "Where you going Bear?"

Bear knelt down to one knee so he could look into the seven-year-old's blue eyes. "I'm goin' to find me a bride, John."

"But you and I live here," the boy protested. "What do you need a wife for?"

"I know ye and I live here, and I'll be back to see ye lad. I do na know how long I'll be gone. Hopefully, the good Lord will put some wonderful lass right in my path and I will na have to look too long."

"Can I go with you?" Little John asked. "I know what lasses look like and I could help you find a pretty one."

Bear cleared his throat and smiled. "Well lad, that would be very nice, and I'm sure ye'd have a skillful eye for spotting a bonnie lass. But I need ye to stay here and help yer mum. Since she's goin' to have a wee brother or sister for ye soon, she may be needin' a big brother like you to help her out."

Little John's forehead wrinkled and he drew his dark brows together. "I hadn't thought 'bout that. I guess she might be needing me."

"Indeed, I will," Catherine said. "You'll be a big help."

"What have ye got there in yer hands?" Bear asked.

"Some shiny rocks. Wanna see?"

They heard a horse nicker. Bear stood and went with Sam to peek out the home's wide entrance.

A lone rider neared the homestead.

Sam grabbed his rifle, leaning near the door and Bear did the same.

"Hello the house," the rider yelled. "I bear a message for Daniel

13

MacKee."

Bear stepped down off the porch, keeping a firm grip on his long rifle.

"I'm Daniel MacKee. What message do ye bear, Sir?" Bear asked.

"Sir, my name is Isaac Ambrose. Colonel Logan has asked that you return to St. Asaph's. He needs to discuss an important matter with you."

"What matter?"

"He did not share that with me, Sir. It's been a long ride," the man said rubbing his lower back. Can I ask for the favor of something to drink and the comfort of your home for an evening?"

"Indeed you may," Sam replied hospitably. "I'm Samuel Wyllie, recently relocated here with my wife Catherine. After you have seen to your horse, please join us inside. This is my son John," Sam said, placing his big hands on Little John's shoulders. "Little John, show the man to the stable and help him take care of his mount. Then bring him into the house."

"Wonder what this is all about," Bear told Sam.

"No telling. The colonel may have word of Indian trouble and is summoning all single men for militia duty at the Fort. Or it may have to do with the new government."

"I hope it's the latter reason," Bear said. "I've had enough of fightin' the natives to last me a lifetime. I'm glad we seem to have finally entered a more peaceful time with 'em."

"Indeed," Sam agreed.

"While I'm at the settlement, what supplies should I bring back?"

"Bear, have you forgotten that you were planning to leave on the morrow and won't be coming back for some time?"

He shook his head, annoyed with himself. "Och, I did indeed. I'll have to get used to the idea, I guess."

Little John brought Ambrose back to the house and Bear followed the man and Sam inside, wondering what Colonel Logan could possibly want with him. The colonel had founded the settlement at Fort Logan many years before and settlers now called the township St. Asaph's—the named suggested by a Welshman in honor of the canonization of a Welsh monk.

When they'd all settled inside by the fire, and Ambrose sipped on his coffee, Bear spoke up. "Well, I was plannin' to leave in the mornin' anyway so yer timin' is ideal, Mister Ambrose."

"Ye can sleep in the nice quarters we built above the barn for our workers when we finally hire some," Sam offered.

"It's considerably quieter there," Catherine added with a side glance at Little John.

"With Bear leaving, we'll need to hire those workers soon," Sam told Catherine. "I'll have to hire three men to do the work Bear accomplished in a day."

"Perhaps Mister Ambrose could spread the word at the fort that we are looking for dependable workers," Catherine suggested.

"They should be single men with a strong back and references," Sam added.

"I will be pleased to do so," Ambrose responded.

"And with yer bairn coming, perhaps ye should consider hirin' a cook too," Bear suggested, lifting his eyebrows at Sam.

"Oh that won't be necessary just yet," Catherine said quickly. "I love to cook. I'm learning more and more every day."

Bear glanced at Sam who grimaced slightly. Catherine couldn't see Sam's face from where she sat, but his brother clearly shared Bear's poor opinion of Catherine's cooking skills.

"We'll leave at first light," Bear told Ambrose. "Sam, will ye keep Mister Ambrose's company while I go pack up me things?"

"Indeed, I'm anxious to hear about everything going on at Fort Logan these days," Sam said. "What news do you have? And do you know anything of Fort Boonesborough? My brother William is sheriff there."

15

FRONTIER HIGHLANDER VOW OF LOVE

Bear waited until Ambrose said he had no news of Fort Boonesborough. Then he walked toward his room located on the other side of the house from Sam and Catherine's quarters and next to Little John's room. He glanced behind him to see Little John tagging along. He took the boy's hand in his.

When they reached Bear's bedroom, Little John pouted his lips and his eyes watered. "I don't want you to go, Bear."

"Ahh lad, I do na want to go. But I must. I'll miss ye fiercely. But I promise I'll visit soon and bring ye a fine surprise."

"A surprise?"

"Aye."

"I like surprises. So do Martha and Polly."

"Then I will find a surprise for yer cousins as well."

He gave Little John an affectionate hug. He loved the boy dearly and it would sadden him to leave. Little John sat on the floor and watched him pack. It wouldn't take long. His few things, mostly an assortment of various types of weapons and an extra buckskin shirt and leather breeches, would fit into one bag. He retrieved his hidden stash of coins—money he'd earned helping Sam raise and sell horses—and stashed it in the bag's hidden pocket.

Kentuckians prized horses, not only using them for transportation through the vast wilderness, but also for sources of farm power, hauling, and racing. He counted the funds. It would take all he'd earned to build a home of his own.

Now all he needed was a bonnie lass who could put up with him.

Bear knew that woman was out there. He just had to find her.

Chapter 2

Roanoke, Virginia, September 1799

A rtis started the new day with hope in her heart for the first time since she left her home in Scotland.

She smiled as she brushed her hair and afterward tied it at the base of her neck. She splashed cool water on her face and removed the sleep from her eyes. As she dried off, she wondered what freedom would feel like.

The last time she was free was the day she arrived in the colonies.

But today she would complete the final day of her seven-year indentured servitude. Her mother's coin had bought her an accommodating passage to the colonies on board the ship Ulysses, but upon arrival in Wilmington, North Carolina, she had no choice but to either sell her body or sell her labor. She would rather have jumped ship and drowned herself before selling herself into prostitution. That left her only one choice— becoming a servant. A slave really. Except, unlike slaves, indentured servants could see an end to their plight.

Along with the others from the ship to be indentured, the ship Captain and several members of his crew took her to the auction taking place in the Cape Fear area known as the Argyll Colony, about an hour from Wilmington. She learned later that the Argyll Colony was named for the shire in western Scotland from which its first residents came. They were the first trickle of what grew into a virtual flood of Highland immigrants. Highland Scots, thought to be at least a third of the Argyll population, earned the bustling colony its nickname—Valley of the Scots.

But she was not to remain there.

The auction, run by a Wilmington company that specialized in selling indentured servants, drew numerous wealthy planters and merchants. She'd signed a contract with a Virginia plantation owner, named Morgan Roberts, whose face and manner seemed kinder to her than the others seeking to indenture servants that day. She sold her labor in exchange for room, board, and what they called freedom dues—what she would receive at the end of seven years. In her case, a land grant of fifty acres in the new state of Kentucky.

That afternoon, she'd bid farewell to the few friends she'd made on the voyage, each of them following separate paths into bondage, scattered like autumn leaves in a hearty gale.

Artis found the long voyage getting to the colonies difficult, but it was of little consequence to her whether she travelled three miles or three thousand. The loss was the same, the pain as great.

Boarding a ship for a foreign shore was for some a new start to life, a grand adventure. But Artis saw it only as being forced to move from a land she loved all her life, a land where she had once lived with a loving mother and father and a large extended family. She'd been born and bred in the Highlands, held for centuries by generations of her ancestors, common folk who fought and, when necessary, died to hold their clan's precious land.

Now, her mother too had died for their land.

Unprepared for the loss and the change in her life, she held on to the bitterness that chaffed against her heart like an iron shackle on delicate skin. A chafing caused by the indelible hatred in her memory for the factor named Steller and his ruthless oppression and extortion of the Highland people. He and the other sheep farmers would forever be minions of the devil in her mind.

That bitterness and hatred often made Artis a spitfire when men neared her. Quick-tempered and sometimes highly excitable, she wanted nothing to do with men. Someday, her mother's murder would be avenged. Until then, all she wanted was to be left alone.

Even now, after seven long years, she could not erase the vivid image of her mother suffering a cruel death right before her eyes. She slapped the towel down on the worn table by her small bed and dressed quickly. The last piece of clothing she donned was her long tartan shawl, which she only wore on special occasions. She pinned it together with a very old family brooch, once belonging to her dear Uncle. He too had died because of Steller and his hard-hearted men.

She hurried from the female servant's quarters over to the landowner's home and, being the first to arrive, a servant ushered her inside. She laid her hand upon the brooch, embellished with a fist tightly clutching a dagger pointed heavenward. The brooch also bore the clan motto—*Manu Forti*—with a strong hand.

As she took the quill to sign her freedom papers, Artis glanced down at her own hands, calloused from the farm work she'd done day after day for seven years. Because she was tall for a woman and appeared well-built, Roberts had assigned her to work the fields and barn instead of inside the main house.

At first, her duties caused painful blisters to form on her hands, particularly the hoeing she'd done, alongside the other servants and slaves, to the seemingly endless rows of tobacco and corn crops on the large western Virginia plantation. The farm owner used the corn crop to feed hogs and to distill whiskey and the tobacco crop brought him substantial income. The blisters finally turned to callouses and protected her hands from further damage.

Artis had learned numerous skills working on the plantation, including how to care for and exercise the plantation horses and how to spin and weave hemp used for cotton bale bagging and rope making.

It had been so long since she held a quill and signed her name, her heart raced for a moment wondering if she could remember how. But for the last few months, she'd dreamed of this moment daily and she wasn't going to spoil it with self-doubt. She gripped the quill a little tighter and with a confident hand and a bit of flourish wrote 'Artis MacKay' on the document.

"Thank you Miss MacKay," Roberts said, "you have been a faithful and hard-working servant. You are now a free woman. My wife and I wish you the best of fortune in your future. Here is the deed to your land, located near Boonesborough, Kentucky. It is part of a larger tract of land that I have divided into several acreages. As soon as you arrive, take this document to the Land Office there, and register it with the Land Commissioner Mister Simmons. He should be able to direct you to its location. I have not seen it, as I acquired it in payment of a man's debt to me, but Simmons has assured me that it has good timber and water and will make a fine homestead. Simmons is also selling the remaining small tracts of land for me."

"Aye, thank ye Mister Roberts. I'll be sure to find Mister Simmons."

"A group of settlers in town are leaving tomorrow morning from the inn for the new state of Kentucky. I suggest you travel with them for your protection. Perhaps there will be a wagon you can ride in."

"Thank ye Mister Roberts. Yer kindness over the term of my indenture was most appreciated. I have heard from others that some landowners are na as benevolent as ye and yer wife have been."

"We are compelled by Christian charity to kind-heartedness. I regret that I am also compelled by necessity to employ the use of servants and slaves on a plantation of this size."

"Perhaps ye could start payin' the workers a fair wage," Artis suggested.

"Maybe someday, when I've paid off my debts," Roberts said, leaning back in his leather chair and sighing. "Until then though, I must travel to North Carolina this week for a new group of servants." He rested his clasped hands on his ample belly.

20

Artis lowered her head and looked at her well-worn boots, solemnly thinking about the men and women who would soon arrive here. No doubt, many would be her fellow countrymen, forced to give away seven years of their life. At least they would be working for a fair man who treated his servants and slaves with compassion.

"I regret that circumstance forced a young woman of your obvious education and charming appearance to spend the first years of her womanhood in servitude."

"I am not a servant anymore," Artis said adamantly. "I never was really. I was just forced by circumstance to work here in exchange for a chance at finding a new home and a future."

"You are right, of course. And at twenty-two, you are still young and lovely enough to marry and bear children. If you can just learn to control your outbursts of temper, I know you will find happiness in Kentucky."

"If I get angry, it's because someone has given me good reason to be," Artis said, setting her jaw and tossing her hair behind her back. "I'll na hold my tongue when someone deserves to be set straight."

"I know, I know. And men especially, often say and do foolish things," he counseled like her father had long ago. "And, some men will do and say cruel things. Like that evil man you spoke of who murdered your poor mother."

Artis peered down at her feet, unwilling to let him see the pain that still made her eyes burn with tears she refused to release.

"But remember this, not all men are like that man. Now, I don't often give my coin away, but time and again, you worked as hard as two servants. And did a better job of it too. I want you to accept these coins as a bonus toward your new life. I wish it were more, but perhaps it will be enough to give you a new start."

Artis glanced up, liking the sound of his words. A new start. "My thanks to ye, Sir." She reached out for the coins, surprised at the weight of the pouch. "You are too generous." She wondered if it would be enough to buy a pistol, lead, and powder. She would need a weapon if she were going to survive in Kentucky by herself.

"You've earned every penny of that Artis."

She couldn't quarrel with the man about that. Her parents had taught her to do a job well and without complaining and, unlike some of the other surly servants, she'd made a point to do just that ever since her arrival at the Robert's plantation.

"Now if you would be kind enough to send the next servant in line into my office, I will leave you to the good guidance of the Almighty and bid you farewell."

"Goodbye, Mister Roberts. And thank ye," Artis said. She would almost miss the man.

Artis' chest swelled with elation and she smiled at the realization that she was now a free woman. Free to find her own happiness, and as Roberts called it, a new start.

With a full heart, she turned toward the door, opened it, and breathed in the smell of freedom.

As she stepped out, a dazzling shaft of morning sunlight fell on her. But its radiance couldn't compete with the joy on her own beaming face.

Chapter 3

Fort Logan, St. Asaph's, Kentucky

After covering the near seventy mile distance to Fort Logan over a full day of hard riding to the north, Bear arrived with Ambrose. The two dismounted and led their mounts through the fort's gates.

The fort, an imposing structure impenetrable to arrows and rifles, had never fallen during an attack. Although not nearly as large as the settlement at Fort Boonesborough, numerous homes and a few businesses sprouted out from the fort in all directions.

Several men waved their welcome toward Ambrose and he returned their greeting. Bear knew few men here besides the Colonel. Both he and Sam had visited the fort when they returned from their trip to Boonesborough for building supplies, but they only stayed overnight. Sam had been anxious to pick up Catherine and Little John—who had been staying with their brother Stephen, his wife, daughters, and new son Samuel—and get his own family back home.

Bear's first order of business was to care for his gelding Camel. He led the tired horse into the center of the bustling stockade.

"The stable and corral pen are located over there on the east side of the Fort, next to the blacksmith's," Ambrose explained, pointing. "I'll take

23

your mount with mine and see that he's well cared for."

"Yer kindness is appreciated. As ye can see, he's tall and stout, so he'll need extra feed."

"After carrying a man of your size all day, I'd say he needs double the ration of most horses," Ambrose joshed.

"Aye, like myself, he's a big eater to be sure. I'll be seein' ye later then," Bear said. "I know where the Colonel's office is." Over the course of the day, Bear had decided he rather liked the short, but stocky, Welshman.

He strode through the stockade and made his way to the blockhouse where Logan's quarters and office were located. He passed a group of men bringing in gunpowder in drum-shaped kegs that fit snugly against the horses' flanks. The keg hoops were made of saplings, rather than metal, to prevent an accidental spark. The precious powder was typically stored in an earthen repository disguised as a root cellar. It didn't surprise him that Logan would keep a substantial supply of gunpowder on hand for the fort. Being prepared before an enemy strikes is often half the battle.

The Colonel was considered to be one of the best rough and tumble fighters in Kentucky and Bear often heard numerous stories recounting his bravery in action. Yet, the man tended to be quiet and prudent, unlike his fellow frontiersman Daniel Boone, known for his oratorical flourish and gregarious nature. Bear held great respect for both men.

Benjamin Logan's imposing figure—just over six-feet tall—towered over most fellows, but not Bear. He stood a good six inches taller and weighed about fifty pounds more than Logan. After he entered the dimly lit room, he peered down at the Colonel who leaned against an artfully carved pine desk reading a paper.

"Good evenin', Colonel. Ye needed to see me?"

Looking up, Logan said, "Ah, Daniel MacKee! Otherwise known as Bear—a fitting nickname for a giant like yourself."

"Aye, the name does seem to suit me. Given to me by me step-mum,

Sam's mother."

"Are you well? And your brother Sam?"

"Aye, we are fightin' fit."

"And Sam's wife and son?"

"Catherine is with child, but she's na due for some time. Little John is growin' taller and smarter by the day."

"Did you and Isaac have a trouble-free journey?"

"It was uneventful, and the weather remained pleasant, so aye, we did."

"I thank you for coming so swiftly," Logan said. "Please have a seat."

He fell into the closest chair, appreciating the chance to rest his tired back. The wooden chair squeaked under his weight as he regarded Logan. The man's eyes held a sheen of purpose. What was on the Colonel's mind?

"No doubt you're wondering what my reason is for summoning you."

"Aye, that I am. And I'm hopin' it is na further trouble with the natives."

"No, we were able to negotiate a peace with the Shawnee. We had to swear that we would never raid their settlements again, and they did the same. I also apologized for the slaying of Chief Moluntha by one of my overzealous men. The last Shawnee raid happened in retaliation for that. Hopefully, this peace will be permanent. I would hate to lose more good men to fighting."

"News of your peace treaty is most welcomed, Colonel. And now that we have peace with the Cherokee as well, Kentucky will hopefully be free of any further strife and bloodshed."

"That is my fervent hope as well."

"Then what is your reason for summonin' me here?"

"Governor Garrard has asked that each of the settlements send a delegate to Boonesborough for a special-called assembly."

"For what purpose?"

"The delegates will discuss and advise the Governor on a number of matters important to Kentucky's future—among them bills to preserve game, arrange for improved roads, and provide for better breeding of horses."

His brows drew together in confusion. "But, Colonel, what does that have to do with me?"

"Bear, the last time we met, you impressed me as a wise and well-spoken man. I've found that most Scotsmen are also well-educated."

"I owe my education to many hours spent with my nose in books in front of a peat fire as a youth. I owe what wisdom I have to God."

"You are also a single man, without your own homestead and family to guard," Logan answered.

"All true, though I am hopin' to change that fact in the near future."

"Are you engaged then?"

"Nay, but I plan to be soon."

"Who is the lucky lady?"

"I do na know."

Logan's laughter filled the room.

Bear sat up straighter and glared at Logan, frowning. He didn't understand why the man found what he'd said so humorous. "I have not yet met the lass," he added quickly.

"Bear, usually men meet a woman, *then* decide to become engaged."

"I know she's out there," he said, still annoyed. "I will find her."

"I wish you God's speed with that, Sir," Logan answered. "Perhaps your assignment, if you will accept it, will aide in your quest. Bear, I want you to be Fort Logan's and St. Elspeth's delegate at the Governor's assembly."

He was too startled by the suggestion to offer any objection. Being caught off guard did not happen to him often, but he was now.

"I can see you are surprised. You shouldn't be. The Governor has asked for men of character and the stamina for hard work. You strike me as just that kind of man."

"Och, Colonel, I am honored by yer words and by yer suggestion that I serve in that capacity, but I do na have experience with government."

As the last of the day's sunlight disappeared, Logan lit a candle and its rays brightened the dim room. The Colonel took a seat behind his large desk covered with several spread out maps and other documents. "Bear, every delegate sent to meet with the Governor will have little or no experience with government. Experience is not what's needed. What is needed are intelligent men who care about Kentucky's future," Logan said, vigorously tapping the tip of his index finger against one of the maps of Kentucky.

Bear glanced up from the finger to look directly into Logan's pale blue eyes. "Men like you, Colonel."

"My career in government is over. As you no doubt know, after serving in Kentucky's House of Representatives for four years, I lost the recent race for Governor. On the first ballot, I received the votes of 21 electors, Garrard received 17, and Todd received 14. Our new state constitution did not specify whether a plurality or a majority vote was required and a second vote had to be held between Garrard and myself to see who could get a majority. Unfortunately, most of Todd's electors supported Garrard, a more skilled orator than I, giving him a majority."

"Do ye support the Governor now?"

"I do, but only so far. What's important at the present time is supporting Kentucky. That's where you come in, Bear."

"Nay, I'm afraid me temperament would na be suitable for such an undertakin. Scots tend to be forthright—so much so we are often blunt."

"Just agree to serve in this one specially called assembly of delegates and I will be forever in your debt, Sir."

Bear's resolve faltered. His mind wavered, weighing what Logan had said. "Perhaps a wee bit of whiskey would help me decide." What he really wanted was a moment to think about the decision while Logan fetched the decanter and a couple of pewter cups from a side cabinet. And the whiskey would be refreshing after his long journey.

"Oh, I forgot to tell you one detail," Logan said, his voice brightening as he poured whiskey into the two pewter cups. "And this may interest you since you mentioned earlier that you were hoping to find a wife and have a home in the near future." Logan handed a cup to Bear. "The Governor's wife, Elizabeth Mountjoy, is using this occasion as an excuse for a party."

Bear swallowed the whiskey in one gulp. "Is that really the lady's name?" he asked, incredulous.

Logan regarded him with amusement, and added more whiskey to both their cups. "Indeed it is, or was, her maiden name. I believe it *actually* refers to a mountain of joy."

Bear's mouth twitched with mirth and then, unable to control himself, his laughter rippled through the room.

Logan joined in, the sound of his laugh deep and jovial.

"Tell me more about this party," Bear said, still chuckling. "Will there be women there?"

"Invitations to Mrs. Garrard's ball were carried, along with the request from Governor Garrard for delegates, to all the interior forts. I believe fifteen men and six women will make the journey from St. Elspeth's. The women will sport their finest clothes. Unfortunately, all the women going from here are married, but I'm certain some unmarried women will attend from other settlements."

Now Bear was intrigued.

Logan continued, "Last time the Governor held one of these events, abundant toddies kept the party going for several days."

"Well, those two facts do sweeten the brew a wee bit. And I would enjoy visitin' my brother William and his wife Kelly and their new wee bairn."

"He's sheriff of Boonesborough, is he not?"

"Aye, and a mighty fine one too!" Bear was proud of what William had already achieved.

"I wouldn't be a bit surprised if he wasn't a delegate too," Logan speculated. "Now, why don't we discuss this further over dinner? My wife Ann has prepared a pork roast."

The delicious fragrance of the meat cooking, in the home adjoining Logan's office, had teased Bear's stomach for some time. Did he also smell pie wafting through the air now too? He loved pie. His stomach grumbled in earnest.

Logan chuckled. "I can hear your stomach agreeing that it's time we enjoyed something to eat."

"Aye. It's time," Bear agreed.

It was time to enjoy many things.

Chapter 4

The size of Boonesborough surprised Artis. It seemed like a town that bloomed right out of the wilderness—for that was all she'd seen on their journey here. The day after she regained her freedom, she left Virginia with a group of settlers headed for Kentucky. The group soon passed through the Cumberland Gap and followed the Wilderness Trail north through miles and miles of pristine verdant forests and colorful rocky hills. The breathtaking scenery was the first she'd seen since arriving in the colonies that could compare to her beloved Highlands. The blue-green mountains reminded her of home.

But the air smelled completely different here. In Scotland, she mostly remembered the distinct salty scent of the nearby ocean, the earthy aroma of peat, and the woody and mossy fragrance of heather. On the Kentucky frontier, the sharp smell of pine and other woods was most dominant, mixed with the fresh fragrance of a nearly blue grass.

As they rode the wagons into the bustling town, the air's fragrance slowly changed, becoming unpleasant. She wrinkled her nose at the pungent odor of hides piled high on carts, horse manure scattered everywhere on the street, unwashed men, and bones cast into the street for dogs. But, now and then, she also caught the pleasant scent of fresh lumber stacked on wagons, several gardens, pots of blooming flowers, and to her astonishment, a bakery.

As soon as they reached what appeared to be the center of town, she bid the kind people she had traveled with goodbye. They all needed to find places for their families to camp and she was too impatient to wait for them.

Straight away, she set out to find the Land Office. After getting directions from a stranger, she hurried toward it, carrying all she owned in her linen bag, the same one she'd carried from Scotland.

Most of the people on the street seemed friendly enough, the men tipping their hats at her and the women smiling. Surprisingly, she wasn't the least bit afraid. She belonged in Kentucky. Here, she would be a landowner once again.

"Miss," she heard a man say from behind her.

Artis turned. A well-dressed, handsome, and tall blonde fellow smiled back at her.

"Can I help you find something, Miss? I've never seen you in Boonesborough before, so I assume you are newly arrived here."

"Aye, I am. Just a few minutes ago. But I already received directions to my destination. I thank ye just the same," she said.

"Are you from Scotland?" he asked.

"Aye, from the Highlands, though I have lived in Virginia these past seven years."

"My adopted brother is from the Highlands, so I recognized your charming accent. I'm William Wyllie, Sheriff of Boonesborough, at your service."

"I am pleased to make yer acquaintance sheriff. My name is Artis MacKay."

"That's a strange coincidence; my adopted brother is Daniel MacKee."

"'Tis the same clan, but a different sept—one from across the Loch."

"If I can help you in any way, Miss MacKay, my office is just inside the fort, on the right side of the enclosure."

"I thank ye for yer kind offer, Sir," she said. "I may need help securin' a horse and a weapon later. Perhaps ye could advise me as to the best place to purchase both."

"Indeed I would be delighted to do so. And my lovely wife, Kelly can offer suggestions for where to purchase clothing or other items you may need."

"Do you think I look like I need new clothes?" she said, irked at his comment. She smoothed her dusty skirt with her free hand.

"I didn't mean to imply that at all," the sheriff insisted. "I just wanted you to know that I have a wife about your age who could be of assistance to you."

"Do ye have an inn here in Boonesborough?" she asked. She felt tired and achy from the long journey on rough roads in the bumpy wagon and it seemed to be making her irritable. She would need to rest soon. Perhaps she just needed to eat something.

"Indeed we do, but it is small and always kept full. I'll be glad when someone builds this town another."

She let out a heavy sigh. "Well where do new arrivals stay?"

"Anywhere and everywhere. Some camp by the fort in oilcloth tents, as you no doubt noticed on your way into town. But most camp on the outskirts in their own wagons. That's what my family did when we first arrived here two years ago. But I would not advise that if you are alone. Are you?"

"Aye, I am. I traveled with some settlers to get here, but they all have large families and have too many mouths to feed as it is. They continued on through Boonesborough to find a place to camp."

"Where are you headed now?"

"To the Land Office. I have a deed to register. In fact, I must be goin'."

"Miss MacKay, I would be happy to escort you to see Commissioner Simmons," Sheriff Wyllie offered.

"Ye are most kind, but I can find it myself. I'm told it is just down the street on the left."

"That's correct. When you're through, come see me and either my deputy or I will help you find a horse and assist with locating your land."

"Do ye do that for other settlers?" she asked, curious as to why he was being so helpful.

"Only the single women who have no one else to help them. I will not allow young ladies to come to harm in my town. It's my sworn duty to protect you and anyone else who needs protection."

The sheriff's words seemed particularly adamant and Artis wondered if there could be a deeper reason for his resolute insistence on protecting women. Perhaps his wife had once been threatened.

"Well, my thanks for yer kindness, Sir. I must be on my way. Good day," Artis said, and turned away.

❧

Bear left for Fort Boonesborough on his own, having no desire to travel with a large noisy group, especially one that included six chattering women. The men and women from St. Elspeth's who were travelling to the party hosted by the Governor and his wife would follow the next day.

With his stops to let Camel rest and water, it took him all day to cover the roughly forty-five mile distance from Fort Logan to Fort Boonesborough.

He spent the majority of the morning wondering if he was doing the right thing by agreeing to serve as a delegate. Well, at least he'd have a chance to see William, Kelly, and the new bairn again. The thought of wrapping them all in his arms made him smile. He'd seen their new daughter Nicole only once when William brought them to visit last spring. The bairn was a bonnie wee thing, bound to be a stunning beauty with the fine-looking parents she had.

As he rode into town, he caught sight of William, a short ways off. His brother stood talking to a woman—a tall stunning beauty herself. As quick as he could manage, he wove his way around wagons, other riders, and people milling about. "William," he called out.

William turned and his face lit up like a brand new sun. "Bear!"

Bear quickly dismounted and tied Camel's reins to a nearby rail. "Come over here and let me give ye a Bear hug," he told his brother with outstretched arms.

The two embraced for a moment and then William asked how Sam, Catherine and Little John were. Unexpected visits on the frontier often meant the delivery of bad tidings. After hurriedly assuring his brother that the three were well, Bear stepped back and looked in the direction the woman took as she had walked away from William.

"And how are you Bear?"

"As fine as frog's hair, but please tell me brother who was that lass ye were just talkin' to?"

"She's a newly arrived settler. I just met her. Her name's Artis MacKay."

"MacKay!" Was it possible she was one of his kinsman? If so, he hoped the family ties were not too close. "Did the lass say where she was from?"

"Indeed, from the Highlands. I didn't ask what village."

"I couldn't quite see her face as she spoke with ye, but from the back she appeared to be a bonnie lookin' lass. Is she as pretty as she appeared from a distance?"

"She was quite lovely," William agreed.

"Where did she go? She was just here. Is she alone?" Bear sincerely wished she was."

"Yes, I believe the young lady is alone. She traveled here with several families, but they are no relation to her. She went to the Land Office to see the Commissioner about a deed in her possession."

"I wonder how she came to acquire land."

"It appears she has somehow. I invited her to come to my office when she concluded her business to help her find a horse and locate her land. She also mentioned needing to buy a weapon."

"Perhaps I could assist the lass as well."

William chuckled. "Could it be that I see a spark of romantic interest in your eyes?"

Bear felt his cheeks burn in embarrassment, but decided he needed to tell William the truth. "Aye, that's the main reason I'm here. I've decided it is time for me to find a bride." He looked in the direction of the Land Office, hoping to spot her.

"All I can say is, it's about time," William said. "You don't know what you've been missing."

"Aye, but I hope to find out." Seeing the amusement in William's eyes, he laughed and then added, "I'm also here on official business for Colonel Logan." He filled William in on the details of Logan's request and the upcoming ball.

"Yes, I'm well aware of the meeting," William said. "In fact, I am the delegate for Boonesborough, appointed by Judge Webb."

Bear leaned forward and lowered his voice. "We can discuss all that later. What else did ye learn about Miss MacKay? I did na get a good look at her face. What color are her eyes? Did she seem nice or a nag? Did she sound like she had a head on her shoulders or would she na know 'sic 'em' from 'come'?" Bear realized he was ticking off all the things he wanted in a woman and his thoughts were racing dangerously. He had only just begun looking for a wife. He needed to slow down.

Williams's eyes grew openly amused. "Whoa, one question at a time," he said, grinning.

"My apologies, William. I guess I've spent so much time alone, now that I've decided I want somethin' else for my life, I canna seem to get it done quick enough."

"Let's go back to my office and wait for her. Or would you rather get an ale first?"

"No, let's just go to yer office. I do na want to risk missin' her. This is one lass I plan to meet. Now tell me all about Kelly and yer wee one. How is Nicole?"

William's face brightened at just the mention of his wife and daughter's names and while they walked, he happily updated Bear on everything going on at his cabin.

Bear half listened, his mind elsewhere. Leading Camel, he walked through town beside his brother. His feet seemed to be drifting along on their own, as he thought about a tall lass named MacKay.

Chapter 5

Artis opened the door and stepped inside the land commissioner's office. She let out the breath she'd been holding as she looked around.

Specks of dust danced in the rays of light streaming in through the window. A thick-necked, pot-bellied man glanced up from his map covered desk. Even more maps hung from nails on the log walls. On a narrow table, a long row of ledger books lined one wall.

"Hello Miss, how may I help you today?" He extended his hand. "I'm Commissioner Simmons."

"Artis MacKay," she said as she shook his outstretched hand.

"Are you here to file a land claim?"

"Nay, I have a deed I want to register."

"I see. How did you come by this deed?" he asked.

"My former employer gave it to me at the end of my indenture—my freedom dues. He urged me to see ye just as soon as I arrived."

"I see," Simmons said again. "Please have a seat. May I see your deed?"

Artis sat and then reached down and pulled the deed from inside her stocking. She handed the wrinkled document to Simmons who examined it for some time. As she anxiously watched him, she pressed her lips shut so no sound would burst out.

"I remember this parcel. No one has ever lived on this land, but Mister Roberts of Virginia is the owner of record. This deed appears to bear his signature. Just let me be sure it matches the signature I have on record."

Artis held her breath, praying this would go smoothly. Roberts did not seem to be the kind of man who would cheat her and she hoped that her instincts were right.

Simmons stood and pulled one of the ledgers off the table and moved it to his desk. After an agonizingly long minute, he located the correct page and compared the two documents. "Everything seems to be in order, Miss MacKay. Welcome to Kentucky. You are now a landowner."

A small cry of relief broke from her lips.

Commissioner Simmons peeked up and smiled kindly.

As she realized she was in fact a landowner, a warm feeling flowed through her. She finally had a home of her own again. After Steller's flames consumed her mother and her home, and the Countess shipped her away, the painful awareness of her losses never left her, even for a day. It felt as though her life had been first trounced upon and then stolen away completely. Her work at the plantation had only camouflaged the deep despair and extreme loneliness she felt. But now, a layer of that despair lifted for the first time.

"And the size of my parcel? Is it fifty acres as promised?"

"Indeed, it is. Would you like me to show you where it is?"

"Aye, I would."

Simmons stood and motioned her over to one of the maps nailed to the wall. "Your property is located north and west of Boonesborough but a short ways—my estimation is that it is about a twenty minute ride by horse at a canter."

Artis studied the map, noting the location of the trail that led northwest. "We are here, and the road is there," she said, pointing with her finger.

"That's correct. Your place is just past a half-circle bend in the road. See it there?"

"Aye."

"It starts here and goes all the way to where this creek runs."

"Mister Roberts said it had good water. Is that stream the source of water?"

"Yes it is. Although you will probably want to have a cistern built to hold rainwater for you during dry spells."

"Aye. That sounds wise."

"Your property is located a few miles closer to Boonesborough than Sheriff Wyllie's place—Whispering Hills." He sat down again, made several notes in the ledger and the deed, and then handed the deed back to her. "Here you go. I believe all is in order now."

"I met the sheriff on my way to yer office. He offered to help me locate a horse."

"Oh, there's no need to bother the sheriff. He's a busy man. I can help you with that."

"Ye can?"

"Just down the street a little further, a horse trader has a sizeable livery stable. His name is James Burdette. He's a short fellow with a big honest heart and a good reputation. Tell him I sent you and you'll get a fair price."

"My thanks to ye Commissioner Simmons. Ye have been most helpful."

"I would advise you to also purchase a weapon if your funds will permit you to do so. These woods are fairly tame now that Sheriff Wyllie has strictly enforced the law for the last two years and put law breakers behind bars. But occasionally we get a dishonest fellow or two passing through. And, of course, you'll see your share of wolves and such. A weapon is a necessity here."

"And where would the best place to purchase a weapon be and what should I expect to pay for one?

Simmons gave Artis the information she needed and she stood to leave, astonished at the sense of fulfillment she felt.

"I wish you happiness in Boonesborough Miss MacKay."

Happiness. The same thing both her dear old Uncle Donald and Morgan Roberts had said she would find. She hoped they were all correct. It had been an exceedingly long time since she'd known what happiness felt like.

"Of course you'll stay with us while you're in Boonesborough," William said. "You can bunk with Kelly's father. We built him a nice cozy cabin next to ours. It has two beds. I made one extra-long to accommodate you when you visit."

"My thanks, little brother," Bear said. "How is Mister McGuffin?"

"He's ornery at times, but still sober, and an immense help. I feel much better with him there to help guard Kelly and the baby when I'm away."

"Aye. That has to be a great comfort to ye."

"It is. Did you bring appropriate attire for the Governor's ball?"

"Nay, I need to find me some. Unless ye think these buckskins will do after a good cleanin'."

"We need to get you to the tailor right away. The ball is in three days. He'll need time to get something made for you. Kelly ordered her gown a week ago and I'll need to pick it up while we're there."

"Nay, ye said that Miss MacKay may come by."

"Yes, I said, she might. Bear, we can't sit here all day waiting for her."

Bear crossed his arms in front of him and gave William a slight smile of defiance. He wasn't going anywhere.

Deputy Mitchell strode in and greeted Bear.

"Tis good to see ye again, deputy. Are ye keeping the sheriff in line?"

"Only Mrs. Wyllie can do that!" Mitchell said, grinning.

"Deputy, will you stay here and if a young lady named Miss MacKay should happen to come by, make her wait and you come and get us. We'll be at the tailor's shop," William said. "And then the barber's."

"But…" Bear started.

"No buts. You're going. For a man with such an eagle eye, I would think you would notice that you're starting to look as shaggy as a real bear. I won't have a brother of mine meeting the Governor, and his wife, looking like he just stepped out of the woods after a year."

"Actually, almost two years. But there's na sense in havin' ye keep blatherin' on about it, I'll go." Reluctantly, he stood. William was right. If he was going to favorably impress Miss MacKay or any other young woman he happened to meet, he definitely needed some sprucing up.

The two slowly made their way to the tailor as many of the townspeople stopped the two to greet them warmly. In the few months that Bear had lived in Boonesborough, before moving with Sam and Catherine to Cumberland Falls, he and his brothers had developed a reputation for bravery and gallantry, making them all favorites of the town's inhabitants. Even the tailor seemed glad to see him.

"Bear! *Hé! L'ami!*"

Bear returned the greeting. "Hello, my friend."

"You're looking well. How is Sam? Is he still wearing buckskins too? And dear Catherine, Kentucky's most beautiful woman?" the Frenchman asked. "I hope you're here to let me make you presentable." The man rattled on, in his heavy French accent, not giving Bear time to answer any of his questions.

"I think a dark green fabric would complement your red hair coloring, *mon ami*. Take a look at this."

Bear began examining the fine fabric but the tailor pulled it away and said, "Yes, that is the perfect color for you. The only question is do I have enough fabric for a man of your amazing stature?"

Bear peered over at William, who just rolled his eyes. His brother, leaning against the wall with his arms crossed, seemed to be overly enjoying Bear's discomfort.

Then William stepped forward and joined in. "Monsieur Beaulieu."

"*Oui?*"

"Can you make a cravat big enough for Bear's neck?"

"*Oui, Monsieur!*"

"I think he needs one made from some of your finest French lace." William held up a frilly bolt of something Bear didn't recognize and then his brother eyed Beaulieu. "Agree?"

"*Oh oui!* I will make it just so."

The Frenchman seemed far too delighted at the idea and Bear could tell William was just getting started.

"The cravat should have several rows of lace to frame his ugly face," William added, amusement flickering in his eyes.

"*Oh contraire, Monsieur*. Bear's face is most magnificent!"

This was getting entirely out of hand. "Ye will make it out of plain white cloth," Bear said firmly. "And only one wrap around the neck and one knot." He gave William his best angry bear look.

Monsieur Beaulieu removed a tape measure hanging from his neck and wrapped it around Bear's waist. "Bear, *mon ami*, your waist is too trim for a man of your size."

"Not enough pie," Bear replied. "Sam's wife Catherine is na much of a cook. I guess because she always had cooks growin' up." He looked over at William. "I predict Sam will hire her a cook before he loses much more weight himself. Did I see a bakery on my way into town?"

"*Oui, Monsieur!* And it has excellent pies."

"While Monsieur Beaulieu is taking your measurements, I'll go check with the barber to be sure he's there and give him time to get his razor sharp. He'll need a keen edge on the blade to take off that beard," William said. "Come to think of it, he'll need to sharpen his scissors too. You have enough hair on that big head of yours for ten men."

Bear could only stare helplessly at the door as William exited.

Chapter 6

The horse trader named Burdette, bent over with a shovel in his hands, had his back to Artis. He scooped up a pile of manure and tossed it into a barrel as he cleaned out one of his stalls. Artis counted ten stalls in the livery and from the smell wafting through the air, it would be some time before he finished the unending chore. That particular task had not been much to her liking on the Robert's plantation, but she enjoyed being around the horses and often took them out for exercise after she'd finished her other duties.

She glanced around, giving the man time to notice her, while she looked over the stalled horses. Most of these likely belonged to someone in town. She would probably have to choose from the horses she saw standing in the large pen she'd passed. She'd spotted a bay mare there that appeared promising.

Burdette finally noticed her. "Oh, hello Miss. I did not see you come in. Welcome. Are you looking to buy or stable a mount today?"

The balding horse trader seemed friendly, smiling at her in an outgoing manner. His relaxed attitude seemed to be one of perpetual merriment. He was considerably shorter than she was and although a smaller middle-aged man, he looked as though he could handle himself when needed.

"Aye. I am in need of purchasin' a mount, Sir. Commissioner Simmons assured me that ye would sell me one at a fair price."

He set his shovel aside. "Indeed. And a woman of your beauty should have a beautiful horse." He turned up his smile a notch further.

Apparently, Burdette was capable of shoveling out more than manure.

Artis followed him outside.

"I'd recommend a mare for you. They are easier for a woman to handle. I have three for you to choose from—a dun, a spotted white, and a bay."

She didn't bother to tell Burdette that she'd exercised several stallions on the plantation, including Roberts' prized stud horse. But he was right, a mare would be easier to handle.

"Which one has a level head?" Artis asked.

"I'd say they all do," the man answered, "but the calmest is the bay."

"I'll na own a lazy horse."

"Oh she's far from lazy. I suspect she's one of the fastest mares in that pen. She's just a sweet gal. And a pretty one too, like you. She'll turn the stallions' heads." He laughed as if he'd sincerely amused himself.

She managed a little chuckle. "May I take a closer look?"

"I'll bring her out." Burdette grabbed a lead rope and approached the mare.

Artis watched the horse carefully to see if she accepted the rope easily and followed Burdette willingly.

"She's got nice hips and a full chest," he said, his eyes on Artis, as he led the mare forward.

Artis wondered if the man was talking about the horse or her.

"She also has excellent feet and sturdy legs. And she reins and stops well. Schooled by one of the area's best horse trainers. He showed me what he taught her before I bought her. Would you like me to show you?" Burdette offered.

Artis studied Burdette's eyes. He seemed to be telling the truth. "Nay, that won't be necessary. I can already tell she's well trained."

She lifted her hand to the mare's nose, letting the animal read her scent, then she gazed into the bay's large brown eyes. She saw kindness, and just as important, intelligence reflected back at her. A smart horse would be far easier to train and ride.

The bay's body color, a reddish brown, glowed in the sun's rays. And her black mane, tail, ear edges, and lower legs made the mare look showy. She ran her hand down the mare's neck and looked her over thoroughly. As she ran her hand across the mare's shoulder and chest, she could feel strength in the horse's muscles. "She seems young. How old is she?"

"Three or four."

Artis suspected that meant five or six, but the mare was still young at that age.

"How much?"

"Well, she's an exceptional beauty, but for an exceptionally beautiful young woman like you...."

Artis had put up with the man's blarney long enough. "I do na want to hear ye flatter me. Just give me that fair price I was promised and be done with it!" She would not be duped by claptrap smooth talk or be taken advantage of by this or any other man.

Burdette hastily named his price and Artis offered to meet his charge if he threw in a good saddle, bridle, and a small bag of oats. "All right, for a woman of your...."

Artis put her hands upon her hips and narrowed her eyes at him.

When he stopped himself and quickly grabbed a saddle, Artis was barely able to keep her amusement from showing on her face.

While Burdette got the mare saddled, Artis stepped back into the stable and reached between her breasts for the handkerchief tucked into her stays. The square of cloth held the coins she'd received from Roberts. The sight of the pink handkerchief would forever remind her of her mother—her mum truly was a beautiful woman, inside and out. She swallowed her grief. Perhaps because of the way her mum had died, Artis thought she would never be able to think about her mother without feeling an acute sense of loss. Especially since her mother's murderer probably became a wealthy sheep farmer by now living off the land he stole. When she thought about the despicable man—which occurred without fail every day, sometimes more than once—she was assailed by a terrible bitterness.

She counted out the amount she needed and carefully tucked the rest away again.

"What'll you name her?" Burdette asked.

"Beautiful."

Burdette threw back his head and a cackle of laughter burst out.

Artis brought her hand up to stifle her giggle.

Bear sat up, yanked the towel from around his neck, tossed it into his lap, and glared up at the skinny barber. "Och, man, yer takin' my neck off with the beard," he grumbled. "Can ye be a wee bit gentler?"

"I'm sorry, Sir, it's just that you have the thickest neck and beard I've ever had to shave. And reddest too, I might add."

"Well, do na send me to our Maker while yer at it!"

"Calm down, Bear. You'll make poor Mister Gerhardt nervous and a nervous barber with a well-honed blade is not a good mix," William said, giving Gerhardt a smile and a wink.

Bear sighed and leaned back again. He tried to make himself relax, but all he could think about was missing the chance to meet a bonnie Scottish lass. What if she left town? He'd never see her again! For some reason, the thought left him feeling an uneasy sense of losing something important. But how could he lose someone he'd never even met?

William insisted on the shave occurring today because he said the skin underneath would be milkywhite and would need a few days to get some color before the Governor's ball. He also suspected William didn't want to be seen walking around town with a scruffy brother who looked like a barbarian.

Since Bear couldn't talk, William took the opportunity to tell him all about the issues the delegates would be discussing starting tomorrow morning. With the occasional comments added by the barber, he heard more than he ever wanted to know about prison reforms, public education, militia restructurings, business subsidies, and legislation favorable to the state's landowners. By the time the barber finished with the shave and the hair wash and cut that followed, Bear had a good understanding of what matters he and the others would need to address.

He paid Gerhardt and gave him a generous tip to compensate for his outburst and the two left to return to William's office.

As soon as they entered the well-organized and surprisingly clean office, Bear asked, "Did Miss MacKay come by?"

"No, Mister MacKee, she did not," the deputy answered.

He turned to William. "Perhaps she's in trouble and needs our help."

"Bear, she was just going to the Land Office. How much trouble could she get in?"

"She should have been back by now!" Inexplicably, worry filled him. How could he be troubled about someone he'd not even met yet? Could she have met another man? Were they getting to know one another right now over an ale or a meal? A strange feeling he didn't recognize gripped him. Then he understood what it was—jealousy. How could he possibly be jealous?

Confused, he wandered about the room, head bent in thought. He found it disturbing that a woman he knew nothing about could affect him so.

"Would you feel better if we went and looked for her?" William asked, setting down the papers he'd been looking over.

Bear glanced up, surprised at how relieved he was at the suggestion. "Aye, I think that is a fine idea."

The two walked out of the Fort and onto the street and swiftly headed toward the Commissioner's office. When they arrived, they found the door locked, but noticed Simmons walking away.

Bear hurried toward the commissioner as if it were a matter of some urgency and William rushed to keep up with him.

"She concluded her business with me. She mentioned needing a horse, perhaps that's where she is," Simmons told them. "I swear, she was the most beautiful woman who ever walked into my office." The commissioner let out a long sigh and walked away.

"Let's go see Burdette," William suggested.

They marched in unison to the livery and found Burdette feeding the stabled horses. Flies buzzed over several barrels of manure lined up outside.

After they exchanged greetings, William asked, "Did a young woman come by here earlier to buy a mount?"

"Yes, and what a beautiful woman she was. She didn't give me her name, but she spoke with a lovely Scottish accent. It was music in my ears."

"Did the lass buy a horse?" Bear asked.

"Yes, a fine bay mare. But she drove a hard bargain. Made me throw in a saddle, bridle, and feed. I didn't have the heart to tell her no. She was just so beautiful…"

"Enough of her beauty, Sir!" Bear snapped. The man was making him irritable again. "Now, where did she go?" He ripped out the words impatiently.

William gave him a reproachful look.

"I have no idea where she went," Burdette said, looking baffled by the questioning. "I only know she was beautiful. Oh, and she named her mare

49

Beautiful. Would be a fitting name, for her owner too," the man said wistfully as he ambled away.

Bear glared at William and scowled to keep himself from biting the horse trader's head off.

"The gun shop?" William suggested.

"Aye!" he agreed and took off, taking long strides.

But they had no luck there either. The shop owner said she had just left and seemed reluctant to say anymore.

The woman was as elusive as a ghost. A 'beautiful' ghost. As everyone kept telling him.

Chapter 7

A rtis had bargained with the owner of the gun shop until she got what she wanted—a fine flintlock pistol along with a shoulder bag that held her powder and lead.

Leaning a bit too close to her, he'd shown her the weapon's sights, and helped her load it. He said she would need to practice using the weapon and he could take her out back and give her some pointers. She politely declined.

Once she was ready to pay for her purchases, she'd turned around and reached into her stays again for her coins. When he implied that she could "work" for the price in a suggestive tone, she'd nearly used her new weapon on the shop owner.

She called him a few choice names in Gaelic and gave him a searing look, before tossing her coins on the counter, and leaving abruptly. She certainly didn't need his help or want his attentions. Her annoyance increased when she found that the encounter had made her hands shake.

Her purchases left little in the handkerchief that held her coins, but she decided to treat herself to a small meal before she set out to find her land. She found a shop that sold bread and cheese and bought a loaf, a little wedge of cheese, a hunk of ham, and an apple. After eating a bite or two, she rewrapped the food in the paper the store clerk gave her and tucked the apple, ham, and most of the loaf of bread into her linen bag and hung it from the horse's saddle. At least she would have some food for the next couple of days if she ate sparingly.

With an abundance of hope in her heart, she set off to find her new home.

The awe-inspiring woods were thick and full of dazzling fall colors that cheered Artis' soul. She recognized black walnut, cherry, maple and red and white oak trees, but didn't recognize the many varieties of wildflowers, ferns, and vines. She would make a point to learn their names later. She loved the beauty of even the most common plants. For those who have eyes to see, and the heart to feel, the forest could be a magical place. Here in the deep still silence of the wilderness, she could feel nature's beating heart just as clearly as her own.

Perhaps because of that very silence, she abruptly felt so alone. She recognized it for what it was—loneliness. A weakness she refused to acknowledge. She'd felt it before and knew it would pass. She would ignore it once again and focus on what she had to be thankful for.

Her heart swelled with the realization that she now owned land, a weapon, and a first-rate horse. It was a fine start to her new life. For the first time since her daydreaming days in Scotland, she wondered what else life had in store for her. The thought barely crossed her mind before another followed that surprised her. Would she meet someone here in Kentucky she could grow to love?

She was anxious to put all the pieces for a happy life together. For the last seven years in servitude, circumstances placed her own life on hold. But now, she suddenly understood that she wanted what her mother and father experienced together. True love. Someone who would cherish her as her father had cherished her mother. Somebody she could depend on as her parents had done for each other. A man who would do anything to protect her in a world that was often cruel—especially to women.

She realized she was setting a high standard—maybe impossibly high—but if she couldn't have a man like that, she would have none at all.

A nervous snort from her horse interrupted her musings. Beautiful had performed well so far, keeping up a steady and smooth canter, and Artis reached down to stroke the mare's moist neck with her palm. She promised herself that she would take excellent care of the horse. Just as she was marveling at how calm her new mount was, Beautiful raised her head and side-stepped. Artis knew this signaled something the mare didn't like and quickly glanced around, searching for the source of trouble.

A bloodcurdling scream, which sounded like a woman, vibrated and echoed through the dense trees.

Beautiful backed up a few steps and pranced nervously. Artis could barely keep the trembling mare under control.

What was it? She'd never heard anything like it in her life. She'd loaded her pistol before she left and feeling vulnerable and threatened, she drew it from her belt. But controlling the mare with one hand was proving challenging. "Whoa girl, whoa now."

Whatever it was out there screamed again. But this time it sounded closer. Artis' heart raced, it had to be an animal of some kind. But what? She'd heard that mountain lions roamed the dense forests of the wilderness and preyed on deer, elk, and sometimes the stock of farmers, particularly sheep, goats, and cattle.

Could that be what this was? *Oh God, please no.*

Should she turn the horse and race away? But she'd also heard from one of the settlers she'd traveled with that mountain lions can run faster than horses. It could spring on the mare's hips or bite her hocks, and Artis would likely take a terrible fall. Worse, the ferocious animal would kill Beautiful or her.

She could try to shoot it, but she'd probably miss, having never shot the weapon before. Nevertheless, she had to try. She located the sights and remembered what the store owner said about lining them up on her target. But where was the lion? She turned Beautiful around slowly in a tight circle and tried to listen for it. But she heard nothing. The cat must still be in a silent, hunting mode. Then she spotted it, crouched down in the brush,

53

staring at her. Was it preparing to attack?

The cat's intense yellow eyes glowed with what appeared to be contempt. It glared directly at her, chilling her to her core.

Her entire body tensed with fear and she could feel the mare quavering beneath her as well.

It was, indeed, a mountain lion. And based on its immense size, she guessed it to be an adult male. The cat's thick coat was a rich reddish brown color and the black mask that encircled its mouth made the animal look even more terrifying.

The lion stayed low to the ground in the gloomy shadows of the brush. Its large long body remained motionless except for an enormous tail that twitched ever so slightly. Then, without warning, it did something Artis found hard to believe. It leapt at least ten feet up and onto a tree branch just above her.

Beautiful reared, pitched her, and took off in the direction of town.

Artis landed on her bottom and quickly scrambled up. Terror threatened to stop her heart. She could barely breathe.

"Bloody hell," she swore. Now it was just her, completely alone, afoot here in the middle of the wilderness.

Facing death.

How could all she'd endured and worked for end like this? The thought raised her ire. Her heart refused to believe she was about to die. She couldn't let her life end like this.

She met the animal's eyes without flinching and took a defiant stance. "Leave me alone or I shall dispatch you to the devil forthwith," she yelled, trying her best to sound threatening.

The lion growled low in its chest, unimpressed by the challenge.

Artis had never heard anything so intimidating, but she refused to give in to her fear. She thought about throwing her ham at the animal to perhaps give him something else to eat besides her, but then realized the ham was in the bag still on Beautiful, racing toward town. Damn.

Her flintlock held only one shot and she would have but one chance to save herself when the cat attacked. Then she remembered her dirk and she unsheathed it with her left hand. The muscles in her arms hardened and she took a firm grip on both weapons.

"Come closer and I will cut off your ballocks and eat them for my dinner!"

The cat opened its mouth and snarled, as if laughing at her ridiculous threat.

She'd run out of ideas. There had to be something she could do. Aim. Aim carefully.

One shot. One chance.

Artis bit her lip, and took a deep steadying breath, fighting to keep her composure. But her terror mounted with frightening speed and she felt her hands begin to shake and her palms grow moist. Both would make it difficult to aim properly.

The mountain lion stared down at her. Something in its cold eyes told her it was ready to kill. The muscles of its massive body tensed.

Then it bared its teeth.

God, help me!

Bear rode beside his brother as they made their way along the trail to William and Kelly's cabin at Whispering Hills. He couldn't wait to see sweet Kelly and their young daughter.

The air felt cool on his newly shaved face and his haircut made the back of his neck feel exposed. He'd taken a bath in a stream on his way into Boonesborough, and the barber had splashed some smell good stuff on his face, so he felt tidier than he had in some time.

He was actually looking forward to trying on the new clothes he'd ordered. Perhaps they would make at least one woman take a second glance at him.

However, he was not looking forward to the rituals of courting. Patience was definitely not one of his virtues and he hoped he would have enough to keep him from scaring off a woman by appearing too eager or forward. But he was committed to the idea of finding a wife and he would see this thing through, come hell or the creek rising.

As if he had read his thoughts William said, "I know you're keen to find a wife, Bear, but you must give it time. The perfect woman comes along only once in a man's lifetime."

"By the Lord in heaven, I pray that *once* is verra soon," Bear said. "Ye know I have little patience for anything, much less courting."

"I do, and I understand that you're disappointed that Miss MacKay never showed up at my office," William said. "We'll be tied up for a couple of days at this meeting with the Governor, but after that we'll find her. Commissioner Simmons at the Land Office will know where she went."

"Och, she's probably betrothed to someone anyway. A woman of her beauty would be."

"Yes, you would think so. She appeared to be between twenty and twenty-five. Perhaps she's a widow."

"But ye said she introduced herself as Miss MacKay," Bear said looking over at his brother.

"You're right. Fear not, if you are meant to meet her, you will," William said.

They heard a running horse and both looked back to the road. A saddled bay raced toward them.

A piercing scream of terror followed by a loud roar and then a gunshot filled the air.

"You go. I'll catch the horse," William shouted.

Bear urged his horse to a full run. A moment or two later, he reached a woman fighting off a wounded mountain lion.

Using her pistol like a club, she clobbered the viciously snarling animal's head repeatedly. Blood dripped from the animal's shoulder, but the ball had not stopped the cat's attack. A long dirk lay on the ground beside her, perhaps knocked out of her hand when the cat struck.

Bear leapt from his horse, yanked his own dirk from its leather sheath, which hung over his sporran. He grabbed the cat by the skin on the back of its neck, heaved it away from the woman, and planted the blade in the animal's chest. It hissed and then died. Bear pulled the knife back and released the beast, letting it drop to the ground. It lay in a heap at the woman's feet, blood spilling from both of its wounds.

The woman just stood there, her chest heaving, her long hair hiding her face as she peered down at the dead animal.

When she glanced up, he set eyes on her face for the first time. He breathed in shallow, quick gasps, more from the sight of her than killing the beast.

The terrified lines on her face began to relax as she stared at him with big luminous green eyes.

She *was* beautiful. Just as the horse trader said. Breathtakingly so. Her waist-length hair, a mixture of reds and golds, reminded him of the color of fine whiskey. It hung loose and in disarray from her fight with the beast. Her still panting chest displayed curvaceous breasts. She wore a plain olive green gown, now torn in a few places by the cat's claws. A wide brown leather belt accentuated her small waist. A timeworn leather sheath hung from the belt. An armorer in Scotland must have made it, for interlocking Celtic knots—symbolizing eternity and something that cannot be undone—embellished the leather.

Was this Artis MacKay?

She stuck the pistol in her belt, picked up and sheathed the dirk, and then glanced up at William who just arrived astride his mount and leading

57

her frightened mare.

William tipped his tricorne at her. "Miss MacKay," he said, "may I introduce you to my brother Daniel MacKee. We all call him 'Bear,' for obvious reasons."

She turned her eyes back to Bear and opened her lovely mouth to say something, but stopped.

He decided he'd better speak up or he might be forever tongue-tied in her presence. He could see a few scratches on her arms, one fairly deep, but her fair face and body held no wounds. "I am most pleased to make yer acquaintance Miss MacKay. How do ye fare? I have some bandages in my saddle bag. Do ye want me to wrap that deep scratch?"

She glanced down at the scratch and took a closer look. "Nay, it just needs a good washing. Thank ye for yer timely assistance Mister MacKee."

"Ye are probably still shaken, but yer goin' to be fine. I assume that's yer horse William is leadin'?"

"She threw me and ran off when the lion came close."

"Horses are na too fond of mountain lions."

"I can na blame them," she said still somewhat breathless.

"Why don't ye mount yer horse and I'll load this mountain lion on mine. Camel is well used to the smell of all the animals I've hunted, includin' big cats like this."

"Why do ye want it?" she asked.

"So I can skin him and give you the hide," Bear answered, surprised that she didn't realize his intention. "These hides are quite valuable, and it is yers if ye want it."

"Aye, I would, it would likely make a nice blanket."

"Indeed, it will," he answered, and stooped to pick up the animal that weighed as much as some men.

She kept staring at him and Bear knew it was likely because of his unusual size. He'd seen the same reaction before from other people.

"Can my brother and I escort you to where you were going?" William asked.

"I would welcome ye, for a wee bit," she said and strode over to her horse. After deftly mounting the mare, she said, "I was on my way to see my land for the first time. From the directions I received from the Land Commissioner, it should be just ahead at the bend in the road."

"I've been wondering who that land belonged to. We'll be neighbors. My wife and I have a place called Whispering Hills, a few miles beyond yours," William said.

While the two spoke, Bear tied the mountain lion to the back of his saddle. "Steady Camel. This big boy is dead. He will na harm ye. Artis and I have seen to that."

He remounted and followed as William led them both to Miss MacKay's land.

Chapter 8

A rtis' heart was still racing. She had never come so close to death. And hoped she never would again.

And the sight of the immense Scot standing before her, after he'd killed the beast, had been nearly as frightening as the lion. He seemed as strong as an oak and almost as tall. And, as he'd slayed the cat in the blink of an eye, she could tell that his fierce face and swift actions revealed but a glimpse of the warrior within him.

His enormous body looked like a virtual armory. Besides the deadly dirk he'd wielded to kill the lion, he kept a smaller knife, called a *sgian dubh* by Scots, tucked into the top of his tall leather moccasins. Another knife hung from his neck in a beautifully beaded doeskin sheath. A hatchet, which appeared as though it might once have been an Indian's tomahawk, stuck out from his belt. Two flintlock pistols, pointing in opposite directions, protruded through leather sheaths. And a Kentucky long rifle hung from his saddle.

When she saw him for the first time, her initial emotion had been relief. But something else quickly followed as he'd intently peered at her. Although he'd acted a gentleman and his words were kind, his eyes had raked boldly over her. When other men did that to her, her only reaction was immediate anger and repulsion. She found their gawking degrading. But for some reason, with this man, she didn't seem to mind. He seemed to be admiring not demeaning her. Perhaps it was his voice that reminded her of her home or the humor reflected in his kind eyes, but she found his charismatic manner exciting. Whatever it was, she had to admit his compelling character intrigued her.

As they rode side by side behind William's horse, she decided she wanted to learn more about this rugged Scot. He was dressed in a buckskin hunting shirt and black leather breeches and looked ready to take on anything and everything.

"Mister MacKee," she said, tingling a little when she said his name, so similar to her own, "where in Scotland was yer boyhood home and how long have ye been in the colonies, if I may ask?"

A sudden sadness appeared on his face. "Please call me Bear, Miss. My parents and I sailed for the colonies right after the first clearance—the bastards took our land and forced us off it. My da and mum both died on the voyage and we buried them at sea." Bear gazed down and she saw him swallow his emotions before he continued. "I was but thirteen years old, although I was already as big as most men."

"What happened to ye?"

"New York was just too sizeable for a boy from the Highlands. I had my father's coins, and used some of it to travel to New Hampshire. I met William's kind parents, God rest their good souls, in church and soon they adopted me. They treated me like one of their own five sons. Durin' the winter, Mrs. Wyllie would insist that I stay with them, attend church, and receive schoolin' with her own boys. But the rest of the year, I wanted to be outdoors. I used the skills me grandfather taught me in the Highlands to become a hunter and rid the area of the threat of dangerous predators, especially bears and wolves."

"Where was yer family's land in the Highlands?" she asked.

He turned toward her. "Grumbeg, on the north side of Loch Naver."

Artis' heart ached within her breast at the mention of her beloved Loch. She could not stop her eyes from watering and she bowed her head as she remembered the clear dark blue water lapping against the Loch's scenic shores. She took a deep breath, looked up, and wiped her eyes.

"I'm sorry Miss MacKay, did I say somethin' amiss?" Bear asked gently.

"Nay, I was just rememberin' our homeland with fondness. Bear, we grew up within a few miles of each other. I'm from Achadh an Eas on the south side of Loch Naver."

His face lit up and a tiny glow cheered her too. To have found a fellow countryman here in Kentucky was not that unusual. Virginia and Kentucky were full of Scots because the blue mountains reminded them of home. But to meet one who spent his youth so close to her own home, she could only call a divine appointment. God must have arranged their meeting. There could be no other explanation.

And he had experienced the same tragic losses—his home and his parents taken from him. And, like her, she could tell it still pained him.

"I remember my father mentionin' that he sold some cattle to a man from Achadh," Bear said.

She smiled at that. "I wonder if it was my Da he sold them to. He owned quite a few Highland cattle. Did yer father raise red or black coated?"

"Black," Bear answered. "Because they were a wee bit harder for thieves to spot in the night."

"My Da's were black too!"

They both laughed and she felt wrapped in the warmth the man exuded.

"I hate to interrupt your reminiscing, but I believe we have arrived at your land, Miss MacKay," William said, tugging on his reins and pointing.

Artis' thoughts came back to where she was. She beheld her land for the first time. It was spectacular. A lovely place, with abundant hard woods and a gentle pasture that slopped upward from the road. And she could hear a creek babbling peacefully on the north line of her acreage. Bear and

William followed as she rode Beautiful a short ways into the property and gazed around her. All the magnificent trees were hers! Each shrub. Every blade of grass. Every single rock and piece of soil. Hers!

She savored the thought. For Artis, like most Scots, land signified life itself. As important as air to breathe or water to drink. Its necessity was absolute. For some, property simply signified power or wealth. But this land meant far more to her. It was her new home—a place where she might live and love with a family—a place for her weary heart to rest.

But it would take a lot to make it a home—for now it was just raw wilderness. She would need to find a job, save enough money to build a house, buy livestock and equipment, and plant a garden. She suddenly felt ill-equipped to undertake such an enormous task, particularly with winter approaching. But she would not let worries dampen her spirits. She had come a long way to get here and somehow, by God, she would make it all work.

"It's a charming place, Miss MacKay. You are fortunate to have it. Land around here is increasingly hard to come by. Were you planning to camp here for the evening?" William asked.

"Yes, I brought a blanket and I have a wee bit of food in my bag too," Artis said, "and I have a pistol, as you saw earlier, and my dirk." She couldn't help feeling proud that she'd actually managed to hit the immense cat, although the lead only managed to weaken and slow the animal's attack, not stop it.

"Och, ye canna stay here by yerself with na protection save a single shot flintlock and an old rusty dagger," Bear declared, shaking his head.

Artis narrowed her eyes at the big man. "Aye, I can, and I will, if I choose to!" she shot back. "And an old dirk it is—for it belonged first to my grandfather—but I carry it proudly."

"My pardons," Bear said quickly, "I meant na offense, so take none. I was just worried for yer safety."

"I thank ye for yer concern. But I have taken care of myself since I was fifteen—seven long years—so I've na need of a man tellin' me what I can and can na do."

"I did na tell ye what ye could do," Bear protested. "Just what ye should na do. That is if ye have any sense at all."

William just sat there watching them, smiling broadly. She gave him a reproachful sideways glance too.

"Bear tends to be on the protective side for all of us, Miss MacKay, not just you. Like a clan chief, he protects and cares for everyone in my family," William explained.

That made Artis feel better. Perhaps she'd over reacted.

"I guard them all like a mother would her babe," Bear said proudly.

"Well, I suppose I should be honored to have someone concerned for my safety. I'm just na used to it. Forgive me for lettin' me temper slip out."

"Since you don't have a shelter built yet, you are most welcome to join us at Whispering Hills for as long as you need," William offered.

"Nay, I do na want to make your home too crowded. You already have Bear to find room for."

"Bear will be staying with my wife's father, Mister McGuffin, in the cabin next door. In my cabin, we have an extra sleeping area in the loft upstairs. I'm certain my wife Kelly would relish the company of another woman for a while."

Artis thought about the attack by the mountain lion and the fact that the woods held numerous other dangers—wolves, bears, and snakes, among them. She quickly decided that she should take the sheriff up on his offer. "Aye, I would love to meet yer wife Kelly and to accept yer kind offer of hospitality."

She peered over at Bear who sat comfortably in his saddle. His smile was so wide she thought his lips might split. His ruggedly handsome face appeared clean shaven, and his dark red hair looked freshly washed and combed. Bushy dark brows framed his bluish green eyes. His strong jaw reflected his inner strength and suggested a stubborn streak. But his demeanor seemed kind.

"William and I will be occupied for two days at a meetin' of appointed delegates gatherin' in Boonesborough, but when we're through with our business, we can help ye build somethin' that will serve as a temporary shelter," Bear offered.

"Och, I would na want to keep the sheriff from his duties, but yer kind offer to help is appreciated, Sir. I imagine a man of your size and obvious strength can cut a tree down a wee bit faster than I." She let her eyes slide boldly over his body, and then felt her face flush when she realized what she'd done. She quickly reproached herself. She couldn't imagine what he might think of her brashness. What was wrong with her?

Bear only chuckled and looked a bit self-conscious. When he smiled warmly at her again, for a long moment she felt as if she were basking in the sun. Her embarrassment forgotten, she decided his nature was not only kind, it was also full of sunshine.

Her life had seen far too many gray clouds over the last seven years. It felt good to feel a little sunshine. But who would have thought it would come in the form of an enormous well-armed Scotsman in the middle of Kentucky?

Chapter 9

Wilmington, North Carolina, Fall 1799

Aconstant reminder of the country he'd lost, Patrick Steller heard the accent of Scotsmen or those speaking Gaelic almost everywhere he went. Today was no exception.

He recognized that he was responsible for a good many of them being here, so he averted his eyes and avoided looking directly at others as he walked. His mouth tight and frame of mind grim, most people would avoid him anyway.

As he brooded over what brought him to this point in his miserable life, he grew even more surly and ill-tempered.

At the direction of his former employer the Countess of Sutherland, he'd been efficient in clearing the villagers off her tens of thousands of acres—opening up the land for more profitable sheep farming. But, in the end, the woman thought his tactics too much.

The Countess had learned of his murder of Mary MacKay from Artis herself. Artis had wasted no time traveling the thirty miles to the Countess' residence, Tongue House, to report the murder and demand justice. He'd learned later that Artis covered the distance to the castle on foot and at night, to avoid being spotted by Patrick or his men.

When she arrived, she described her mother's slaying in gruesome detail and told the Countess of the death of her uncle as well. The devious girl tried her best to convince the Countess that Steller should be tried for murder. She'd also demanded that her family's land be returned to her forthwith.

The Countess refused to give her land back, ordered her carriage brought up, and told the driver to straightaway take Artis to the port. She also sent another man along with the driver and told them to be sure the girl caught a ship leaving soon for the colonies.

Glad to be rid of the haughty trouble maker, Steller had tossed Artis and her bag into the carriage himself and felt a sense of satisfaction as they took off. He'd kicked her dog when the animal growled at him. Then the dog took off chasing the carriage.

Steller angrily recalled the events that led him here. After she sent Artis away, the Countess ordered him to his quarters and questioned his men without him present. She soon verified Artis' story. Afraid of scandal amongst her circle of high-born friends, she didn't have him arrested, but that same week, she had banished him to the colonies. The ungrateful bitch. Trying to keep her hands clean, she had blamed him for the evil deeds done at her direction. She even had the audacity to say that if he didn't leave the country, she would have him tried for murder.

But it wasn't murder it was justice, Steller reasoned. Mary MacKay had poisoned Artis' mind against him. She thought her daughter too good for him. The widow should have wished for her daughter to marry someone like him; after all, people considered him handsome and he was a factor responsible for managing the entire enormous estate. But when the impertinent widow had refused to leave her home and shown such insolence, he had no choice but to kill the stubborn woman.

The Countess stripped him of his rank in the Sutherland household and summarily dismissed him. He'd been disgraced in front of his men and treated like a criminal. Instead of gratitude and reward for clearing her land of the primitive crofters, she gave him just enough money for passage on a ship leaving the next month.

67

On the dreadfully long voyage, and during his interminable indenture, he'd deliberately let his hair and beard grow long to hide his identity.

He also let his hatred for Artis grow. If she hadn't spurned him, he would never have killed her mother, and he would still be factor of Sutherland's estate. If only she'd done what he asked and agreed to marry him!

After seven years of indentured servitude, he was now free to walk about the city. As he strode by the town's docks, the buzz of activity amazed him. Dock workers hurried about loading cotton, tobacco, lumber, and other goods onto ships. Newly arrived slaves stood waiting to be auctioned to a gathering crowd of farmers and planters. Scottish merchants manned stores where they sold imported British goods. The city appeared far busier now than it did upon his arrival seven years ago.

But Patrick's mind was focused on finding only one of the many Scots in North Carolina—Artis MacKay.

Now that he was free of his demeaning indenture—serving as a butler for Robert Murray, a Wilmington official, merchant, and planter—he could, finally, find Artis.

Find her and make her pay for ruining his life.

First, he would defile her—ravishing her hard and repeatedly. Then he would kill her, slowly.

Fortunately, colonists kept excellent records and it was only a matter of time before he determined her whereabouts. His first order of business was to visit the main office of the firm that sold his own indenture. The same company had likely sold Artis too.

The clerk glanced up from his ledger as he walked in. "May I help you, Sir?" the polite young man asked.

"Indeed ye may," Steller replied. "I am lookin' for my wife—Artis MacKay. I believe she became an indentured servant upon her arrival here in Wilmington. I was forced to remain in Scotland for a while before I had the funds to join her here."

"Yes, many new arrivals from Scotland take that course. Usually, though, it's the husband who comes first."

"I rue the day her indenture separated us. I would like to learn where she went to serve out her contract. I hope to find her and be reunited at long last."

"Do you know when she arrived in North Carolina, Mister MacKay?"

"Aye. It was seven years ago—midyear. I miss her so." He did his best to make his voice sound sincere and woeful.

"In 1792 then?"

"Aye."

The clerk hauled a thick ledger from a dusty shelf and flipped through a few pages before he finally stopped. The man ran the tip of his ink-stained finger down a long column. Then he did the same on the next page, and the next.

Steller's stomach knotted as he awaited the information. He'd waited seven years for this moment, but now, each second made him grow more impatient. "Is she there or not, man?"

The young man's finger finally stopped, and Patrick let out a sigh of relief as the clerk read aloud. "Artis MacKay, female, age fifteen..."

"Bloody hell, I know she's female, where did she go?" he demanded.

The clerk frowned with silent indignation, but continued, "from Sutherland Estate, Scotland..."

Patrick slammed his fist down on the counter, making the clerk jump. "And I know she's from Scotland. Where the hell did she go man?"

"Indentured, August, 1792, at Argyll Colony, to Morgan Roberts, Roanoke, Virginia." He looked up, his expression one of pained tolerance.

Triumph flooded through him at the man's words. "Anythin' else?" he pressed.

"That is all the information I have."

"How far is it from here to Roanoke?"

"Close to 300 miles. Good luck to your wife," he said smoothly and closed the ledger with a thud, causing dust to fly into the clerk's pocked face.

Patrick didn't miss that the young man failed to wish him good luck. He wanted to reach out and throttle the bugger.

He turned abruptly and left, letting the door slam behind him. "Churlish fool," he muttered as he marched away.

After hastily buying a few supplies for his journey—a blanket, a pot, coffee, dried meat, a small tinderbox containing flint, fire steel, and tinder, and a few other necessities—he made his way to the livery. He had stabled and ordered feed for the horse he'd bought earlier that morning with part of his freedom dues. He'd also bought a saddle and he quickly saddled and loaded his supplies on the gelding. With a harsh jerk on the bridle, he turned the horse's head toward the road out of Wilmington, and gave a hard kick with his boot heels to the gelding's sides.

So, Artis was no longer in North Carolina. She was three hundred miles away in Virginia. At a steady canter, his mount could cover the distance in three or four days. He didn't care how hard he pushed the animal. He'd could always buy or steal another mount if he wore the gelding out.

When he got to Roanoke, he would find out where Morgan Roberts lived and question the man as to her whereabouts. And woes be to the man if he failed to cooperate.

His mouth curved into a smile at the thought of soon getting his hands, and his body, on Artis. He hoped she was still untouched. Taking her virginity was just one of the punishments she'd earned. As he rode, he savored malicious thought about how she would die.

Chapter 10

It took only a few minutes for Artis, Bear, and William to reach Whispering Hills, an enchanting spot on a rise that overlooked the higher hills rolling toward the distant horizon. The beginnings of a colorful sunset lit the sky with reds, corals, and golds—colors that matched the fall leaves on the endless trees covering the darkening hills.

As they rode up, Artis could hear a dog barking loudly inside the cabin. A moment later, she heard a door open and a tail-wagging large dog dashed out and ran toward William.

William stepped out of the saddle, and bent down to pet and rub the handsome blonde-furred dog. "This is Riley," he said, introducing the dog, "the fourth member of our family. Kelly treats him like a child."

"I had a dog in the Highlands that I loved greatly," Artis said, looking down at her feet, "but I was forced to leave him behind." She still pined for the huge black dog with white on his chest and front paws. He'd followed her to the Sutherland estate when she reported her mother's murder, but when Steller flung her in the Countess' carriage, he would not let her take her dog. The poor fellow had followed the carriage for miles until, exhausted, it finally gave up. Despite her desperate pleas, the carriage driver would not stop. Heartbroken yet again, she'd pounded on the carriage wall until her fist hurt, but still he refused to stop. "I'll always miss him."

"What was yer dog's name?" Bear asked.

"Wilson," she answered with a catch in her throat.

Riley hurried over to Bear's horse and eyed the mountain lion strapped behind Bear's saddle. A deep growl rolled from the dog's chest.

"Na need to worry Riley," Bear said, "Artis and I already killed him for ye."

While William unsaddled, wiped down, fed, and put the three horses up in a pen made of logs, Artis decided to watch Bear skin the cat in the dim light.

Before he started, he took a moment to admire the mountain lion. "Tis a handsome and powerful animal. I'm sorry we had to take its life." He gazed up at her. "But I'm immensely thankful I came along when I did."

"It did na look so handsome lecrin' at me from the tree limb above my head," Artis declared. "It looked more like a devil's minion, waitin' to rip the skin from my throat." She put her hand to her neck and shuddered.

"Tis the way of the wild. The big and mighty eat things smaller than themselves. And little animals eat what's even tinier than they."

After gutting it near the tree line, and firmly telling Riley not to touch the pile of innards, he hauled the animal back near where Artis stood. While she stood petting Riley, Bear cut and then tugged the hide off the back legs. Then, he used a rope to hoist the carcass by the skinned hind legs to eye level and hung it from a study tree limb. After making a few more cuts, he fisted the rest of the hide off. She was shocked at how quickly Bear was able to accomplish the skinning.

Artis heard the cry of a hawk above them and glanced up. The soaring hunter probably smelled the blood of the remains.

Bear held the heavy fur out for her to touch. She ran her fingers over it as the breeze rippled the thick hair. Never had she touched anything so soft. "Can ye carry it?" he asked.

"Aye."

He hiked toward what he called a smokehouse carrying the meat and she carried the beautiful fur. William headed to the creek at the bottom of the rise to bring back a bucket of water for Bear to wash in.

She followed Bear inside the smokehouse, intrigued by its unique fragrance—both sweet and charred—it smelled like blackened oak and burnt sugar.

"Is mountain lion enjoyable to eat?" she asked.

"Oh, aye, some think it the best meat there is," Bear answered. It took him several minutes to get the carcass hung from the ceiling with a chain.

William stepped inside the smokehouse with them. "It's been a long time since I've had any mountain lion," William said, "but from what I remember, it was quite good."

"How does your smokehouse work? They had smokeries in Scotland in the larger towns but they were used to smoke salmon," Artis asked.

"Aye, I remember," Bear said, "The smokeries gave the salmon a unique flavor. The Gauls called salmon *salmo*—meanin' leaper. Tis said that salmon hold mysterious knowledge because they are as ancient as time and know all the long forgotten past and the unknown future."

"Aye, tis also said that eating salmon can teach you how to get in touch with the knowledge of yer ancestors," Artis added.

"Well, here we use the smokehouse mainly to keep meat from going bad and to store it for the winter. We cure pork, but it can be used for other meat too," William explained. "We slaughter pigs after the first real cold norther, usually in December. Hog-killing day. After the animals are dressed and cleaned, they're cut up. We heat water to boiling in Kelly's washtub hung over a fire. The chunks are dropped in the boiling water to scald the hair off. Then, any hair that's left is scraped off. The meat is layered in a barrel with sugar cure salt and it sits for several days and then more salt is added and we wait a few more days. The salt pulls the moisture from the meat and the water drains out a hole in the bottom of the barrel."

"What happens next?" she asked, anxious to learn all she could about how settlers survived in the wilderness.

"After that step, we remove most of the salt and hang the meat from the smokehouse rafters so it will be safe from predators and vermin. We build a small fire here in the center of the smokehouse," he said, pointing to a fire pit in the center of the dirt floor, "and let the wood, usually oak or maple, turn to coals. We keep the coals burning and let it smolder for a couple of weeks. The smoke goes out that little hole in the center of the roof."

"How long will the meat last?" Artis asked.

"Dried, the smoke-flavored meat is long-lasting. It can remain in the smokehouse for as long as two years. It's so tasty, it never lasts that long though," William answered.

The three stepped out into the cool evening air again. At once, Bear sat the bucket of water on a stump and scrubbed his hands and the edges of his shirt sleeves. She could see he was a clean man. Many men, as she saw on the wagon train west, would have just wiped their hands on their pants.

"Your smokery is marvelous," Artis said. "But you won't leave the skin in there will you?" She didn't want it to smell like smoke.

"Nay," Bear said, I just hung it in there to keep other animals from draggin' it away tonight. We'll scrape and salt the skin soon to dry it out."

"Sam told me that the natives believe an arrow quiver made from a mountain lion's hide will protect the bearer," William said.

"Perhaps Artis would like it if I made her a fine cloak with it," Bear said, glancing at her. "With winter comin', you'll need someone to keep ye warm *and* protected." He eyed her and the meaning of his gaze was obvious.

Bear's words shocked her, but left Artis feeling the oddest tingling in the pit of her stomach. What would it be like to have a man like Bear keep her warm? And the thought of him always being there to help protect her was certainly comforting.

"Bear! Didn't you mean something?" William asked pointedly. "Not someone?"

"Aye, of course, that is what I meant," he said, smiling. But he did not apologize for his slip of the tongue. Instead, he softly took her elbow and guided her toward the main house.

The impact on her body from his gentle grip shocked her. Her heart thudded for a few moments and her stomach felt like something tickled it from the inside.

In the darkness, they headed for the main house. The structure looked quite large and Artis could smell the welcoming fragrance of food cooking and a wood fire in the cabin's hearth. She was anxious to meet Kelly. It had been a long time since she'd enjoyed the companionship of another woman her age.

William opened the heavy plank door and ushered them inside. A beautiful young woman with straight hair the color of butter stood near the hearth stirring something in a pot. Her violet-blue eyes glanced up, and at the sight of William approaching, her face seemed to blossom like a new flower. Then she glanced behind William and spotted Bear.

"Bear!" Kelly cried and darted for him, leaving William looking foolish when he kissed nothing but air. "Oh, my Lord, it is so good to see you again my wee friend."

Artis chuckled inwardly at Kelly's affectionate greeting.

Kelly gave Bear a big hug and then asked, "And who is this beauty?"

"This is Miss Artis MacKay," Bear said, "yer new neighbor. She's from Scotland too." Bear set her bag against the far wall.

Kelly embraced her warmly. "Welcome Artis. Please, take a seat at the table. You must be worn-out from your trip here. It looks as if your journey was a rough one. How did you get those terrible scratches on your arms? They're fresh, did this just happen?" Kelly asked, sounding concerned. She held Artis' arm to inspect it

Before Artis could answer, Bear began relating the story, embellishing it only slightly when it came to the size of the beast. She was pleased when Bear said she'd courageously fought the animal off, first shooting it and then clubbing it silly, until he arrived to just finish it off.

"Dear God, it's a wonder you weren't killed. As long as I've lived here, almost two years now, I've never seen a mountain lion. But William has me well trained, and I always carry a pistol and sometimes my rifle too whenever I'm outdoors."

Kelly poured Artis some tea and added cream and sugar.

"Just the way I like it, thank ye," Artis said, and smiled at Kelly. "Who is this young lady?" Artis asked, pointing at the child playing on the floor.

"This is Nicole," William said, picking her up. Pride lit up his face.

"She's a year-and-a-half old," Kelly said. "And becoming a handful."

"She's so lovely," Artis said. She couldn't remember ever seeing a prettier little girl.

"Let me clean those scratches for you," Kelly said, retrieving a bowl, water, and a cloth. "Then I'll put some ointment on them. Tomorrow, I'd be more than glad to help you mend your gown."

Artis' felt drawn to Kelly. Her genuine warmth and concern was something she hadn't felt since her mother's death.

While Kelly cleaned her wounds, Bear went outside, retrieved a massive log, and then threw it in the hearth to warm the room. Then he turned to Kelly. "I hung the mountain lion meat in the smokehouse along with the skin. Perhaps yer father can get it salted tomorrow mornin'. Tomorrow evenin', I'll scape the hide and then we can dry it."

"Tomorrow evening? Where will you be all day tomorrow?" Kelly asked. "Are you going to the Governor's meeting?"

"Aye. William and I are both delegates," Bear answered.

"Judge Webb appointed William," Kelly said. "Did Colonel Logan appoint you?"

"Aye."

"Logan made a wise choice," William said.

Artis could sense the camaraderie and love between the three and wondered if the rest of their family was equally close. "You mentioned you had two other brothers," Artis said. "Where do they live?"

Bear and William glanced at each other and Artis recognized a hint of grief in their eyes. But neither one offered an explanation.

Kelly spoke up. "Actually, they have three brothers. Two here in Kentucky and one in New Hampshire. He chose not to make the journey to Kentucky."

"Aye, Sam, the oldest, lives south of Fort Logan, as does Stephen and his family," Bear said. "Sam is married to Catherine, and Stephen to Jane. For two years, I've been helping first Stephen and Jane, and then Sam and Catherine build fine big homes. We started with Stephen's house first because Jane was about to have a bairn. And she delivered a whopping lad before we even finished. His name is Samuel."

"It must be nice to have a large family," Artis said. "I was an only child."

"Artis, how did you come to be in Kentucky?" Kelly asked.

At the question, Artis stared silently at the flames in the hearth. The fire triggered recollections of her home burning. She couldn't help tightening her fists and biting her lip.

"Perhaps you're too tired to tell us now," Kelly said quickly. "We should enjoy our dinner before it gets cold. William will you go fetch Papa?"

After William left, Artis stood and helped Kelly set the table for their dinner, while Bear played with his niece outside on the porch. The tantalizing aromas from the food made Artis' mouth water. "Ye must be a good cook, the food smells wonderful."

"I do hope you enjoy it."

Artis reached into her bag and pulled out the ham. "Here, let me add this to the meal. We need to eat it before it turns bad. I also have some bread and an apple."

"It may have been the smell of the ham that drew the mountain lion to you."

"I'll never carry meat on my horse again!" Artis swore.

"We'll put the ham into the beans I made, but keep the bread and apple. You may need it later. Will you be going to the ball that the Governor's wife is hosting?"

"I knew nothin' of it."

"You must come. I would love to have your company. I don't know many of the ladies in Boonesborough."

Artis realized a ball would require elegant attire. "I do na have anythin' suitable to wear."

Kelly looked her over. "You're about my size, but a little smaller in the waist. Having a baby added a few inches to mine. I have an exquisite gown that would be perfect! Catherine bought it for me to wear to Sam and Catherine's wedding and it's a bit too tight on me now. Since you are taller than me, we will need to add a row or two of lace or ribbon to the bottom…"

"But…"

"And I have a lovely roll of ribbon and maybe enough lace," Kelly continued without pausing. "Or we can go to town and buy what you might like to add length."

"But…"

"Please, it would mean a lot to me. I can't wear it anymore anyway and you would look so lovely in it. I already ordered a new gown for me."

Artis could see the earnestness of her request and the thought of a party did hold appeal. She couldn't remember the last one she'd been to. "All right. If it pleases ye, it pleases me."

Kelly squealed with delight.

Bear came back inside carrying Nicole in his muscular arms. The grinning child's hands pressed against Bear's cheeks, making his lips pucker. "She's goin' to learn how to say 'Uncle' while I'm here," Bear declared.

"Un," Nicole murmured.

"That's a fine start," Artis told the child. "How long will ye be here, Bear?"

"I have na home—yet. And na obligations. So, I do na know the answer to yer question just now."

William and Kelly's father entered. Nicole squealed with glee at the sight of her grandfather.

After William introduced the middle-aged but robust man to Artis, Mister McGuffin stole Nicole out of Bear's arms. Artis could tell that the two would take turns spoiling the darling blonde-haired child.

Kelly fed Nicole and after showering her with affectionate kisses, she laid her in a crib tucked into the corner by her parents' bed. Artis could hear the child happily cooing to herself before drifting off to sleep.

While Bear told Mister McGuffin the story, even more embellished this time, of the mountain lion attack, Artis helped Kelly serve dinner. They ate amidst a lively conversation between the men about the topics to be discussed at the meeting.

Artis found every topic interesting and asked a number of questions that Bear patiently answered for her. Then something occurred to her. "Are women permitted to attend the meetin'?"

Bear raised his brows and looked to William, who just shrugged his shoulders. They both seemed surprised by her question.

"Wouldn't you rather stay here with Kelly?" William asked.

"I would enjoy her company, but I think I would also find the meetin' interestin' to observe. I'd like to learn more about Kentucky and how it's governed."

"Why don't we both go?" Kelly suggested. "I can leave Nicole with her Grandpapa. Would that be all right, Papa?"

"Well, I guess," he said, with a jolly grin, "I can force myself to take on the task." Everyone chuckled. "While she takes a nap, I'll quickly salt the cat's carcass. I can get the skin stretched and salted here on the porch so I can hear her when she wakes up."

"It's settled then," William said. "I suggest we all retire for the night so we can get an early start. The town will be crowded with visitors coming from all over Kentucky."

Artis was already excited about attending the meeting. She'd always enjoyed learning new things.

"I'll show you upstairs," Kelly told Artis. "Just let me grab sheets and a blanket from my trunk. I have a small pillow you can use too."

"Before ye retire, give me yer dirk and I'll sharpen it for ye tonight," Bear volunteered.

She handed him the blade. "My thanks, Sir."

After Kelly got the bedding and gave it to Artis, Kelly climbed the stairs leading to the loft and Artis followed. With one arm, Kelly carried a bowl with a pitcher of water in it. A towel hung from her other arm, which also carried a lit candle. Artis clutched her bag and the bedding.

Before Artis ascended completely, she glanced back at Bear to find him watching her, holding her dirk in his hands. They exchanged a brief smile. But it was the look in his eyes that caused her pulse to quicken as she took the final steps to where she would sleep. Or at least try to sleep. She was exhausted and ready to collapse, her body weak from the day. But today had been so exciting—finding her land and meeting new friends—she thought she might be awake for a week.

She was surprised to see how large the room was—the same size as the lower floor, but with a pitched roof above that made the room cozy. They made a pallet against the log wall.

"I'll put your bowl to wash in over here," she said, setting it against the opposite wall. And there's a clean chamber pot. Be careful not to hit your head when you rise in the morning. That ceiling is close."

"Thank you, Kelly, for your warm welcome. You've made me feel at home for the first time in a long time."

"You are home Artis. Kentucky is your new home. Goodnight then," Kelly said before leaving.

Artis removed her clothing, leaving only her shift to sleep in, and washed up. Drained, she decided to forego her usual Bible reading and blew out the candle. She laid her head against the little pillow and breathed in the clean scent of the pine logs. The one deep scratch burned and she could feel nicks and abrasions on her other arm. She also ached from her fall from the horse and fighting off the mountain lion. She would definitely have sizable bruises by tomorrow. But it could have been so much worse.

Remembering her terror, she gave thanks to God for letting her live. And for sending Bear. *A mountain lion's no match for a Bear*, she thought smiling.

She closed her eyes, and was not surprised when the first image that popped into her head was his handsome face.

Chapter 11

E arly the next morning, to the sound of Kelly's rooster crowing and hens cackling, Bear assisted William with harnessing two horses to the wagon. The women soon joined them and William helped Kelly onto the driver's seat beside him as Bear lent a hand to Artis who climbed into the back of the farm wagon, carrying a tartan shawl. His mother had worn a similar blue and green plaid shawl and it caused a tug at his heart. He still missed the dear woman.

As he took Artis' hand, something surged through him that he didn't quite recognize. It wasn't just desire—it was far more than that. It felt as though her touch triggered an awakening within him. Something dormant that was now fully alive.

If just the touch of her hand were enough to do that, what would a kiss do to him? He intended to find out.

He hopped in behind her. His weight caused the wagon to wobble a bit and he took her hand again, this time to steady her. He spread a blanket out for her to sit on and she settled in.

As William took off for town, they all waved goodbye to Nicole, held in Mister McGuffin's arms.

Bear could see how much McGuffin cherished Nicole just by the look on the man's face. "Sir, load yer weapons," he yelled to McGuffin, as they pulled away. "And keep a careful watch."

McGuffin waved and nodded his understanding to Bear.

Artis' long locks hung behind her back, neatly clasped by a silver hair ornament decorated with Celtic knots. She wore another gown today, this one equally as simple as the one she wore the day before, but dark blue instead of green. Her simple gowns did not detract from her attractiveness—if anything they revealed more of her alluring figure. But Bear couldn't help but wonder what Artis would look like in some of the gowns he'd seen on Catherine. Sam's wife was a keen follower of the latest fashions and she regularly ordered gowns shipped to her from a Boston dressmaker.

Artis shivered a bit and reached for her tartan shawl, about three yards in length. She donned the garment, letting it fall gracefully around her.

Bear took notice when she pinned the shawl closed with a brooch, embellished with their clan motto. He hadn't seen the symbol of their clan for almost two decades. He recognized it right away and it brought back both memories and pride. He cherished the MacKay clan name—a proud name—a gift from his ancestors. He vowed he would keep the name highly regarded as a gift to his descendants. Perhaps he would start spelling it the traditional way—MacKay—instead of MacKee. The spelling had gotten changed somehow after the voyage to the colonies.

For propriety's sake, he sat across from her, even though what he wanted to do was swing her into the circle of his arms, and have her sit next him. Or perhaps on his lap. The delightful thought made him smile at her.

He'd spent a restless night lying awake wondering what it would feel like to hold her against him. When he did finally sleep, he *was* holding her in his extremely pleasant dreams.

He sat his rifle down beside him and bent his long legs at the knees to fit the width of the wagon, being sure not to touch her. The last thing he wanted to do was scare her off or offend her.

83

"How are the scratches on yer arms this mornin'? Better?" he asked.

"Aye, Kelly's ointment has already started them toward healin'," she said. "They'll be just fine in a couple of days."

"Did ye sleep well in the loft?" he asked, trying his best to make polite conversation.

"Indeed. I was so exhausted, I fell asleep directly and slept quite well."

He noted her eyes dart down as though she wasn't being completely truthful. Perhaps she'd spent a restless night too. He almost hoped she had and that the reason was the same as his.

For a while, they just sat in comfortable silence behind William and Kelly listening to the two chatter, but only able to catch a few of their words here and there, with the noise of the wagon and horses.

But sitting this close to Artis was proving a challenge. Her beauty was overwhelming. When she nervously moistened her dry lips, a tremor heated his groin. He was dismayed at the magnitude of his desire. He hardly knew the woman. Yet he already felt a tangible bond between them.

His heart seemed to beat faster with each turn of the wagon wheels. By the time they reached town, it would be racing. Clearly he was physically attracted to her—more so than he could ever remember being with a woman. But he knew virtually nothing about her, save for the fact that she was raised in the Highlands. He needed to get to know her better.

"Artis, what made ye leave Scotland?" he asked, trying to keep his voice gentle and soothing, remembering how she'd reacted to Kelly's question the night before.

Anger flashed in her eyes. An inner fire hardened her exquisite features, followed by raw hurt. Her mouth tightened, but she said naught. She lowered her head and studied her calloused rough-skinned hands.

Where had she worked so hard that her hands would appear as hardened as a man's?

"Sometimes talkin' about a pain will lessen its ache," he said. He

84

quirked an eyebrow at her questioningly, trying to get her to open up to him.

She peered up at him, her face full of remoteness, and then her eyes seemed to see something horrific. He could almost see her troubled spirit fighting to control her emotions.

"Were ye forced to leave by the clearances too?" he asked. "I heard that they have gone on for some time."

"Aye, durin' *Bliadhna nan Caorach*, 'the year of the sheep'."

"I've heard others call it that. What happened to your parents?"

"Da died of a fever the year before the clearance. The Sutherland estate factor killed my mother right in front of me." She paused to regain control of her emotions.

"Och, lass, I'm so sorry. What was the bastard's name?"

"Steller." She hissed the name. "I know he murdered her because I would not accept his attentions. If I'd been more agreeable to him, she might still be alive."

He heard guilt in her tear-smothered voice.

"Not only did he kill her, he and his henchmen set fire to our home, our village, and many other townships along the Strath. My dear aged Uncle was caught in his blazin' home. Some of the men plucked him from the fire, but he died shortly afterward."

"How long ago was this tragedy?"

"Seven years."

"Oh, Artis. I'm sorry for all yer sufferin'. Tis clear it still pains yer heart even though it's been some time."

Her anguish evident on her face, she said, "It will always pain me. Because I have done naught to appease my anger. If I could, I would go back to Scotland and kill him. That would ease my pain. *An Diabhal air na Sutharlanaich*."

After damning the Sutherlands, she crossed her arms in front of her, and stared off into the forest. Her blazing eyes filled with moisture, and hate.

"And I would go and do it for ye—if it were the right thing to do. But it is na."

"Aye, it is."

"Artis, ye and I are descendants of a race of whom we have abundant cause to be proud. We are not murderers. But this Steller is. And, *'...there is nothin' covered that shall not be revealed, neither hid, that shall not be known.'* When the time is right, Steller will pay for all the evil he committed. I promise you."

"But he stole my home and land and the land of many others. Our beloved Highlands will become a howlin' solitary wilderness, from which our pride and love are fled forever!"

"Aye, he and others like him did steal our land. And the passionate notes of the bag-pipes will be replaced by the bleatin' of sheep. But we did na lose what is most important. We carry the pride of our ancestors and our love for Scotland with us in our hearts. It is na left back in the Highlands. The Almighty sent us both here for a reason. It's yer duty to learn what that reason is."

"He certainly put me on a cruel path to get here."

Bear was glad Artis opened up to him but wanted to know more. "Where have ye been for the last seven years?"

"When I arrived, I was forced into indentured servitude."

"Did ye work on a farm or in a household?"

"On a large plantation in Virginia, near Roanoke. I worked in the fields and in the stables. At the end of my contract, the planter I worked for gave me a deed to land located here as my freedom dues."

Coincidentally, they were passing by Artis' land at just that moment. "Tis a grand place," Bear said, gazing around at her magnificent trees and lush grass covered land, brushed by the brilliant rays of the morning light.

"It is beautiful," she replied reverently. "Someday I hope it will be a happy home too."

"Fear not, it will come to pass. God is never deaf to the desires of your heart."

Reaching out, he took her hand in his and kissed the top of it. He could see her uneven breathing in the rise and fall of her chest as he gently caressed the top of her hand with his thumb until her eyes no longer held heartache. Until they filled with life, warmth, and unspoken desire.

After a moment, he asked, "Artis, do ye think ye could let yer land truly be yer *freedom* dues? Can ye let the beauty ye see before ye heal the bleeding wounds of yer past?"

Artis stared at him, her mouth hanging open, her eyes glittering and thoughtful.

Could Artis let her land release her from her tragic past? Would she claim the happiness she deserved? "Let the future free ye of yer sorrow and release yer life to happiness," he urged.

Her face showed some indefinable emotion. A few tears slipped down her pink cheeks. She quickly swiped them away.

"Weep na more, my lady," Bear said. "Today, yer life starts anew."

Chapter 12

Roberts Plantation, Roanoke, Virginia

Steller felt every one of the three hundred miles he'd traveled in the muscles of his aching back—now as hard as solid rock—as he turned his weary horse onto the road leading to the plantation's main house.

A wide green expanse welcomed visitors to the sprawling farm. He passed a fine-looking black stallion nibbling on verdant grass. He decided it must be the stud for what looked like blooded mares grazing with the big horse in the fenced pasture.

He decided he'd switch his horse for the stallion on his way out. He still had a little sweet feed left and he'd use that to coax the beautiful horse close enough to slip a bridle over his head.

In the distance, he saw rich river-bottom land and hilly pastures. He also noticed that the plantation supported a large-scale tobacco and corn crop.

As he neared the two-story main house, painted white and trimmed with black shutters, he could see dense woods directly to the rear of the enormous home. A handful of outbuildings stood some distance from the house. Two of them appeared to be simple frame buildings that perhaps housed servants and slaves. The board buildings were no doubt icy cold in the winter and blistering hot in the summer.

Was that where Artis had lived for the last seven years? He hoped so. Residing with the African slaves and other servants was all Artis deserved after all. At least he had been given private quarters in a fine mansion, even if his bedroom was in the home's attic.

He took the stairs leading up to the porch two at a time and knocked. A dark-skinned male servant answered the door and, after Steller asked to speak to Mister Roberts, ushered him inside. The servant told him to wait and proceeded down the hall, on the right side of the carved staircase, to a set of double doors with brass handles. The servant disappeared inside.

So that was where Roberts was. If the plantation owner refused to see him, at least now he knew where to find him.

After a moment, a short man, with a belly that threatened the strength of his silk vest's buttonholes, strode up. "I'm Morgan Roberts. How may I be of service to you, Sir?"

"My name is Patrick Steller. And I am lookin' for my wife. I was told she was indentured to ye seven years ago. I am hopin' she is still here."

"I don't remember having a servant by the name of Steller," Roberts said, wrinkling his forehead.

"Perhaps you knew her by her maiden name—Artis MacKay."

"Yes, indeed. Artis was a faithful and cooperative servant here until recently."

"Where did she go?" Steller asked, a little too anxiously and forcibly than he wanted to sound.

"Before I tell you, I must have proof that you are indeed her husband. Do you have your marriage license?"

"Nay, it was lost on my voyage here," Steller lied. "I assure ye, we are indeed married. But on the day of our weddin', the Highland clearances caused us to become separated. Wealthy landowners sent both of us to the colonies, but on different ships. I just finished servin' my indenture in

89

Wilmington."

Roberts peered deeply into his eyes. Steller tried to keep his expression calm and nonthreatening.

"Come into my office," the planter finally said.

He followed the man, down the carpeted hall and into a magnificent room. He could tell that the portly fellow was a pampered child of fortune.

Roberts sat down behind his ornate desk, looking as if he needed the piece of furniture for protection. When Roberts hauled out a pistol and laid it upon his desk, he realized he'd seriously underestimated the man.

"I don't know who you are or what you want with Miss MacKay, but I will not give you the location of her whereabouts without proof of your relationship to the woman. I suggest you go find that proof and bring it back to me."

Steller glanced around the room. It contained an impressive library of perhaps a thousand volumes. A portrait of a distinguished looking man, probably a Roberts ancestor, hung above the brick fireplace. This farmer was wealthy and a gentleman. He was used to people following his orders without question and he expected Steller to just leave without pursuing the matter further.

He would soon learn otherwise.

"Ye have an extraordinary library, Sir," Steller said. "Ye must be a well-educated man. And I can see that ye keep careful records, judgin' from the numerous ledgers on the shelves behind ye. I'm certain one of those account books contain yer slave and servant records. Would ye be so kind as to show me Artis' signature. Then I will know for a certainty that the Artis MacKay who worked for ye is indeed my dear wife."

Steller wouldn't recognize Artis' signature. He'd never even seen it. But if he could get Roberts to open the correct ledger, he was certain he could find out where she went.

Roberts hesitated a moment, and then stood. Instead of grabbing a ledger from the shelf behind him, he picked up his pistol. "I must ask you to leave now, Sir. You have over stayed your welcome."

"I think not," Steller said. He picked up a hefty brass candle stand, holding a burning candle, from the left side of the desk. "What would a fire do to this fine library? What would the flames do to your family in the rooms above? Do you have young children? Or perhaps an elderly parent?"

"You can't be serious!"

Steller moved closer to a stack of papers. "Do ye really want to risk shootin' me? These papers will make excellent kindlin' as will this fine wool rug beneath my feet." He picked up the matching brass candle holder on the other side of desk, its candle also burning brightly. "I assure you I am serious—*deadly* serious."

He held one of the candle holders closer to the papers. I few drops of hot wax dripped off the candle and onto the papers.

"Please no, I beg you not to."

Roberts sounded contrite now and the hand that held the pistol was shaking slightly. The wealthy man sat the weapon down again and frowned in exasperation. "What do you want with her?"

Steller sat one of the candle holders down, went around the desk, and slapped Roberts, hard. So hard, he could feel the burn in his own hand. "That, Sir, is none of yer business."

The force of the blow caused the man to bend over on his side. He slowly raised up, holding his hand against his cheek. "You, Sir, are nothing but a thug," he growled.

"Tell me where she went, you bastard, or I'll change your home to smolderin' cinders. Believe me, I have some experience with that." He put a thin mirthless smile on his lips.

Recognition and then shock shown in the man's eyes and sweat popped out on his shiny forehead. The farmer's round face became grim. "You're the one who murdered Artis' mother, aren't you?"

"It was na murder. The stubborn old witch refused to leave her home. I had na choice."

"There is always a choice."

"Then choose to tell me where Artis is, or ye will watch yer home, and all within it, burn to the ground."

Chapter 13

T he noisy conversations grew quiet as Governor Garrard marched in. The sizable room at the fort was Boonesborough's largest meeting place, and the same one that would be used for the ball, Kelly had explained. A flag hung in one corner that Artis assumed was Kentucky's new flag. In the other corner, the flag of the United States bearing fifteen stars and fifteen strips added festive color to the otherwise unadorned room.

Over the last half-hour, dozens of delegates and a few observers including Artis and Kelly, the only ladies there, stuffed the room chock-full. They both quickly took seats on a long bench next to a side wall. Bear and William sat next to each other in the center of the room.

From the way he walked and held himself with authority, Artis suspected the thick-necked and rather rotund Governor was a strong leader. He swiftly called the meeting to order and another gentleman with spectacles took a seat beside the Governor. She presumed the man would record the proceedings.

"Good morning gentlemen, and, ladies," he said, looking over at Artis and Kelly and giving them a nod and smile. "I want to thank all the delegates for agreeing to assist me today and tomorrow. My goal is to prepare a list for the legislature of priorities for Kentucky's future with the help of your valuable guidance."

The men in the room all clapped their approval.

"Shall we begin then? I encourage you to speak freely, but I ask one thing of you. We have no time for prideful posturing here. Do not offer an opinion unless you have some expertise and a strong feeling on the subject—or we will all be here till Christmas."

After a few chuckles and a hearty laugh from William, Garrard continued. First, he asked their opinion of penal reforms. Garrard advocated for the abolition of the death penalty except for crimes of murder.

William spoke up, supported the Governor's proposal, and added that assaults on women and children should also carry extremely harsh penalties.

"Thank you, sheriff," Garrard said. "Duly noted, and I agree with you wholeheartedly. We will introduce a bill to ensure that becomes the law of our land."

Beside her, Artis could sense Kelly stiffen as she heard William's words. It made her wonder if the reason William seemed so adamant about protecting women was that something had happened to Kelly.

When the Governor introduced the next topic—reforming and expanding the militia—another gentleman stood to speak.

"That's Colonel Byrd. He's in charge of the militia here in Boonesborough," Kelly whispered.

The Colonel offered at least a half dozen suggestions and urged that the number of militia in each of the Forts be doubled because tensions with Britain and the French remained high.

Next, the delegates discussed a proposed law to deal with the surveying and registering of land claims with the registrar of the state land office. "Our goal is to forestall additional lawsuits, which are already numerous, related to land claims," explained the Governor.

After hearing that discussion, Artis was even more pleased that she had a clear title to her land. But she was beginning to tire of sitting on the hard bench, until the Governor mentioned one that raised her interest. She noted that Bear sat up straighter and lifted his jaw as he listened closely to the Governor too.

"I want to introduce legislation that will forbid the unjust removal of squatters from land they have lived on for more than three months," Garrard said.

Several men called out their scoffs and nays, but Garrard refused to be browbeaten.

"As you all know, land claims here in Kentucky are a source of confusion and conflict. Many settlers unknowingly become squatters or are labeled squatters when they are not. Dishonest landowners let these so-called squatters remain on the land just to take advantage of the improvements these people make. Fairness demands that if the squatters have made substantial improvements to the land they should not be forcibly removed. Powerful landowners are running too many people from their homes, sometimes even at the start of winter, *after* they have invested back breaking labor and their resources into improving said land. I have no quarrel with property owners wanting to protect acreage they have legal claim to, but the landowner should take action without delay or no later than three months of the squatter's arrival. After three months, I believe they should file a petition with the court and prove just cause for removal. And, landowners should pay for any improvements made to their land."

Many of the men in the room appeared to be wealthy landowners themselves. Everyone started to talk at once and, as far as Artis could tell, the topic appeared doomed, buried in confusion and controversy.

Bear stood, standing tall and straight, like a towering pine. The entire room seem to take note of his size at the same time. The very way he stood there spoke of his commanding air of self-confidence. Before he said a word, he looked directly at Artis and smiled. His compelling eyes and handsome features caused a flush to race up her neck and face that she hoped would go unnoticed.

Bear's expression stilled and grew serious. He turned back to face the Governor, his face filled with inherent strength and pride.

"Fellow delegates, my name is Daniel MacKee, and I represent Fort Logan and the St. Elspeth's settlement. I rise today to address this topic because..." He paused to look at her again. "...it is dear to my heart."

Artis felt a flutter in her own heart.

As Bear spoke, his voice deep and his lilt melodious, every man turned their ears his way. "The forced removal from one's land is one for which both I, and Miss Artis MacKay, newly arrived from Virginia, both have some knowledge." He inclined his head toward Artis and everyone peered at her, including Kelly.

Now her face felt like she had a fever. She locked her eyes on Bear and he looked back with both eagerness and tenderness. She felt her pulse quicken and she held her breath.

Bear turned his gaze back to the men in the room and continued. "Some of you have undoubtedly heard of the infamous Highland clearances—a dark page in the long and proud history of Scotland. A wealthy landowner from the glen my family had occupied for many generations expelled my own parents from their land when I was but thirteen because raising sheep became more profitable than crofters. Had I been just a wee bit older, I would have sheared the man top to bottom like one of his bleatin' sheep."

The entire room erupted in laughter, breaking the tension Bear's words had fostered. Bear waited for the room to quiet.

"But I wasn't," he continued, "and along with my parents, and so many others driven from their land, we boarded a ship and sailed for the colonies. Unfortunately, my parents did not survive the voyage." He placed a hand on William's shoulder. "Sheriff Wyllie's parents later adopted me. But my story is an easy one, compared to Miss MacKay's."

Again, all eyes turned toward her. She was tempted to threaten Bear with the fate all men most dread. She did not want to be the center of everyone's attention. She had just come today to learn more about

Kentucky. Was he about to tell everyone here her story? Surely not.

"I will na tell ye the details of how Artis came to be in Boonesborough, as they were confided to me in confidence, but I will tell ye what I know to be the truth. Tens of thousands, maybe hundreds of thousands, of Scots, includin' Miss MacKay, are here in this country because of clearances. Although they were not squatters, they were crofters, on land held by chiefs, landowners and lairds. Like squatters, these crofters were unjustly forced from their homes after years, nay, generations of workin' to improve the land. Why? Because someone placed more value on profit than people. Because someone chose to exploit the situation.

"From what the Governor described, it seems that is exactly what is happenin' here in Kentucky.

"Land is a precious thing and those who are blessed to own it, have the right to protect it. And government should strive to help them protect it. But people are also precious and worthy of protection. Powerful landowners should fairly compensate people who have invested labor and resources into improvin' land they thought was theirs, through na fault of their own. Land titles are in a state of confusion, and fairness demands that we all work together to ensure justice and evenhandedness.

"Kentucky should offer *all* of us—rich and poor—a chance for a better future. Not a future handed to us on a silver platter. But a future for those willin' to work hard for it. We must na let what happened in Scotland—hardworkin' people defrauded and treated less than animals—happen in Kentucky!"

The room erupted with cheering and all but a few men stood and clapped enthusiastically.

Bear looked over in her direction.

When he did, she stood and joined the others in clapping for him, her chest swelling with pride.

&

Bear was oblivious to all the commotion in the room as the delegates decided to take a much needed break, since nearly all were already standing. As he and William made their way toward the two women, he could not take his eyes off Artis.

Tragedy had etched strength and dignity into her beautiful face, but now he perceived something else there too. He hoped his speech was to her liking. Perhaps she was impressed with the support he had inspired for the squatters' law.

When she smiled warmly at him, a breath of relief broke from his lungs. He'd been afraid that he offended her by using her name in a public proceeding. He should have checked with her first to be sure it would be all right. But he'd had no idea that the topic would be one the delegates would address today.

"Bear, you make an impressive statesman!" Kelly declared, when they reached the two women. "Perhaps you should think about running for office."

"Och lass, this will be my one and only attempt at statesmanship."

William took Kelly's arm and the four stepped outside into the fresh air and sunshine. Bear filled his lungs with air that smelled like the fall leaves scattered beneath their feet.

As the four of them strolled away from the others, Bear glanced down at Artis who hadn't said a word. But she carried herself with an air of dignity and confidence he had to admire. Artis was a woman who knew her own worth. He could tell she would have little tolerance those who didn't respect her.

What was she thinking? When he could no longer keep silent, he said, "Artis, I hope I did not offend ye with my mention of yer name and circumstance."

"Nay," she said at once. "Ye made me proud to be a Scot again. To hear your strong voice and impassioned thoughts stand out among such distinguished men was truly a pleasure to behold. Thank ye for sayin' what ye did."

Powerful relief filled him and his confidence spiraled upward.

"But I came close to threatenin' to geld ye!" she quickly added, with a wide grin and a hand on the hilt of her long dirk.

"And, fool that I am, I just sharpened the blade for ye," Bear replied.

William and Kelly both laughed and joined in teasing him.

As the four of them enjoyed ribbing and jesting each other, an indefinable feeling of rightness filled him.

Perhaps he belonged here with William and Kelly...and Artis.

Chapter 14

After breakfast the next day, Bear and Artis sat on the porch together drinking coffee and talking endlessly. The more they talked, the more he wanted to talk to her. Conversation between them came easily and they chatted about anything and everything and laughed often. The warmth of her laugh sent joy to his heart.

Already, Bear sensed a bond with Artis that he'd never felt with anyone else. They shared the same feelings about so many things—among them the need to be outdoors more than indoors; a love of horses; a strong faith; and a love of Scotland, particularly the Highlands and the way the music of the bagpipers stirred their deepest emotions.

Just looking at Artis while they talked stirred his emotions now. His instinctive response to her was potent and made a shiver of wanting fill him. He felt an easy affection coming from her too and sometimes he even saw a smoldering flame in her striking green eyes. And after he'd reached out for her hand and told her how beautiful she was, he caught a sensuous aura passing between them.

Could that attraction grow into love? In truth, for him it was already more than attraction. He felt as if he'd found his soulmate—the other half of his soul. Someone meant just for him. His pulse quickened at the realization. Then the thought that flashed through his mind startled him.

Kelly came out, interrupting their conversation and his thought. She said that Artis was tired from her journey and the two days spent in town and needed her rest. Despite both of their protests, Kelly shooed him away. The conspiratorial look in her eyes made him think there was something she was keeping from him, so he decided to do as Kelly suggested and went to find William.

His brother kept him busy the rest of the morning with chores, taking full advantage of having someone around with Bear's strength. But he was happy to lend William a hand.

He and William had a quick lunch with Mister McGuffin in his small cabin, and then he left for town, telling William he would meet them all later at the ball.

His new clothing was supposed to be ready by one o'clock, so he hurried to the tailor's shop to try the garments on in case they needed any final alterations.

"Mon ami, it is magnificent!" the tailor exclaimed after Bear had donned the new garments.

Bear wasn't sure he wanted to look 'magnificent' but as he admired the clothing in the mirror, he did think he now had the appearance of a proper gentleman for perhaps the first time in his life. He hoped Artis would like the new look. But what if she didn't? What if he she thought he looked like a dandy? He frowned at himself in the mirror.

After several minutes of encouragement from the tailor, he decided there was only one way to find out. He would wear the new clothing to the ball. He paid the tailor and told him he'd be back later to put the clothing back on after he went to the bath house and the barber again.

Next, he left his tall brown leather boots at the cobbler for new soles and a good polish. The cobbler assured him that in short order he could make them look like new. He preferred wearing moccasins for hunting, but boots were better for other chores and more formal dress.

Then he set out for Henderson & Co., the general store. His last task was the most important. If he could, he wanted to find a luckenbooth brooch. The heart-shaped pin was the traditional Scottish symbol of love and the emblem of commitment and union between a man and woman.

Tonight at the ball, he would ask Artis to marry him.

He realized he'd only met her four days ago, and that was counting today, but he was certain he could spend four years getting to know her, and he would not love her any more. Not only did he love her, he liked her—a lot. Their friendship had blossomed along with their love.

His heart told him Artis was the woman he'd been looking for. They were destined to meet and destined to be together. He'd set out on this quest, with the desire for a wife in his heart, just one week ago. And God wasted no time in answering. He wasn't jesting when He said, *'Ask and ye shall receive.'*

He had always been an excellent judge of character and Artis showed every indication that she was a person of virtue and goodness. As he rode over to the store, he mentally itemized her traits. His heart thumped a little quicker with each quality he listed. He arrived at the general store, even more convinced that she was the love of his life. A quiver of affection for her filled his chest as he reached for the store's door.

"Good day, Mister MacKee," the apron-wearing shop owner Daniel Breedhead called as he entered. "What can I help you with today?"

Bear had purchased several items from the man in the past and enjoyed visiting the teeming shop that smelled of cinnamon, coffee, leather, and a dozen other scents blending together in a way unique to this particular establishment.

Shelves, crammed full, held an enticing array of commodities and several glass cases contained Breedhead's most valuable items. Bear approached the cases. "Mister Breedhead, I have what may be an unusual request. I am lookin' for a luckenbooth brooch. Do ye happen to have one?"

"I do. And a lovely pin it is. There are so many Scots in Kentucky, I make it a point to always have one on hand or on order." Breedhead took it out of the glass case and handed it to Bear.

The gleaming silver brooch could only be described as stunning—the design consisted of a crown, symbolizing loyalty to the loved one, just as a Scot pledged fidelity to their king or queen. The crown rested above two intertwined hearts. The silversmith's work was skillfully done and several stones of blue and green added color. The stones would match the MacKay tartan of her shawl!

"It's perfect!" he told Breedhead.

"Who is the lucky lady?" the store owner asked.

Bear didn't want to mention a name until he'd asked Artis. News traveled fast in town. "She's the most beautiful woman in the world."

"No wonder you need a gift this exquisite," Breedhead said.

"Aye, she deserves this and more. And if she says yes, I intend to give it to her."

The door slammed open and banged against the wall. Breedhead and Bear both looked up.

Three men stomped their way into the store, pistols drawn, their manner threatening. The features of the balding man in front twisted with menace. The grimy faces of the other two appeared just as sinister.

Bear tossed the brooch down and reached for his pistols.

All three men raised their weapons and pointed them directly at Bear. He froze and held his hands steady, just above his flintlocks. He clenched his jaw and narrowed his eyes as he stared at the three, studying each one. He sensed an undercurrent of wildness and cruelty coming from all of them, but especially the balding man.

None of the men bothered to threaten Breedhead, who stood cowering nearby. "What do you want?" the shop owner asked, his voice shaking.

The robber who remained standing near the front door answered. "We want your currency, powder, lead, and whatever else you have of value,"

103

the man with greasy black hair said.

The one with a balding head came close to the display case Bear stood next to. "And we'll take everything in these two cases, including this pretty bauble," he said, picking up the luckenbooth Bear had just held, and examining it.

Bear felt his jaw tighten a little more. "I think not."

"You think not?" the third man said mockingly, inclining his curly-haired head toward Bear and moving closer. "Do you not see there are three of us?"

"Aye. And the three of you could drop your balls and let them hang, but even then ye will na take that brooch, or rob this store this day."

Breedhead reached over and placed a hand on Bear's arm. "Mister MacKee, that brooch is not worth losing your life, Sir. And neither is anything else I have. It's my loss and I'm willing to take it. If you gentlemen will just wait right here, I'll go get all the money I have in the store and a bag for the other items." Breedhead left for his back room.

Bear continued to keep his eyes trained on the three men, his hands hovering just above his pistols. He towered over the three thieves, but they all looked rough and well-seasoned to fighting. They'd probably been roaming Kentucky, settlement to settlement, robbing as they went, and who knows what else.

"What do you say we have a little fun and cut this one up a bit while the shopkeep is getting our money?" the bald one suggested to his cohorts. "Put your weapons on the floor, giant, including the one in your boot. We'll take your weapons too."

The other two drew huge skinning knives with their free hands and stepped a foot or two closer, their eyes gleaming with open hostility.

Bear glared at the men letting the venom of his wrath leak from his eyes.

The robbers instinctively stopped in their tracks.

He left his hands, and his weapons, where they were. "I'd advise ye three to leave now. Unless, of course, ye have a yen to die today."

"Is that your great big horse tied out front?" the balding man asked. "I could use a horse like that."

Bear didn't respond. He just narrowed his eyes at the man and waited.

The balding fellow shook his head and told the third man, "This giant's so dumb, he doesn't know if he's horseback or afoot." Then he picked up the pin and held it in front of Bear.

"Put the brooch down," Bear warned through clenched teeth.

"No," the man countered with a mocking smile on his face.

"I've given ye three brigands fair notice," he growled. "Leave or die. I will not let ye take that brooch, my weapons, or anythin' else from this store."

"So you like this pretty trinket do you big fella? Here Roger, take this for your lady friend. Maybe it'll get an ugly chap like you a willing instead of a forced frolic in the hay." The man tossed the pin across the room to the laughing dark-haired man.

As the brooch left the man's hand, Bear's right pistol flew out and powder exploded from the weapon's pan. The lead hit the balding man in the side of the head before his hand tossing the brooch fully dropped down.

Bear's left pistol followed the other instantly, killing the still chuckling dark-haired man before his outstretched hand could catch the luckenbooth.

The stunned third fellow fired his weapon just as Bear dropped to the floor and rolled. He came up with his hatchet drawn and planted it in the man's chest. "*Manu Forti*," he hissed into the man's face, "with a strong hand."

A gasp escaped the dying man and his eyes drained of life before he dropped to the floor.

Breedhead appeared at his storeroom door and eyes wide, gawked at Bear. He swallowed hard. "I didn't think you would still be standing. I heard the shots and was sure you would be dead."

"Nay," he said and began reloading his pistols.

"I'm glad I was out of harm's way, but I wish I'd been here to see that," Breedhead said, his voice unsteady. "How did you get them to leave? Did you fire three warning shots?"

"I sent them to hell," he replied. "Tis where the weasels belong."

The shop owner took a few steps forward and caught sight of the bodies bleeding into the wooden floor of his store. He took in a quick breath of utter astonishment. "My God!" he whispered, and held a shaking hand to his mouth. Breedhead stepped over the dead bodies as he made his way to the front door and turned the 'Open' sign to 'Closed' and then pulled the door's simple curtain together with his shaking hands.

"Mister Breedhead, help me haul these bodies out yer back door. There's na need to frighten the women and children on the street. We'd better slip an oil cloth under them or yer floor will be further stained with blood."

While Breedhead got the oil cloth, Bear reclaimed his hatchet and wiped it well on the dead man's breeches.

The two of them soon had the bodies laid out and covered behind the Henderson & Co. building. Bear scowled as he stared down at the three. The only thing he hated more than killing was dying.

"Go tend to moppin' yer floors before a customer arrives, and I'll fetch Deputy Mitchell. Sheriff Wyllie is at Whisperin' Hills just now and is not due to come into town until just before the ball."

"How will I ever repay you?" Breedhead asked, his pale forehead and upper lip covered with sweat.

"Could ye find that pin and save it for me until I get back? The bald man tossed it toward the dark-haired man by your front door."

"Of course, and there will be no need to pay for it. You saved me far more than the price of the brooch today."

"Nay, I'll pay for it. But ye can bestow what it costs upon the needy and elderly if ye like."

"Indeed, I will Mister MacKee. Indeed. And I'll polish the pin up and put it in a gift box for you. Do you want a ribbon on it?"

"Aye."

"What colors?"

"One green and one blue, if ye have them. I'll be back shortly," he said and turned toward the Fort.

Bear could not believe he'd just had to kill three thieves. This day was not going as he'd planned. Now he would have to spend at least an hour explaining to the deputy what happened and help the young man take care of the bodies. And his buckskin hunting shirt and leather breeches were a mess too. Splattered blood covered his clothing. He growled to himself as he walked.

But he cheered when he remembered he'd found the ideal gift for Artis when he proposed tonight.

A smile replaced his scowl.

Chapter 15

Bear heard snores even before he unlatched the door and stormed into William's office. "Deputy, wake up!" he roared.

The young man sat with his legs propped up on William's desk and his tricorne covering his face.

"Yer sleepin' on the job man, and the sheriff will na be too keen on that!" Bear knocked the deputy's feet off the desk and gave the fellow a severe scowl, but instantly regretted it. He often found it easier to stand up to his enemies than he did to his friends.

Mitchell's shoulders slumped. His slouching body proclaimed his embarrassment.

"Do na worry, I will na tell the sheriff. But don't ever let me, or William, catch you sleepin' on the job again. There's a world of bad men out there and ye must stay alert and watchful. In yer profession, ye must be vigilant and ready for anythin'. And trust na one except those whose hearts ye know well."

"I didn't expect any visitors," Mitchell stammered, his discomfiture still obvious.

"If yer na busy, then ye should use this time for self-betterment and education. It would na hurt ye to read a book man!"

"I do not own a book."

"Och, we will have to change that!"

"I thought all of you would be coming in later today for the ball."

"Well, I came ahead of time. The good news is that since I was here early, I prevented a robbery of Henderson & Co. The bad news is that ye have three bodies to take care of."

"You killed three men?" Mitchell asked, his eyes widening. "Not again!"

Bear sighed heavily, remembering what the deputy referred to. Shortly after their arrival in Boonesborough, he and Sam had to deal with a bunch of unruly murdering buffalo hunters. The battle cost his family, and the buffalo hunters, dearly.

"Aye, again." He filled Mitchell in on the details of the shooting and suggested that he go search the bodies for identification and then go find the undertaker, and have the man bring his wagon to haul away the bodies. Bear promised to meet the deputy at the store in a few minutes. "I'll go see if I can find Lucky McGintey. Maybe he'll know who those three scoundrels are."

"That's a good idea. Lucky knows everybody in the state I think."

"Any idea where I might find him?"

"This time of day he's usually back from hunting and relaxing at the Bear Trap Tavern."

After using William's wash basin to clean up a bit, Bear stepped out into the bright sunshine, made his way through the fort's gates, and then headed for the tavern. He wished he were going there to get an ale, not to find Lucky. He could use a pint and maybe a wee drop of whiskey too. Maybe he'd have time before the ball for a nip or two to ease the tension he felt in his shoulders. It was never easy to kill men, even those who asked for death.

A woman operated Lucky's favorite alehouse. Christiana Campbell was the proprietress and ran the attached eatery as well. He'd heard she planned to add a distillery to the back of the place. It would not be the first in Kentucky. Years earlier, Elijah Craig, a Baptist minister, opened a distillery in Georgetown. The distillery's name—Heaven's Hill—had always amused Bear.

He made his way through town, amazed at the number of women he witnessed busily earning a living. He caught sight of women working in virtually every trade, including one woman who worked at the blacksmith's as a nailer of horseshoes. Several other tradeswomen were helping to construct a building. But most worked in less physically demanding jobs such as milliners, seamstresses, shoe and boot repairers, dyers, weavers, spinners, candle creators, basket makers, and bakers.

Except for the few gentry, who made their living with their minds instead of their hands, the men of the town made their livelihood as cabinet makers, brick producers, founders, blacksmiths, silver and gold smiths, shoe makers, tailors, printers, gunsmiths, and wheelwrights. Others made livings as craftsmen and housewrights, who built and repaired houses and buildings. Bear would need to find a skilled housewright to help build a home for Artis and him. That is, if she accepted his proposal.

He spotted Lucky in his usual spot by the tavern's hearth. The seasoned and aging longhunter, who traveled great distances for game, had once been a companion of Daniel Boone. After their arrival in Boonesborough, the crusty old fellow quickly became a good friend to Bear and his brothers.

He hoped Lucky would have some knowledge of where the robbers came from. If they were wanted for crimes in other towns, sheriffs and militias would want to know that the three were dead so they wouldn't waste time looking for them. Lucky knew more about the Fort and Kentucky than anyone in Boonesborough did.

As always, the hunter's well-worn Kentucky long rifle leaned on the table next to him. The rifle and Lucky's skill at shooting it had once saved Bear and Little John's father during a surprise attack by a party of renegade natives.

"Bear!" Lucky exclaimed, and stood. The many wrinkles on the hunter's weathered face turned upward with his welcoming smile. "You're a pleasant sight for my old eyes my friend."

Bear shook the man's hand warmly and patted him on the back as gently as he could. Forgetting his own strength, he had been known to accidentally knock a man or two down when his greetings were too enthusiastic.

"What brings you to Boonesborough?" Lucky asked, as he sat down.

"I've been at the Governor's delegates' meetin' the last two days, at the request of Colonel Logan. Believe me, I'm glad that's over with. I'm not cut from politicians' cloth."

Lucky sniggered for a bit. "I heard the bellows and debates there caused a rumble as loud as thunder to echo through the fort."

"Aye, it did get loud a few times."

"Are you goin' to get fancied up and go to the Governor's wife's ball too?" Lucky asked.

"Aye. Are ye?"

"I just might go to the party, if they'll take me as I am. I'm too old to change my look."

"I do na think yer too old to do anything ye set yer mind to. But if they give ye any trouble when ye arrive, have them come and get me."

"With your esteemed reputation, just asking that should be enough to get me a place at the Governor's table!" he cackled.

Bear smiled for a moment, but then his thoughts turned solemn when he remembered why he was there. "I must talk to ye about a serious matter. I need to get yer help with somethin'." He lowered his voice and leaned closer to Lucky. "Just a few minutes ago, I had to kill three weasels at Henderson & Co."

Lucky raised his thick gray eyebrows.

"They were about to rob the store and steal Camel. Breedhead was willin' to give them all he had and went to the back to retrieve his currency. I wouldn't lay down my weapons, as they demanded. They threatened to cut me, and I'm sure that would na have been the end of it. As soon as the opportunity presented itself, I dispatched them all to meet the devil."

"What'd they look like?"

"One had greasy dark hair parted down the middle, the second was baldin', and the third, well, he had hair as curly as lamb's wool. They were all ugly to the bone."

"I think I know who they are. Let's go have a look see."

Bear threw a coin on the table to pay for Lucky's drink.

"Thank you kindly," Lucky said.

"It's the least I could do since I pulled ye away from a nice brew."

They marched rapidly over to the back of the general store and Lucky drew back the oil cloth and took a look at the three men.

The one that Bear had shot in the head was more difficult to look at, but Lucky seemed to recognize him too. "They're the three of the no goods who've been robbing all over Kentucky. The long hunters and militia have all been rattling on about it. I've heard descriptions of these thieves from several men. I'd say good riddance, Bear."

The deputy, who had been standing nearby, said, "I found this in one of their pockets."

Bear took the handbill from the deputy. "It's a proclamation from Governor Garrard offerin' a reward for capturin' or killin' four thieves. It describes these three men and one more. It says they stole gold from the state's treasury."

"That thief must have kept it as a keepsake," the deputy said, pointing to the one whose pocket had held the handbill.

"You'll be entitled to the reward, Bear," Lucky said.

"I did it to defend a friend's store and to keep from gettin' killed myself." He didn't mention being unwilling to let the robbers take Artis' brooch. But that reason was the flint and steel that lit his anger. "I'm not interested in any reward. I'm na damn thief-taker makin' a livin' by roundin' up criminals," he said.

"You didn't round them up," the deputy pointed out. "I'd say you rounded them down." He pointed to the three bodies sprawled out before him and shook his head decisively, causing his hair to fall in his eyes.

Lucky chuckled. "I'd have to agree with the young fella. These three are ready to go six feet under in an eternity box."

"I'll go see the undertaker and take care of arranging that. Then I'll start writing up the report so Sheriff Wyllie won't have to when he gets into town," Mitchell said eagerly.

Bear nodded. "Thank ye deputy. Yer doin' a fine job in my brother's absence."

"Wait till the sheriff hears about this," the young man said as he marched away.

"Lucky, this handbill describes four thieves. That means there's one more still out there somewhere."

"Well, there's any number of explanations. The fourth man could have been killed in one of their robberies. He could have decided to take off on his own. Or, he could be hold up somewhere protecting the gold they stole from the treasury."

"What makes the most sense to ye?" Bear asked.

"No way to tell. We just have to wait and see what your brother thinks."

Bear decided Lucky was right. There was naught he could do about the fourth man now. He'd wait until tomorrow to discuss it with William. There was no sense spoiling the evening for all of them.

He looked up at the sky, still free of clouds except for a few on the horizon. It was mid-afternoon judging by the position of the sun. He had time to go back to the tavern before he got his shave and bath and then changed into his new clothes and polished boots.

"Can I buy ye another ale?" he asked Lucky.

"Indeed," Lucky said. "And then I'll buy you a whiskey. I think you've earned it."

"Wait," he said, and turned toward the store's back door. "I need to show ye somethin' and I need to buy a book or two for the deputy."

Chapter 16

He studied his reflection in the mirror. "Och man, are ye sure I do na look like a big green peacock?"

"Oh oui!" Monsieur Beaulieu said.

But Bear wasn't convinced. The cut and the quality of the fabric were excellent, but he knew nothing of current fashions. He was glad Sam wasn't here to see him like this. His oldest brother would be laughing his head off. Like him, Sam dressed for the wilderness and was more comfortable wearing buckskins and moccasins than anything else.

William, however, had always enjoyed wearing fine clothing. Both William and the tailor had insisted that well-tailored trousers tucked into tall leather boots had replaced breeches. And when combined with a fine linen shirt, cravat, and a coat—cut-away in the front and long tails draping in the back—Bear would be wearing the latest fashion.

He sighed, afraid that if he took the garments off, he would offend the tailor. He put the matter aside with sudden good humor. "Ah well, there's naught to be done but to go make a fool of myself in front of everyone. I appreciate yer help, Monsieur."

Bear tucked the luckenbooth's gift box into his vest pocket and left his other garments with the tailor's wife for a thorough cleaning. With his heart beating unusually fast, and a tingle of excitement in his stomach, he headed for the ball.

The fort's enclosure was teeming with horses and carriages and a huge campfire blazed in the center to provide light. He could hear violin music playing, the elegant notes gliding through the cool evening air. As he approached, the sound of many voices mixed together with the joviality of a party.

His excitement grew even stronger. He hadn't been to a party, other than weddings, since he and his brothers were boys. He hoped he would know how to act. He decided he would just follow William's lead. His likeable brother seemed to have a natural affinity for social settings.

He wondered if William, Kelly, and Artis had arrived.

He stepped into the room and was shocked at the transformation. The Governor's wife and the town's ladies managed to transform the rustic meeting room into a festive and elegant ballroom. The flickering lights of candelabras danced in every corner. Cloths with fancy stitching covered the tables. Garlands of ribboned pine draped the log walls. Couples wearing the most elegant attire he'd ever seen stood everywhere holding glasses of fine beverages. Most of the men were dressed much like him. It made him glad he'd worn his new clothes after all.

He looked everywhere for William, Kelly, and Artis and disappointment filled him when he realized they had not yet arrived. He decided to speak to the Governor about the three thieves. He filled Garrard in on the details and the Governor was so relieved he insisted that Bear take the generous offered reward and promised to have the funds delivered to him within the week. He reluctantly accepted saying he would put the funds to good use. Building a fine new home for Artis, after all she'd lost, would certainly be a good use.

Bear's stomach growled as he smelled the aroma of the feast prepared for the guests. He decided to excuse himself to survey the refreshment tables. A long food table bore an assortment of fresh meats, including beef, goose, ham and turkey and a seemingly endless number of vegetable dishes. They all appeared extremely appealing. But when he caught sight of the dessert table, his stomach growled loud enough to turn the heads of two women. Loaded with mincemeat, apple, and peach pies, little cakes, gingerbread, and brandied peaches, the tantalizing display made his eyes widen.

In addition to a rum punch, the beverage table offered wines, brandy, and whiskey. A servant, who presumably worked for the Governor's wife, offered him his choice.

"I'll just have a wee bit of whiskey," Bear answered. He took the beverage, swallowed it in one gulp, and sat the cup down.

He glanced around the room again, still not spotting Artis, but he did notice Lucky sitting in a corner, leaning on his rifle, watching the people move about the room.

He asked for another cup of whiskey and then strolled over to Lucky. "I brought ye a wee bit of *uisge beatha*."

"The water of life."

"Aye."

"Where's your brother and his wife? I'm anxious to meet this woman who has clearly stolen your heart."

Bear shrugged. "I do na know. But I wish they would arrive soon."

As if a higher power granted his wish, at just that moment Artis followed Kelly through the door. At least he thought it was Artis. She seemed so different he did a double take, and then lost his breath for a moment. Her locks, woven into rows of glowing reddish-gold curls, hung down her slender back in a long cascade. Wisps of hair, loosened on their wagon ride here, framed her face.

She was dressed in a spectacular gold gown that revealed her neck and shoulders. The gown looked familiar to him. It must have been Kelly's. Her tartan shawl draped gracefully across her arms and lower back, and was pinned with her clan brooch. But the fabric could not hide her slim, seductive body. She appeared tall and graceful as she strolled in, her cheeks pinker than normal and her eyes sparkling. The corners of her mouth turned upward as she smiled and nodded to the admiring onlookers she passed.

He just stood there, unable to make his feet move, paralyzed by her beauty.

Lucky raised up from his chair and peered in the direction Bear was staring. "I'd bet my good ole gun that she's the one you've been talking about all afternoon."

"Aye...that's Artis," he murmured.

"Well, don't just stand there like a frozen deer. Let's go greet the pretty thing."

With some difficulty, Bear managed to make his legs work and he and Lucky made their way over to the three.

Artis stared at him with wonder in her eyes.

He was certain he was doing the same thing to her.

"I must say, you do clean up well," William said to him. His brother sat the fiddle he was carrying down on a nearby chair.

A flash of humor crossed Artis' face. "I have to agree with yer brother," she said, "you look quite dapper and dashin' in yer new clothing."

"I agree," Kelly said. "William, why don't you introduce Lucky McGintey to Artis?"

William made the introductions and then suggested that the three of them go find the beverage table, leaving Bear to visit with Artis.

Bear realized he had yet to say anything, but could not seem to find his tongue. He also could not keep from staring at her. In the dim candlelit room, she looked almost unreal, a dreamlike vision. But his imagination could never have created a woman so beautiful.

His reaction to her seemed to amuse her. "Bear, ye look like ye've seen a ghost."

"A verra lovely ghost," he said, letting his r's roll on his tongue. He'd finally made his mouth work.

"Thank ye very kindly, Sir."

"Can I get ye somethin' to drink?"

"Maybe in a while. Can we sit down somewhere?"

Bear spotted two chairs in the far corner by the sparkling candles. Perfect. He took her elbow and guided her over to the seats.

She gazed up at the soft lights of the candles. "Do ye remember the Mirrie Dancers?"

"The northern lights. Aye, they often lit up night sky in the Highlands with their magical dancin' lights. I miss seein' them."

"There are many things about Scotland I miss," Artis said wistfully, looking down at her feet.

"Do na look down at yer feet, my lady. Here we look up at the stars."

She eyed him with an intense but secret expression.

"We do na have to leave all our traditions behind, Artis. In fact …"

He heard the violin player brush his bow across the strings of his instrument, filling the room with music again. He stopped to listen for a moment. The violinist seemed to play the sound of his emotions, from hope and expectation to need and desire. Sometimes the violin whispered like the wind and then it would get higher and higher until it nearly screamed, and then it would whisper softly yet again. The melody's romantic notes gave him the courage he needed.

He reached for her hand. "Artis, one of our traditions is the luckenbooth. Do ye remember?"

"Aye, the symbol of the union of two people."

"And I have one for ye." He pulled the little gift box from his vest and handed it to her.

Artis gasped and put one hand over her mouth. She kept her eyes on his and didn't look down at the box.

"I love ye, Artis."

She flushed, but remained silent.

"I love ye, and want ye to marry me."

"Bear, ye have only known me but four days now. Can ye be sure it is love ye feel?"

"I know I love ye because we are two halves of one soul. For the first time in my life, my spirit feels whole. My heart na longer feels hollow. It's full—full of my love for ye." He eyed her with a probing squint. "Can ye be sure it is *not* love ye feel?"

He watched her expression change from surprise to desire. "Aye, I'm sure."

His heart trembled. "Sure of what?"

"That I want to marry ye." She spoke in a tremulous whisper.

His face could not contain the width of his grin. She had just made him the happiest man in the room. Nay, the happiest man in Kentucky.

"May I kiss ye?" he asked.

"Aye. Kiss me now and forever."

And he did, enfolding her in his arms for the first time.

Chapter 17

B ear's kiss sent gusts of ecstasy and desire whirling through Artis. But his proposal brought more joy to her wounded heart than she ever thought possible. The magnificent man who held her in his arms wanted to marry her! In a moment of loneliness, she had dared to hope for love only once—when she'd longed for what her parents had together. But she truly didn't expect to find it. And certainly not marriage. In fact, she presumed that she would never find the kind of man that would measure up to her high standards.

Mentally, she acknowledged his qualities. He was funny, honest, kind, honorable, and clearly possessed an unfailing sense of family. She also admired his strength and compelling intelligence. And he had a spirit as strong as hers. The will and determination he possessed was astounding.

Was this really happening? And how did it happen so quickly? Yet as she gazed into his eyes, the same beautiful color as the waters of the loch she'd missed so dearly, she knew for a certainty that it had. Her heart slipped completely into the embrace of love.

She loved this big bear of a man.

"Tha gaol agam ort."

Bear's Gaelic was rusty but he said it right.

"I love you too," she whispered, placing a hand against her heart.

His smile broadened and they just gazed at each other, relishing the shared moment.

"Open yer gift, my love," he finally said.

Her hands trembled as she untied the ribbons—blue and green, the colors of their clan. Yet another example of Bear's thoughtfulness.

She hadn't received a gift since she was a young lass, and her excitement left her breathless. She giggled a little as she removed the lid.

Artis stared at the grand luckenbooth. She had never seen a prettier brooch in her life. "Ah Bear, it's so lovely!"

"As it should be for a woman of your beauty."

She felt her face color. She wished she had a gift of equal measure to give him. Her thoughts brightened when she remembered that she did have something!

She laid the luckenbooth back in the box and unpinned her clan brooch. "Tis yers now," she said, pinning it to Bear's coat. "Several generations of men in my family have worn it with pride. Ye are my new family, so it gives me pleasure to give it to ye, Daniel MacKee."

"As of tonight, I am Daniel MacK-a-y, and I shall also wear it with great pride."

"Aye, that is the customary spellin'. Let's go tell the others. If we stay here, I'll be wantin' more kisses from ye and we'd create a terrible scandal because I'm sure ye would oblige me."

He gave her a roguish smile and said in a low lusty voice, "Indeed, I would! But it would na be a scandal if we were married."

"Aye, but we're na married yet!"

"William is a justice of the peace now. And he can make it legal. But first we can honor our heritage and marry ourselves by a bindin' vow of love." He bent to his knee and pinned the luckenbooth on her. "I pledge to protect you with all the strength and spirit within my body. I pledge my love to ye for the rest of our lives and, if it be possible with God, for all eternity, forever, and ever, and ever."

He stood and reached out for her hand and she stood as well.

Artis placed her palm against their clan's badge. *"Tugaim mo chroí duit go deo*—I give my heart to you forever. I promise I have loved and will love only ye. And my love will be given with all my heart and all my soul, forever."

He gazed lovingly into her eyes for a moment. The tenderness of his expression made her heart jolt and her pulse quicken. Her feelings for him were intensifying with every second that passed.

Then his face lit with sudden joy. "Ye said forever, but I must protest. Forever is na long enough! I want yer love for wee bit longer!" he said with a glint of humor in his eyes. He wrapped her in his arms and kissed the top of her head.

She was too emotion-filled to speak. She laid her cheek against his muscular chest, feeling his heart pound against her skin. His powerfully built body was a virtual fortress capable of protecting them both. The warmth of his arms was so male, so comforting, she did not want to let go of him. How long had it been since she felt loved?

And she had never known the love of a man. She was astonished at the way it made her feel—valued, cherished, and dear. Her chest swelled with love for Bear, making her feel flushed and warm. And his nearness was making her senses spin. Her clothing rapidly became heavy and constricting. She needed air. "Can we go outside for a while?"

"Aye, let's stroll under the stars for a wee bit." Bear took her hand and led her outside.

She took a deep steadying breath of the cool evening air. Her hand was still in his and it felt like it belonged there—as though together their hands formed a perfect union. She glanced over at him and wondered what it would be like to join with him as man and wife—would their bodies also form a perfect union? The thought made her heart race and she found herself feeling hot again.

Her insides seemed to pulse and throb as though liquid fire surged through her veins. She had never felt like this before. Why was she feeling so strange? Was he feeling the same way? She stopped and he did too. He gazed down at her. She needed him to kiss her. Gripped by desire, she reached up and drew his mouth to hers. A sizzling aura of unspent passion swirled around both of them.

He put a hand on her waist and guided her to the fort's stable. He searched for a minute or two until he found where the hay was stored. She understood what might be coming. Could she deny herself his touch? A battle raged within her. She wanted him. That much was clear. In fact, her own compelling need shocked her.

She also knew Bear would not force her. He was a gentleman. But was she enough of a lady to stop herself?

Reaching for her hand again, he tugged her inside and gently eased her down on the fresh-smelling straw.

She looked up at him. The pulse of her throat leapt with excitement. She found his undeniable strength and power so alluring. This was a man who could safeguard her from the cruelties of the world.

He took his place beside her and gathered her in his arms. He held her snugly as he kissed her until the blood pounded in her head and other places on her body warmed and tingled.

His hand slid the top of her gown off her shoulder exposing one of her breasts to the cool air. His lips trailed down her throat and made their way to her bosom. Almost reverently, he kissed the mound of her breast while his big hand caressed the lower half. The sensation was extraordinary and seemed to make her insides pull together.

Her womanhood was aflame and she grabbed his broad shoulders with her hands, needing to hold on to him. She slid closer to him, compelled by her own desire and a need to feel all of him against her. His clean scent made her heart hammer.

His open palm seared a path down her abdomen and he reached under her gown and lightly ran just the tips of his fingers up and down her bare thigh, just above her stockings.

The gentle massage sent her desire soaring even higher. She would not be able to stand much more. She wanted something, something she didn't understand. And her whole being seemed consumed with finding it.

Her mind told her to resist, but her rebellious body refused to listen. Her body only wanted to feel, not think. She gave herself fully to his embrace, burying her face in the center of his broad chest. Her fingers touched the clan badge she'd pinned on him. She could not dishonor her clan.

"Bear, we're not yet married." Trembling with longing for him, she couldn't keep her voice from quaking. She struggled to clear her mind of the lust that swirled through it. She had to regain control.

His breath was warm against her ear. "When it's consummated, we'll make it legally bindin'," he breathed, in a husky whisper.

He kissed her again, deeper and possessively. The passion in the kiss almost made her change her mind.

She placed her hands on either side of his adorable smooth face. "Bear, look at me."

He opened his eyes and she saw desire burning in them so hot she could almost see flames.

"Nay, Bear, we canna do this yet." She beseeched him with her eyes. "As much as I want ye, my faith demands that I wait until we are married before God and man." She spoke the words quickly, over her rapidly beating heart, wanting to get them out before she could change her mind. And there was a strong possibility that she would. She wanted more of what Bear did to her. Much more.

"All right lass, but I swear, ye'll not regret it if you want to go ahead. We're married right enough."

"Nay, we are by Scottish tradition, but na by Kentucky law. And we're

Kentuckians now," she said. "We must marry legally. I'll na have our marriage questioned by anyone, especially God."

He sighed deeply and kissed her again, but this time his lips were soft and tender, conveying only love, not passion.

Recovering, he gently stroked her cheek with a finger and said lightly, "Ye are the most beautiful woman here. Maybe in all the colonies. Can ye blame me for wantin' ye so terribly?"

It thrilled her that Bear found her so desirable. "Nay, I do na. And ye are the most handsome and braw man here. And I want ye just as much. Maybe even a wee bit more," she added with a smile at him.

He took one long last look into her eyes and then stood and offered his hand. "Come, Artis, we must go back before I lose what little control I have."

Laughing, they dusted and plucked the straw off each other before they left the stables. "Did ye get it all out of my hair?" she asked, when they reached the light streaming through the windows.

Bear gave her locks a thorough examination and found two pieces he'd missed. "I will dispose of the evidence of our wickedness," he said, tossing the straw aside.

They were both giggling with happiness as they went back inside.

Tugging her behind him, Bear found William and Kelly, who were still speaking with Lucky.

"Pardon the interruption, but we have exceedingly important news," Bear declared. "Artis and I are now married by pledge, in keepin' with Scottish tradition. But we want ye to perform the ceremony William, to make it legally bindin' in Kentucky."

Kelly let out a cry of joy. "That's wonderful news!"

Lucky gave Bear a slap on the back as he chuckled. "I could see that coming," the old friend said.

Then, to Artis' horror, Lucky plucked a piece of straw that she's missed off the top of Bear's tall back. Her eyes widened for a moment, but he said nothing, and winked at her.

She could feel her throat and face flushing and quickly glanced away.

"It would be my honor," William said, "when do ye want to marry?"

"Right now!" Bear said as though William had asked an inane question.

"Well…" Artis started. She stopped, as the Governor and his wife strode up to the five of them.

"A good evening to you," the Garrards both greeted at once.

"Good evening. Sir, Madam, we are about to have a wedding," Kelly blurted out at once, her voice bubbling with excitement.

"A wedding!" Mrs. Garrard said. "How romantic!"

William introduced everyone to Mrs. Garrard.

"Miss MacKay, I do greatly admire your gown," Mrs. Garrard said.

"Thank ye, Madam. I have Kelly to thank for it," Artis replied. She smiled toward Kelly, showing her gratitude. She'd felt like a princess in some romantic tale from the moment she slid into the gorgeous gown.

"You will make a stunning bride," the Governor told her. "We were about to start the dancing, but let's get everyone's attention and we will hold the wedding first."

"Nay, if ye do na mind Governor, my wish is to wed Bear later tonight on my new land. I would like Bear's brother William to marry us under the stars of my, nay *our,* new home." Bear was right. It was time for her to look up at the stars, not down at her feet. And she would start tonight.

"Of course, dear," the Governor said.

"Whatever makes you happy," Mrs. Garrard agreed.

She glanced at Bear, hoping she would not see disappointment in his eyes. But he looked back at her with only love, and it made her feel wrapped in his warmth again. Her body ached for his touch.

"As far as I'm concerned, our pledges bound us in marriage. So we will do whatever ye want to make it a formality. We can marry after we leave here."

"Thank ye," she said, feeling her desire for him grow even stronger.

"Well, Sir, can we toast to the bride and groom at least?" the Governor asked.

"Aye, and we would be well pleased to have ye make the toast Governor," Bear said. "Just let me get us a drink."

Bear quickly grabbed two glasses of the rum punch from the beverage table and gave one to Artis, while William made sure the Governor and his wife were served more punch. Then the Governor's aide called for everyone's attention and the room quickly quieted down.

"Ladies and gentlemen," he began, "Mrs. Garrard and I thank you all for coming and we both hope you enjoy the ball enormously. I want to thank all the delegates for their willingness to come to Boonesborough for this assembly. Your help is beyond measure. And, I have two items of wonderful news to share with all of you. First, I am delighted to report that this afternoon, Daniel MacKee, whom most of you know as Bear, succeeded in killing three villainous thieves in the process of robbing Henderson & Co."

Men cheered and women, including Artis, gasped. She'd had no idea.

The Governor continued. "These same thieves were responsible for robbing gold from the state treasury and for many other robberies in Kentucky settlements. We are exceedingly grateful to Mister MacKee for his bravery and for riding our state of these lawbreakers.

"Last, and most important, I am pleased and honored to announce that Mister Daniel MacKee and Miss Artis MacKay will be married later this evening by Sheriff William Wyllie."

Everyone in the room clapped and several called out their

congratulations. Bear waved with a sheepish grin on his face.

"I am also honored to say a toast to the happy couple. Will you join me please?" The Governor raised his glass. "May green be the grass you walk upon, may blue be the skies above you, may pure be the happiness that surrounds you, may true be the hearts that love you."

They all raised their cups and took a drink.

"*Sláinte!*" Bear proclaimed, and raised his cup to the Governor. "Cheers to our fine Governor."

They all raised their cups again. The punch tasted delightful and Artis swallowed the rest of it.

When she grasped that Bear killed three men that day, and could have been killed, she asked for another cup.

"Let's eat!" Bear declared. "All this romance has made me ravenous." He didn't want to say he'd been starving since he first arrived at the ball.

"You're always hungry," William said.

Bear's belly rippled with amusement. He couldn't deny it. He was hungry more often than not. He took Artis' elbow. "A joyful heart creates a hungry belly," he said, guiding her to the food tables.

After they ate, he sampled a small piece of every pie and drank a few more cups of punch. Just when he was thinking about leaving, William picked up his fiddle and joined the violinist and another musician. They performed a number of jigs and reels. The loosely structured dances, derived from the dance traditions of the Scots, kept the area set aside for dancing full and surrounded by clapping onlookers.

Bear noticed Artis tapping her toes to the lively music and humming along happily, as she watched the jubilant party goers dance.

She gave him a vivacious smile and told him, "*O my luve is like the melodie, that's sweetly played in tune,*" quoting the popular Scottish poet

Robert Burns.

"Would ye like to dance to sweet tunes for the rest of our lives?" he asked.

"Aye," she said, "and a wee bit longer!"

He took her hand and they made their way to the dance floor. He had not danced since he was a young lad and wasn't sure he could make his big feet cooperate, but for Artis' sake he had to try. Her nearness and beauty made his heart race and that might also prove to make dancing gracefully difficult. He took a deep breath to calm himself.

"Watch out for yer toes," he warned, "me boots are quite large and my dancin' skills are quite dull."

"Then we are even more ideally suited than I thought, for my boots are quite small and my dancin' skills are well honed. I used to love to dance at our village's celebrations."

They danced as though they'd been dancing together all their lives, but occasionally his feet found it difficult to keep up. Smiling people gathered around and kept pointing to him, apparently astonished or amused that so large a man could be so lively.

"*A Dhiabhai!*" he swore, when she winced after the first time he stepped on her toes. He hadn't forgotten how to say damn it and a few other choice swear words in Gaelic and feared he would need to use of them all before she grew tired of dancing.

He could tell that she would not grow weary of dancing anytime soon. She clearly loved to dance and she seemed filled with irrepressible joy. When she wasn't smiling, she was grinning. And when she wasn't grinning, she was laughing. The sound of her laughter was something he wanted to spend his whole life hearing.

They had both been smiling when they started dancing and still were when his feet finally compelled him to stop. "Ye must let me rest wife."

"Aye, husband, ye will need yer strength later." She eyed him impishly, her expression hungry and lustful.

He decided it was time to leave. "Let's find William and Kelly," he said quickly. He grabbed her hand and in his rush practically yanked her away from the dance floor.

"My pardons," he said, realizing what he'd done.

"Do na be troubled, I'll keep up with ye."

Chapter 18

B ear spread a blanket out in the back of William and Kelly's wagon and then helped his new wife to seat herself. But this time, he sat down next to her, wrapped an arm around her shoulders and snugged her up against him. It felt so good to hold this magnificent woman in his arms. He glanced down and caught the gleam of her eyes and the sparkle of the stones in her luckenbooth. Both shimmered like stars. His sheer joy made him look heavenward.

"Look up," he said. A clear sky left the stars free to glisten in an unveiled pageant of nature.

"It's on the darkest nights that the stars are their brightest," she said.

He was about to agree with her when a bolt of lightning streaked across the horizon illuminating shadowy clouds gathering in the distance. He counted the seconds until he heard the thunder that followed. Good, it was some distance away. Maybe the storm would turn and miss them altogether. The late fall night was cool, but not uncomfortably so. But a storm, especially one that left them all soaked, could make the journey home miserable.

"Are ye sure ye do na need yer shawl?" he asked. She had lain it in the corner of the wagon along with William's fiddle.

"Nay, I have ye to keep me warm now."

William snapped the reins and the four took off toward Whispering Hills, with Camel tied to the back of the wagon.

"I'm sorry it is na a fancy carriage to carry ye tonight my beautiful bride," he said.

"Och, we have na need of fancy. We only have need of each other," Artis said, looking up at him.

"Aye, and we will always have that." Bear exhaled a sigh of contentment. He couldn't believe the gorgeous woman sitting next to him was his wife. He pressed her a little closer and gave her a soft lingering kiss, relishing the softness of her lips.

His calm was shattered by the hunger he felt in her kiss.

"Husband, will we be able to…to be together tonight?" she whispered.

He caught her meaning and smiled. "Nothing of this world could keep us apart this night."

"But where? We have only have this one blanket. It will na be enough to keep us both warm."

"Oh, I promise ye I can keep ye warm."

"But how will ye stay warm?" she asked, and then kissed his neck.

He found it hard to think clearly, but she had a point. He quickly devised a plan and shared it with her. "We'll let William marry us, then we'll go back to Whisperin' Hills, change our clothes, and get everythin' we'll need. Then, if the weather is still fair, we'll come back to yer land and make a camp for the night."

"*Our* land."

"Aye, our home." He sat up straighter. "Speakin' of home, I'm goin' to see if the land next to yours is still for sale. If it is, I'll buy it with my funds."

"That would be wonderful." She placed a palm against his chest and gazed up at him.

"Then with my reward money, I'll hire a housewright and craftsmen to help me build our home. If we hurry we can get it finished before the first snowfall."

Joy bubbled out of her in a wide grin and happiness shone in the sparkle of her eyes. Even in the darkness, he could see the warm glow that lit up her ecstatic face. She leaned against him, her softness melting into his body. He could feel her breast pressed against his chest and it made his desire flare and a smile spread across his face.

Satisfaction made him smile too. His heart swelled at the realization that he'd made her so happy. He pressed her against him again, wanting to always keep her as happy.

"Halt!" a man's voice yelled from the darkness. "I've got one of your women in my sights and she dies if one of you men makes a single move. Throw out your weapons."

William instantly shoved Kelly's head downward and slapped the reins of the horse team, urging them to a fast run. "Hah!" William yelled to the horses.

Bear pushed Artis' entire body down and, as best he could, entangled in her skirts, he tried to move in front of her.

A ball of lead exploded the rear boards, sending splinters of wood flying over both of them.

Artis screamed, but Bear kept his eyes on the attacker, trying his best to aim his pistol with the wagon bouncing violently.

The horseback man gave chase, hunkering down low on his horse.

Bear fired his pistol, but a lurch of the wheels as they hit a rut in the road caused the lead to miss its target. "Damn it to hell!" he swore.

The man ducked his horse into the safety of the dark forest before Bear could fire his second weapon. He could hear the rider having to weave his horse through the woods. That would slow him down.

"He's following!" he yelled to William.

William leaned back and crouching down low, extended one of his two pistols toward Bear. "Shoot him, first chance you get."

"Here," Bear said, exchanging weapons. "Have Kelly reload it."

Bear peered into the darkness, trying to spot whoever it was. Dark clouds obscured the stars and moon now and all he could tell was that it was a lanky man.

"You killed my brother and my friends you bloody Scot," their pursuer yelled from what seemed like a good distance away.

So that's who this was. The fourth wanted man listed on the handbill. Bear knew the man probably had another pistol and would take his shot soon. He had to do something before the man shot Artis, Kelly, or William. He stuck his and William's loaded pistols back in his belt. "Stay down as flat as ye can," he told Artis. Between the utter darkness and the bouncing wagon, he could barely see her.

He crawled to the back and, ducking below what was left of the wagon's rear boards, he untied Camel's reins. Slithering forward on his stomach, he led the horse alongside the wagon up to the front driver's bench.

"Keep it straight," he yelled to William.

William glanced back and nodded.

"Steady now, steady Camel," he told the gelding. With one giant leap, he swung his leg over the horse and managed to almost land on the saddle. Leaning hard to the horse's right side, he was in danger of falling under the wagon's wheels.

Gritting his teeth, he reached up, gripped the pommel, and heaved himself fully astride the gelding. Breathing a sigh of relief that he'd tightened the saddle well, he bent low on the horse's neck, and pulled up next to his brother. "Keep goin'. Get the women to safety," he yelled.

"Nay, do na leave him!" Artis cried out.

Thankfully, William ignored her and kept the wagon thundering down the road away from him.

With a tug, Bear turned Camel around and, pistol drawn, headed down the road toward where he'd last heard the pursuer. He approached cautiously and slowly and led Camel into the safer area of the woods on the side opposite of the path taken by their pursuer. He was still out of pistol range, but the man might have his rifle loaded. He'd wrongly assumed he wouldn't need his own rifle and foolishly left it in McGuffin's cabin. He would never make that mistake again.

Bear dismounted and tied Camel. He needed stealth if he was going to catch the man unawares. Listening, he heard the rider's horse making its way through the thick brush and timber. The robber was about twenty yards away on the other side of the road.

Bear waited, hidden in the trees, until the man's horse passed by on the opposite side. Holding both his and William's pistol, he silently stepped to the other side and came up behind the horseback man.

"Come out of the woods and fight like a man, if ye are one!" Bear bellowed. Nearly all men will respond to a threat to their manhood.

A dark figure, emerged from the woods, turned his mount, and headed toward him. Brandishing his own pistol the man glared at him. "You killed all three of them! The shopkeep told me it was you before I knocked him out."

Bear drew his brows together in an angry frown. "Did ye kill him?" he asked, concerned for Breedhead.

"No, the coward told me where I'd find you."

"A man who threatens innocent women from behind could be called a coward too," Bear said, deliberately trying to make the man angry. Angry men were never very good at aiming their weapons. "Why didn't you just call out for me and voice your grievance to my face? Why sneak up from behind? Because yer na more than a devious coward, that's why." The man must have waited outside the ball and overheard the Governor lavish praise on Bear, then followed them when they left.

"I may be a robber, but you're a murderer," the man growled through clenched teeth.

"Aye, I killed them, because they deserved it." Bear felt a muscle of his jaw quiver as his mind raced. If he could disable him, but not kill him, they stood a chance of recovering the state treasury's gold. They would just have to get this thief to divulge where the gold was hidden. The funds would allow Kentucky to address the many needs discussed at the delegate's assembly.

The enraged man's face twisted in anger and he dismounted and marched closer to Bear. "You deserve to die for killing my brother and friends!" The hand holding a pistol burst upward as he took aim.

Bear fired first, aiming for the thief's shoulder.

The man squealed as the lead penetrated his right shoulder and sent his body sprawling backwards. Unable to hold onto his pistol, the weapon dropped to the ground.

Bear kicked the flintlock away from the moaning man.

He glanced up when he heard noise on the road. He peered ahead, into the darkness, and aimed his second pistol toward what sounded like footfalls. But the night was black and he couldn't see a thing. The stars now lay hidden behind a veil of dark clouds. Bear held the unfired pistol up, pointing it up the road toward the sound but lowered it at once when he realized who it was. William was running up the road toward him at full speed, weapon drawn.

"Ye can slow down now," Bear yelled, then looked down.

The bleeding fellow had regained his feet and, holding one hand against his shoulder, was charging him head first.

Bear head-butted the robber and the man collapsed to the ground again, this time knocked out completely.

Bear turned to William who had just reached his side. "That's what we call a Scottish kiss."

William grinned and nodded his approval.

"Where's the wagon?" Bear asked.

Breathing hard, William said, "Artis kept telling me to wait, but I made Kelly promise she would take them both to safety. I gave the horses a slap to hurry them along, and then I took off at a run toward you."

Bear smiled, amused, at the thought of William sprinting in his fancy clothes. "I thank ye for runnin' to me aid. But I managed to get the best of the fellow."

"Who is he anyway? Just a bandit?"

"Nay, he's the fourth robber described on the wanted handbill I told ye about. He was comin' after me for revenge for killin' his brother and two friends."

"I suspected he'd show up sooner or later, but never suspected he would show up this soon seeking revenge. I should have been more on guard," William admitted.

"Aye, Sam would be disappointed in both of us for not expecting that. In fact, Sam would probably have predicted it."

William grunted. "You're right. Sam is always on high alert. The Revolutionary War made him that way."

"And it saved us all more than once," Bear reminded him. "What will ye charge the robber with?"

"I will not make it easy for him since he threatened Kelly and Artis," William said. "Attempted murder at the least."

"Aye, the despicable coward."

"I'll be sure to recommend the maximum sentence to Judge Webb."

"Ye might be able to get him to tell ye the location of the gold they stole from the treasury in exchange for gettin' the doc to dig that lead out. Kentucky needs those funds."

"Splendid idea," William said, looking down at the now moaning man.

"I'll go get the man's horse, he's just over there."

"Do ye need help gettin' this robber tucked safely into yer jail, before I go back for my bride? I will na let this fool spoil my weddin' night."

"No, I can handle one wounded man and use his horse. But you can help me tie him up. Then we'll throw him over the back of his horse and lash him on well behind the saddle."

"Aye, I'll help ye put the horse's ass on his horse's arse."

Chapter 19

Artis' head felt light. She could feel warm blood seeping through her fingers now. The gown's fabric around the wound had absorbed all the blood it could. She pressed her sticky fingers even harder against the puncture to slow the bleeding. But that made the wound even more excruciating. And each bounce of the wagon caused a sharp pain to radiate up her left side. The robber's one shot hit her. In the darkness, no one had realized she was wounded. She'd tried to get William's attention, but he just took off running back to Bear. And Kelly couldn't hear her above the clamor of the bouncing wagon and horses running a full speed.

She was nauseous. Whether it was from the pain or the jolting lurching ride, she didn't know. She closed her eyes trying to shut out the queasiness.

"We're almost there!" Kelly yelled back to her. "Jump out and run in as soon as I pull up to the cabin door."

Artis turned her head toward Kelly and tried to speak, but didn't have the strength. In a blur, she saw the smokehouse, followed by the barn, and then the creek. Then the horses swerved severely as Kelly raced the horse team up to the cabin.

"Get out!" Kelly cried. "We need to get into the cabin where it's safe."

Artis put her free hand on the side of the wagon. It was all she could move. Even that movement caused her to whimper.

"Artis! What's wrong?" Kelly cried and peered over the side. "Oh my Lord, you're bleeding!"

"Aye," Artis said weakly. Then, against her will, her eyes closed.

&

"They're here," Steller told the older man. "Do na say a word or, as I warned, yer granddaughter dies first."

McGuffin's eyes darted toward the bairn and then held Steller's eyes. "I don't know who you are or what you want with Miss MacKay but, as *I warned*, you'll never get Artis past my son-in-law or his brother. You'd be wise to leave now."

"I'll leave when I get what I've come for. They'd never shoot a man for simply tryin' to find his long lost wife. And if they do give me trouble, I can handle a couple of Kentucky farmers."

McGuffin's mouth drew into a sour grin for some reason.

&

The door burst open. "Papa, come quickly…" Kelly stopped, unable to believe the sight before her eyes. A tall large man stood by her father, a pistol held in his hand. The cabin was in disarray as though there had been a terrible fight. Worse, her father, who sat at the table, was bleeding from numerous scratches and cuts.

"Nicole?" she asked, looking at her papa, her voice near breaking.

"Remarkably, she's still asleep in her bed," her father said, pointing. He sounded weak and defeated.

Kelly marched to Nicole, ignoring the man with the pistol for the moment. Her child appeared unharmed. *Thank you God.*

She glared at the man. "Why have you hurt my father?"

"He would na tell me where Artis was," the man said.

141

"Who the hell are you?" she asked.

"Her husband."

Kelly felt as though her stomach dropped to her feet. Could it be possible? Bear had only known Artis for a few days. Perhaps he'd rushed into something he should not have. This would break his heart. "What is your name?"

"Patrick Steller. I would like to say, at yer service, but I regret I must claim my bride and be on my way. What's yer name?"

"Kelly."

"Where is she, Kelly?" Steller's voice was challenging, his eyes dark and penetrating.

He would be a handsome man were his face not so malicious.

"I miss my wife and want to find her as soon as possible. When I got my shave and haircut in town, the barber said the woman I described had been seen in the company of William Wyllie, his wife, and his brother at some meetin' with the governor. A woman like Artis tends to stand out and his customers had been talkin' about her. He told me ye were all likely to be at the ball. So I asked him where ye lived and came here to wait. I thought it would be a more private place to reunite with Artis than the fort or the ball. Fewer people, ye understand."

His words did not ring true to her. "I repeat, why did you beat my father? Why did you simply not wait for Artis?"

Steller advanced toward her, his lips pressed together as though he were trying to hold in his anger. He stopped right in front of her.

Her papa stood. "Don't you touch my girl!"

Steller's face hardened. "Remember what I told ye old man."

Kelly studied her father's eyes. She saw both rage and fear. It was the first time she'd seen either one on her father's face. Why was he so afraid? It was unlike him.

Steller turned back to her. "Where's Artis?"

"I don't know," she lied.

"Why did ye come back alone?"

Kelly tried to think of a plausible explanation. "I wanted to get back early to be sure my little girl was all right. It's the first time I left her for any length of time. You know how mothers are—always worrying."

"Are the others still at the ball? Are they on their way back?"

The desperate need to help Artis, and trying to stall this awful man until Bear and William returned, warred within her. But what if they took the man who was chasing them back to town? They could be gone for some time. She had to help Artis. She could be bleeding to death. Her face had been so pale.

Steller reached out and slapped her cheek. "I asked ye a question. Answer me!"

Kelly's eyes burned with her wrath. "I won't tell you." She wanted to tell him to leave, but she couldn't. He'd find Artis.

Steller strode to her daughter. He pointed the pistol at Nicole's sleeping form. "She's a pretty thing. Too bad she has to die."

"No! Wait!" Kelly screamed. She ran to Steller and pushed him away from her child. "What kind of a demon are you?"

"The kind that wants his woman back. Are ye ready to tell me where she is?"

Never in her life had Kelly met anyone as cruel. He was even more vicious than the men who had attacked her back in her old cabin. She found it difficult to believe this kind of man was Artis' husband.

Kelly glanced down at her daughter. She swallowed her reluctance. It left a bitter taste, but she had no choice. "Artis is in the wagon outside. She's been shot. We were attacked and chased by a man on our way here. You must help me to get her inside."

Steller just stood there. Eyes glaring, his expression taut, he stared at the door but didn't move. The tension in the room mounted with every second.

Fear and anger knotted inside Kelly's stomach. Would this news cause the man's mind to crack? Would this heartless man kill them all? A shiver of panic raced through her. "Please, just help me get her inside. I'll take good care of Artis. You can come back later for her."

His eyes turned her way. Derision and mockery filled his stare. "She's comin' with me."

"She's in no condition to travel. You'll kill her," Kelly argued.

"Sir, taking a wounded woman away on horseback is no way for a gentleman to act," her father declared in a forceful condemning tone.

"Who said I was a gentleman?" Steller roared. "And another word and ye will be a dead gentleman. What I do with my wife is my business, not yers."

Her father was shaking with impotent rage. He pounded his fist loudly against the table but kept quiet.

The noise gave Kelly an idea. If she could provoke Steller into a shouting match, it might wake Artis and she might have time to hide—if she was strong enough.

"Where are you taking Artis?" Kelly demanded, making her voice as shrill as she could.

Annoyance crossed Steller's face. "Get some food and water ready. And I'll need several blankets."

"Do I look like your servant?" Kelly bellowed.

"Do it. Now!" Steller shouted.

He strode over to the weapons sitting on a table by the door. "And I'll take these weapons, lead, and powder too."

Taking food and blankets was one thing. Taking her weapons was far worse. It made her furious. "Not only are you not a gentleman, you're a thief!" Kelly yelled, watching him to be sure she didn't push him too far.

"Oh, ye underestimate me. I am far worse than a mere thief," he hollered. "Ye'd be wise to remember that." After checking to be sure the weapons were loaded, he put the leather straps of the powder horn and lead pouch over his head.

"I don't underestimate you. I know exactly what you are—a devil in a man's clothing," she shrieked.

"Just get the damn food!" Steller howled.

Kelly turned and gathered the provisions, feeling Steller's leering eyes on her back.

&

The sound of loud voices coming from inside the cabin woke Artis. She was groggy and hurting. Where was she? Then she remembered. The man who had chased them had shot her. She put her hand to her wet side. The bleeding seemed to have stopped or slowed. Why was she still in the wagon? Where was Kelly? She heard more shouting coming from inside. It was Kelly's voice, and then a man's. The man's voice sounded familiar. And angry.

She tried to remember where she'd heard it before.

Oh, God.

She stiffened at the horrible realization. It couldn't be. He had to be back in Scotland. How could he have found her here? Maybe the loss of blood was making her delirious. She did feel woozy and dizzy. Then she heard the voice again and was certain it was him.

Fear overflowed from her heart, spilling into her entire body. She gritted her teeth against the hurt in her side and the greater pain in her heart. He would kill her. He'd promised to make her pay for spurning him. Wasn't her mother's life enough?

Sobbing, she realized she had to hide. She wasn't strong enough to fight him now. She had to get away before Steller came out. She wanted to live for Bear.

She rallied what little strength she had and crawled toward the back of the wagon. She knew she was ruining the beautiful dress Kelly had given her. The dress she'd worn when she said her vows to Bear. At least they had pledged to be married. Now, she would never be able to marry Bear under the stars on their land, as she so desperately wanted. Tears flowed from her eyes, at much from that realization as the terrible pain in her side.

She reached the end of the wagon bed and let her legs fall off first. She was able to support herself enough to keep from falling entirely, but she could not stand up straight. The dizziness was overwhelming. Bent over, and clutching her wound, she limped toward the smokehouse. She would hide there. The small fire within would help to keep her warm. She was so cold, so dreadfully cold.

Was she leaving a trail that would lead him straight to her? She glanced behind her. The full skirts and long petticoats of the fancy gown were erasing her tracks.

Still clutching her side, she stumbled a few more feet. Sweat broke out on her forehead and her head began to spin. She forced herself to take the next step and then the next. She was almost there. The dizziness grew worse and threatened to make her swoon. She took a deep breath and blew it out slowly. She leaned against the smokehouse door, taking a moment to steady her quivering nerves. She lifted the latch and used the door to support herself as she stepped in and then pulled the door closed behind her.

She coughed a time or two, causing an agonizing stinging to rip through her side. She closed her eyes and waited for a little strength to return before taking a step. The smoke from the fire's coals was not thick, but it made the air heavy and difficult to breathe.

When she opened her eyes, the first thing she saw was the mountain lion's carcass hanging from the rafter. It swayed, ghostlike, as she watched it. Was it moving or was she?

146

Then she spotted the mountain lion's hide laying on a small table nearby. Could it really protect her, as the natives believed?

She took a few tentative steps toward it, frantically gripped it, and then clutched the pelt against her stomach.

She closed her eyes, thought of Bear, and wrapped her arms around the soft fur as her legs collapsed and her head hit the hard ground beneath her.

Chapter 20

S teller could not believe his bad luck. He'd crossed an ocean, albeit against his will; traveled three hundred miles to Roanoke; and then another three-hundred and fifty to Boonesborough, through some of the roughest and most isolated god-forsaken country he'd ever seen. Only to find Artis shot.

It served her right, but it would make taking her, as he'd wanted, difficult. He'd planned to tie her, rape her repeatedly, and then take his time killing her. He'd never raped a woman who had been shot. Perhaps it would add something unique to the experience.

"Your supplies are ready," Kelly told him.

Her voice was belligerent, her expression thunderous. But she was a beautiful spirited woman. Her hair was straight and blonde rather than wavy and reddish like Artis'. Her eyes were lovely too, but violet instead of green. Her figure was equally appealing. For a moment, he considered taking her with him instead of Artis. But then he remembered how much Artis deserved to be punished. It was Artis who had ruined his life. And she would be the one to pay. He could always come back later for this one.

"Carry them outside," he told her. "Then saddle Artis' horse. I assume she has a horse?" He didn't want to take the wagon. It would just slow him down and give the farmers a reason to come after him.

Kelly nodded. "She does."

He snarled at the grandfather. "Stay here."

Holding his pistol to her back, Steller followed Kelly out the door. He told her to lay the supplies on the porch. Then they both took the steps down and stepped past the lathered horses to the wagon. Finally, he would see Artis. He hoped she would be alert enough to recognize him. He couldn't wait to see the look on her face when she realized it was he who stood before her.

But it was his own face that registered shock.

Artis wasn't in the wagon! He turned his rage on Kelly. "You lied. What did ye do with her?" He smacked her across the mouth, hard. He'd teach her not to lie.

Kelly's face reddened and she clenched her fists. "I didn't lie. She was hurt."

He bared his teeth at the deceitful woman. "You lied to me and you'll pay for that." He reached for her throat with his free hand and pressed hard.

She tried to pull away and struggled to breathe. "I didn't lie. Look at the blood," she said in a choked voice and pointed.

He turned and looked. She was right. There was just enough light coming from the gun porthole in the front of the cabin for him to see that a large pool of blood had soaked into the dry graying floorboards and a part of a crumpled blanket that she must have been sitting on. Perhaps Kelly and her father were right. A wound that severe would make it near impossible for Artis to travel horseback even if he tied her on.

He stomped up the stairs and paced the porch, the veins in his head pulsing and feeling engorged. He pounded his fist against the cabin's log wall until it hurt. He'd never find Artis in the dark before Kelly's husband and his brother got back. There were too many places to hide here and in the woods surrounding the place. He would just have to wait and come back for her later.

He could be patient when he had to be. After all, he'd already waited seven years for this.

"Load the supplies on my horse," he commanded. "He's tied just around the corner."

Kelly retrieved the big stallion and tied him on a post supporting the cabin's porch. Then she loaded the animal with the food, blankets, and water. When she finished, she turned around and hurled a cold look at him.

"Don't let anyone follow me, or I *promise* I will come back and kill your wee bairn and yer father."

Kelly gasped.

"If ye don't think I'm capable of that, just ask Artis…if she lives."

He could see fear for her loved ones on the woman's pretty face.

With a threatening sneer at her, he stepped down from the porch and glared back at Kelly. "And if Artis lives, I'll be back for her. And maybe you too. That's another promise."

He mounted the stallion and took off for the hills he could see in the distance. It wouldn't take long to disappear in the thick darkness of the forest.

જ

Kelly dashed back into the house, her heart still galloping within her chest. "He's gone. But I have to find Artis. She slipped away somehow."

"Good for her! You stay with Nicole. Let me look for Artis," McGuffin said.

"No, I need you to protect Nicole. Stay here. I'll be all right. Steller headed toward the hills to the north."

Kelly snatched her tin and horn lantern from the mantel. The lantern had been a gift from William for her birthday. Struggling to still her shaking hands, she lit the candle secured within the lantern. It glowed through window panels made of thinly carved horn. She grabbed her hatchet since Steller had stolen her weapons.

"Be careful, and I hope you find her," her father said.

"Bar the door and don't you dare open it for anyone except me, William, or Bear!"

Kelly raced to her father's cabin and threw open the door, the hatchet held firmly in her upstretched hand. She wouldn't put it past that man to sneak back and try to catch her unawares.

"Artis," she called. She quickly searched the small cabin and decided that Artis must be hiding elsewhere. The smokehouse was unlikely since her father had started smoking the mountain lion. It would be hot inside.

Her heart beating rapidly within her chest, she decided next to search the storehouse where they kept their winter food stores. Again, she found no one. The barn with its stalls and hay loft took a good while to search, but Artis was not hiding there either.

She grew more concerned with each minute that passed. She needed to locate Artis soon. Her move from the wagon to hide somewhere undoubtedly caused the bleeding to grow worse. Artis had already lost a lot of blood. If they didn't stop the bleeding soon, she would certainly die.

Bear would be devastated. They all would be.

Then she remembered Steller's claim that he was Artis' husband. That news would destroy Bear even if Artis lived. It was clear that Bear loved her deeply. And she thought Artis loved Bear dearly too. How could such a lovely day end so tragically? Kelly wanted to weep, but she didn't have time for such nonsense.

She had one last building to search—the smokehouse. If Artis wasn't there, she could be hiding anywhere in the woods. She would be easy prey for animals of the night and with the dropping temperature, she wouldn't last long. She raced for the structure, praying she would find Artis within, and alive.

Chapter 21

Bear was glad to finally mount up again and be on his way back to Artis. Of all nights for something like that to happen. Och! They should have been officially married by now and on their way back to Artis' land for their first night as man and wife.

But, he thought philosophically, all things happen for a reason and it was not for him to question why. He nudged Camel to a slow lope and made his way toward Whispering Hills. The night seemed especially black and it was only the lighter color of the dirt road that enabled him to see where to go.

He decided to spend his time in the saddle thinking about all the wonderful and exciting things he was going to do to his bride tonight. At the stable, he'd given her a proper taste of what was to come. But there would be so much more. The sensuous thoughts soon had his breath quickening and warmth flooding his frame. His fingers ached with the need to touch her magnificent body.

He suddenly wondered if she were a virgin. He'd just assumed she was. But having spent a sea voyage alone without an escort, and seven years as a plantation servant, it was entirely possible that she wasn't. It didn't matter to him. Artis was Artis. And the only thing that did concern him was her future—not her past. But, he hoped, for her sake, that no man had ever forced her to his bed.

He thought about how stunningly beautiful she was earlier at the ball. Kelly must have spent the day fixing her hair that fancy way and the gold gown made her shine with the radiance of a new sun. She was the loveliest woman at the ball. And she'd waltzed into the room full of strangers with all the confidence of a high-born lady. How proud he was of her!

And she was pledged to him. He still found it hard to believe. Even though it was not official, they were married as far as he was concerned.

He gloried for a moment in his recollection of her pledge. Her words spoke to his heart and made him nothing short of jubilant. Especially when she said, 'I promise I have loved and will love only ye.' He hoped his pledge brought her happiness too. Judging from the passion she put into their kiss afterwards, his words must have pleased her. And she appeared to be thrilled with her gift. The luckenbooth would forever symbolize the unity and loyalty of their hearts.

Now he understood what Stephen, Sam, and William must have felt on their wedding days. He attended all three weddings and witnessed their joy. But it is one thing to see happy—it is quite another to experience it. He couldn't stop smiling. In fact, his cheeks were growing sore from grinning all evening. Even now, he smiled as he remembered their wanton behavior in the stable. And dancing with Artis was so extraordinary. He'd never danced with so much joy in his life. He'd been left breathless, but with a lightness of limb and heart he'd never felt before.

He absolutely could not wait to see her again. His hands tingled at the thought of embracing her again. So much love filled his heart that his eyes watered with tears of joy.

He felt moisture running down his cheeks and scolded himself for being so emotional. Or was that rain? He stuck a hand out and when several drops landed in his palm, he realized that it was indeed raining. He'd been so lost in his blissful thoughts, he hadn't even noticed.

Lightning cracked just above him and both he and Camel startled. The boom of thunder that followed almost instantly did not make Camel any calmer. It fact, he'd never seen his trusty horse made so nervous by weather.

The light rain intensified quickly to a heavy deluge that poured from the sky.

Bear slowed Camel's pace to be sure they did not slip in the thickening mud. When the wind coming from the north grew stronger, he pushed his tricorne down firmly on his head, hoping it would not blow away. He wished he'd brought his cloak, but when he had left for town right after noon, it had been so warm it never even occurred to him to bring it. The rain soon soaked through his jacket and into his shirt, making the linen fabric stick to the skin of his back.

He tried to judge where he was and how far ahead Whispering Hills was, but he'd been so lost in his thoughts, he had no idea how far along the road he was. He couldn't be that far away. He'd soon be with Artis again. But their night camping in the woods on her land was no longer going to be possible. Maybe he would ask Kelly's father to give his cabin to them for the evening. Perhaps Mister McGuffin would even continue to stay in the main house's upstairs loft so he and Artis could have the cabin until he got their house built.

The torrential rain refused to let up and the air grew colder with each passing minute. And the northerly wind continually whipped pieces of bark, pine needles, and leaves at him and Camel.

He suspected William would decide to stay in town until the terrible storm blew through. Storms like this could cause low water crossings to flood faster than Bear could skin a rabbit. It always amazed him how normally tranquil streams and creeks could suddenly transform into raging torrents, spreading far from their banks, their depths bourgeoning tenfold or more.

Flood waters could also turn deadly in a flash.

Within minutes, Bear grew concerned. The downpour caused water to stand in the road, making it difficult to even see the road. Worse, the terrain was gradually sloping downward. Sooner or later, he was going to encounter all this water running downward.

It was sooner. He found himself standing on the edge of a low water crossing or swiftly moving stream. He wasn't sure which. In the extreme darkness and heavy rain, he couldn't even see to the edge of the other side. If he tried to cross it without knowing its depth, the swiftly moving water could carry both him and Camel downstream into rocks or other treacherous debris. It wouldn't be as bad in the daylight, but in the dark, he had no way to know what the water could hurl them into.

"Steady Camel, I'll figure this out boy," he said trying to soothe the horse. Camel was still acting particularly nervous. It was more than the storm. Something else was out there.

Then he remembered that it was near here where Artis encountered the mountain lion. This must be the stream that ran beside Artis' property. It had been a brisk, but little, stream the day he'd met Artis. But it was far from that now.

Without warning, Camel decided it was time to make a move. The horse leapt into the moving waters. Bear jumped off the saddle, knowing Camel stood a much better chance of making it across without his heavy weight. The water pushed him into the panicky horse. Bear extended his legs against Camel's side to keep from sliding underneath the gelding. Darkness and water enveloped him and he went under. He prayed he was not under Camel's hooves. He pushed against the current, trying to stay oriented. When his feet touched bottom and he could tell which way was up, he used his big hands to pull his way through the muddy water until he burst through to the air and took a much needed breath.

Freezing, he began to shake. He had to get to the opposite bank soon. Artis was on the other side. Artis would help to warm him. He repeated that over and over, as he struggled through the water, swimming and then being pushed or tossed by the current, and then swimming again.

It seemed to take forever, but he soon felt the bank against his body and he scrambled up clawing into the mud until he found purchase. He gripped what felt like a root and was able to get enough traction to haul himself out of the rushing water. He spit muck and dirt out of his mouth and crawled a few feet before he stopped, breathless and spent. He took a few deep breaths, and felt better, and mercifully, the heavy rain abruptly lessened.

He tried to stand, but his boots were full of water and heavy. He took them off, poured the water out, and put them back on. So much for the shine he had the cobbler put on his boots, he thought grimly. His new tricorne was long gone. But after wearing it all evening, he didn't like the hat anyway. It was too tight on his big head.

His eyes widened and his breath caught as he remembered Artis' pledge gift. He slapped his palm against his upper left chest. The clan crest was still there. He let out a long sigh of relief.

Then worry grabbed his mind again as he remembered Camel. The horse had been his loyal companion for more than a decade. "Camel!" he called, as he quickly stood up. But he heard nothing to indicate that the horse was out there.

But he did hear something else.

Another mountain lion. It must be the mate of the one he and Artis killed. The animal's scream echoed through the darkness and the rain, chilling him further. He reached for his pistol, but it wasn't there. It must have washed away. He'd given his other one to William so he could give it to Kelly to reload and he'd returned William's pistol to him.

He reached for his knife that hung on top of his sporran. As always, his trusted blade was there. He'd almost left both behind, thinking they did not complement his new clothes. But the sporran was the only item he wore regularly that represented his Scottish heritage. In the end, he could not part with them. It had been a wise decision.

He tightened his grip on the knife, as best he could with wet hands. The best defense against a mountain lion was to make it think you were not easy prey.

156

He extended his arms above his head and yelled, "Come out ye bloody girl. Aye, I'm the one who killed yer mate. Let's have this fight and be done with it. I'll not have ye stalkin' me half the damn night!"

Bear heard the sound of an animal walking through the trees. It wasn't the cat. Thick pads kept a mountain lion's tread so silent it was undetectable to human ears. He peered into the darkness, hoping it wasn't a bear he'd heard. Och! That was all he needed now.

He was not a man to back down from either man or nature's challenges, but this evening's events were beginning to wear on his nerves.

He couldn't see anything. Then to his great relief, he heard Camel's familiar snort. The sound warmed his heart as nothing else could have. "If yer done with yer swim, get over here ye big ugly fellow."

At the sound of Bear's voice, Camel hurried over and stood next to him, nearly leaning into Bear's chest. He stroked the gelding's long neck and, as best he could in the darkness, checked him over. He appeared to be unharmed.

"Let's go find Artis," he told Camel, "my wife."

Chapter 22

Kelly threw the smokehouse door open and stepped inside. She held her lantern high, lighting up the black interior walls. Disappointment filled her when she didn't find Artis. She lowered the lantern, and it illuminated the floor, as she turned to leave. There she was, crumpled in a heap on the dirt next to the table, her face on the fur of an animal's pelt.

Kelly rushed to Artis' side and turned her over. Despite the warmth of the glowing coals, Artis' skin felt icy and her beautiful face appeared strained and drained of color. Was she still alive? Her own heart beat furiously as she tried to find a pulse on Artis' neck.

Thank God. It was there, faint, but steady.

The side of the gold gown Artis wore was soaked with dark bloodstains. At least the bleeding looked like it had stopped. For that, she gave thanks.

"Artis, can you hear me? It's Kelly. You are going to be all right. I'll help you. Don't leave us, please. Bear needs you. I need you."

Artis did not respond and Kelly decided to go get her father to help. She opened the door to the smokehouse and started to step out, but rain was pouring down. No wonder it had been so dark as she had searched for Artis. She made a dash for the house, nearly slipping twice. By the time she reached the front porch, her gown was soaked.

"Papa, I need your help. I found Artis in the smokehouse. She's won't wake up, but she has a pulse."

"I'll pull the wagon over there and we'll load her in the back. But we need something to cover her with. It won't do to get her wet."

"How about my bear rug?"

"That's exactly what we need. No rainwater will get through that big hide." Her father had bought the fur in town and given it to her for a wedding present.

He helped Kelly grab the black rug from the floor in front of her bed and carry it to the door.

"Let me turn the wagon around and then you come running and hop up by me. Do you think you can carry the heavy fur?"

"I've had to move it several times, cleaning."

Moving a little gingerly, her father pulled on a jacket and hurried out the door. It made her angry all over again to see evidence of the thrashing Steller gave her father.

Kelly grabbed one of William's extra tricornes, twisted her damp hair up and tucked it inside, and nestled the hat snugly on her head. It would keep the rain off her face at least.

She watched a curtain of rainwater pour off the roof of the porch while he got the horse team facing the right way, then she darted out, carrying the bulky fur with some difficulty.

A spectacular bolt of lightning lit up the sky, illuminating the black clouds looming overhead. "This is going to be a bad one," her father said as she climbed up to the seat.

He pulled the wagon close to the door of the smokehouse and Kelly and her father jumped down.

Within a few minutes, they were back inside the house. Kelly helped her father lay Artis on the bed she and William shared. Her father barred the door and then took Artis' boots off while Kelly blotted her face and long hair, the only part of Artis that got wet. She handed the towel to her father and he dried his own hair and face.

Kelly carefully removed the luckenbooth and set it aside. Then she began removing the filthy gown. With some difficulty, she was able to get it off Artis, while her father added logs to the hearth fire and heated some water.

"One of us will need to get that bullet out of her," McGuffin said.

She halted, shocked. "Can't we wait and get her to the doctor in town?"

He put his hand on her shoulder. "The way this storm sounds, the creeks will rise and will be impassible, near impossible to get a wagon through. I don't think she'll last through the night if we don't get that lead out of her."

"Have you ever removed a ball from a wound before?" she asked.

"Yes. I have." He didn't elaborate further and turned his face away.

Kelly wondered when her papa had to do such a thing. But now was not the time to discuss it.

"Surgery is perilous, but not as risky as letting the wound fester any more than it already has. It has to come out. Do you want me to do it, Kelly girl?"

"Oh, I wish Bear and William were here. It should be Bear's decision, not mine. Where are they anyway? I pray to God that man chasing us didn't catch up with them."

The frightening thought hung in the air between them.

"Let's not borrow any more trouble than we already have. I'd say we have more than enough as it is. They probably both took whoever it was to William's jail and wisely decided to wait out the storm in town."

"Are you sure you're up to helping Artis? You look in pretty bad shape yourself."

160

"I'm well enough, but she isn't. Let's get started."

Kelly cut open Artis' shift above where the blood had soaked through and laid the fabric to each side of the wound. She gasped at the sight of Artis' torn flesh. It was the first time she had ever seen a bullet wound up close. She stood and stared down at the blood on her own hands and felt a sudden coldness hitting her core.

McGuffin sat down on the bed next to Artis and bent his head over the injury. His fingers gently probed around the wound. "I was hoping the lead was near the surface. But it's not. Get William's bottle of whiskey, some fresh cloths, and the water I warmed. First, we have to get this clean. I need to pour whiskey into the wound."

Kelly jerked her head up. "Won't that…hurt her?" she asked, worried as she set about getting what her father needed.

"I hope so. That means it's cleaning it out." Her father dipped one of the cloths into the warm water and washed away most of the blood. Then he poured a little whiskey directly into the hole left by the lead. "It's a good thing she's passed out. That whiskey stings a fair bit. But what I'm about to do will hurt a good deal more if she wakes. If she does, have her bite down on a clean cloth. Roll one up and have it ready."

Fear and apprehension coursed through Kelly. What if Artis died? God forbid. What would Bear do? Would he blame her father? A wave of panic swept through her confused mind.

"Kelly, we can do this. Trust me girl. But, I will need your help. Get your sewing kit—I'll need a strong thread and a sharp needle. And I need your smallest knife."

Kelly swallowed the panic rising within her and retrieved the items her father asked for. "Should I thread the needle?"

"Yes, but first thrust that knife into those hot coals in the hearth for a moment or two."

Kelly did as he asked and then drew the blade from the coals. Her hand shook as she gave him the knife. Then she grabbed the needle and thread and took several deep breaths to still her trembling hands. It took her several attempts to get the thread through the needle's tiny eye.

"This knife will do nicely, it's long but narrow." He rinsed the ashes off with clean water, letting the liquid spill to the floor, and waited a moment for the blade to cool. Then he inserted the blade tip into the hole on Artis' side.

Kelly thought she might swoon. She was more shaken than she wanted to admit at the sight of the blade point entering Artis' soft flesh.

"How deep do you think it is?" she asked. She turned away without waiting for a reply.

"Don't know yet." He gritted his mouth tighter and leaned in.

She took a deep steadying breath and turned back. She had to do her part to help Artis. "What can I do?"

"Soak a cloth with that whiskey and be ready to apply pressure with it when I get the ball out," he answered. "I think I feel the lead." Kelly held her breath.

He edged the knife deeper, without haste, but with purpose.

Blood began to gush from the wound.

"Kelly, soak up this blood. Don't use the cloth soaked in whiskey. Get another cloth," he said. His voice and face were still calm and full of strength and determination. "Get as close to the hole as you can, without touching the knife or my hand, and apply some pressure."

Kelly had to admire her father's composure. Now, she was sure he had done this before, maybe many times. But she was far from calm herself. Her mouth felt parched and her throat tight. And her heart ached with worry. She had to bite her lower lip to keep from crying.

She positioned herself by Artis' head and reached down toward the draining blood. Artis could ill afford to lose much more blood. If her father didn't locate the lead soon, Artis might be in serious trouble. She was even more certain of that when the cloth quickly became soaked.

Kelly startled as someone tried to open the latched cabin door. Then impatiently pounded on the heavy door.

Fear filled her instantly. Was it Steller? Had he come back to torment them further? Or to get Artis?

The noise woke Nicole and she started crying.

"Artis! Kelly! Open the door for God's sake," she heard Bear shout.

"Don't move," her father told her firmly "He'll just have to wait. I'm almost there."

"Are ye all right?" Bear yelled. "Answer me!"

Chapter 23

Bear pounded the heavy plank door. Why weren't they answering? He could hear the wee bairn crying. His mind searched for a plausible explanation. Perhaps they were up in the loft.

"Kelly," he bellowed again. "Artis!"

"Bear, wait a minute. I'm coming soon," Kelly finally yelled.

Bear was relieved to hear Kelly's voice and assumed Nicole was keeping her occupied. He reached up and wrung the water out of his hair and stomped his feet on the porch to shake some of the moisture off his clothes. Then he removed his boots, poured a little water from both, and sat them by the door to dry. His entire body was chilled. He was looking forward to the warmth of the hearth fire and some hot coffee.

When Kelly unbarred the door a moment later, Bear's throat closed up and his heart nearly stopped. Kelly's bloodstained hand held a cloth soaked red. But it was the look on her face that chilled him to his very bones.

"What happened?" he asked before he could take a step.

"Artis," she replied in a small frightened voice.

"Artis what?" he demanded. Panic rampaged within him.

Kelly was on the verge of tears. "Bear, she was shot by the man who chased us. I didn't realize she was hurt until I got here. I'm so sorry. I would not have driven the wagon so hard had I known. All those bumps." Kelly looked wretched and miserable.

"Shot!" Was Artis dead? *God forbid.*

"She couldn't get out of the wagon. Then I noticed all the blood." Kelly glanced uneasily over her shoulder then back at him. "What happened to you?"

He ignored her question, pushed the door aside, and stomped in. The sight before him weakened his knees. He took a quick breath of utter astonishment. Artis lay on William and Kelly's bed. Blood soaked rags and clothes were everywhere.

In two long strides, he stood by Artis' side. The scene before him ripped his heart apart. Blood was everywhere. Her face was pale and she seemed to be barely breathing. And the sight of a needle entering her skin above a heinous wound made his limbs start shaking. He had to hold back a cry of panic. Instead, he growled with despair. He glowered at Kelly. "Holy God, what's happened?" he demanded.

Kelly didn't answer him. Instead, she quickly moved to pick up her crying daughter.

Mister McGuffin, bent over Artis' stomach, did not look up. "I'm just finishing the last stitch now. I got the lead out!" he said, triumphantly.

"Lead? No. No!" The shock of the news hit him full force. He could only stand there, blank, and shaken.

"Rest assured Bear, if the wound doesn't fester, she'll be all right," McGuffin said.

"That's not reassurin'," he managed, growing angry now. "Wounds often fester." He knelt down next to her and bent to one knee. He put a hand on her forehead. At least she had no fever yet. "Artis," he breathed. He had to swallow the emotions tightening his throat.

McGuffin withdrew the lead from a pocket and handed it to Bear.

His breath caught in his lungs for a moment as he scrutinized the small ball. A tiny thing—nonetheless so often deadly—capable of stealing life from the living. Traces of her blood still clung to the metal, painted on like tiny strokes of red paint. It made his own blood boil.

He stuck the lead in his sporran and fixed his gaze on McGuffin, his eyes searching, imploring, hoping.

McGuffin's voice sounded tired as he said, "I did all I could to reduce the likelihood of the wound festering. I cleaned the wound carefully with whiskey and we heated the knife in the coals to cleanse it. The lead did not hit any of her organs, but Artis lost a significant share of her blood. Nevertheless, she's young and healthy and with Kelly's help and good food, she'll heal fast."

"Why did ye na take her to Boonesborough? To the doctor?" he asked. "Was it the storm?"

"Yes. The way that cloudburst came down, I knew the creeks would rise and be impassible. She would not have lasted through the night, Bear," McGuffin explained. "Besides, she was bleeding too much to withstand another rough wagon ride into town."

"But what do ye know of surgery?"

"I know enough." His tone was patient and calm.

But calm was the last thing Bear felt. He seethed with mounting rage. "That damn thief. If I'd known the whoreson shot her, I would have killed him instead of just woundin' the man," he swore.

"Who was he?" McGuffin asked, as he pulled a clean sheet up to Artis' neck and then laid a blanket over her.

"The fourth robber of the state's gold," he answered abruptly. "He was after revenge because I shot his brother." He didn't want to talk about the robber. He's was too worried. Only once before had he experienced worry this deep and overwhelming. It happened on the journey to Kentucky with his brothers. And that did not end well. A deep foreboding erupted within him.

"Where's William?" Kelly asked.

"In town, lockin' the bastard up in his jail."

"I can see that you got caught in this terrible storm," Kelly said, putting a now quiet Nicole back down on her bed. "You look a bit worse for wear." She handed him a towel to dry off.

He ran the towel across his face once and then tossed it aside. "Aye. Camel and I had to swim across high water. But that does na matter now."

His mind burned with worry. He could think of nothing else.

"Nevertheless, I'm glad you're here and that you are all right," she said, gathering up the bloodied cloths and Artis' soiled clothing. She tossed the cloths into the fireplace and put the gown into a bucket full of water to soak.

The sight of the gown made his belly knot. Like Artis, its beauty was made heart-rending by blood.

Bear towed a chair up next to the bed and just stared at Artis. He loved her. He couldn't lose her. Not now. Not ever. He struggled to hold his raw emotions in check as he gently stroked the top of her head.

"Talk to her," McGuffin urged kindly. "Sometimes the voice of a loved one will keep them from slipping to the other side."

A startling realization washed over Bear as he realized *he* was her only 'loved one'. The thought filled him with an overwhelming need to help her. He leaned closer to her ear and spoke in a soft whisper. "Ye've got to get better wife. As soon as ye do, we'll start buildin' our home. We'll put it right on top of that hill on yer place—I mean *our* place—we'll call it Highland House." He heard his own voice break, as was his heart, but he forced himself to continue. "And we'll build it just as ye want it. With lots of room for all the wee bairns we'll have. You'll find happiness there for many years to come. Remember my pledge. I'll love ye forever, and ever, and ever…and a wee bit more."

He had also pledged his protection. But he'd failed her already. They hadn't even been married one evening, for heaven's sake. She'd lain, all alone in the back of the wagon, with her lifeblood spilling out of her while he'd been gone. How could he have been so negligent? Yes, it was dark, but he should have made sure she was all right after the robber fired his weapon. His carelessness filled him with self-loathing and sent his temper soaring.

Vexed, he clenched his hand until his nails bit into his palm. He wanted to hit the man that did this to his wife. Aye, they were married right enough—and always would be, by God. He stood and pounded his fist on the nearby table, turning over the candlesticks Kelly had just righted.

The sudden noise caused Kelly to jump a bit and then she started straightening things again. He sat down again and watched her for a moment. The candlesticks were not the only things in disarray. A bucket by the door was knocked over, a stool lay on its side, and several trenchers and tankards were scattered on the floor. A few of the strings of dried apples, peppers, and ginseng roots, hanging from the ceiling lay on the floor. Everywhere he glanced, something was out of place. Normally, the cabin was neat and organized.

He abruptly realized Mister McGuffin looked like someone had beaten him. He'd been so troubled about Artis, he failed to notice the man's scrapes, bruises, and torn clothing.

Kelly was acting strangely too. She was normally a strong woman, but he could see her hands trembling.

He sprung up, realizing something else was terribly wrong. "What happened here?"

He stared at McGuffin expecting an answer, but the man just cleared his throat, scrubbed a hand over his face, and looked away.

A brittle silence enveloped the room and the air grew tight with the tension he sensed from both Kelly and her father. Had the man started drinking to excess again?

"Kelly, stop what yer doin'. I asked ye both a question. Answer me

168

lass. What happened here?"

Kelly peered up at him, but still didn't answer. Her words seemed stuck in her throat.

"Damn it! Someone tell me what the hell happened."

"Bear, please sit down. I'll tell you everything from the beginning," Kelly said. She appeared tired and haggard and let out a long sigh.

"I do na want to sit," he growled.

She bit her lip and stared away, her eyes sparkling with tears demanding to be shed. She poured a cup of coffee and handed it to him. "You must be cold," she said, her words and her hands shaky.

"Nay, na longer."

Kelly was clearly distraught. Why? He sat down, not wanting to upset her further, but the muscles in his arms and shoulders tensed even more.

Something else had happened and they didn't want to tell him about it.

Chapter 24

Williiam arrived at the Fort in a foul mood. He did not like riding a horse he was unfamiliar with. And riding the mount in terrible weather, with a thunderstorm booming overhead, and the gelding bearing the weight of the prisoner too, made the trip back to Boonesborough slow and far from pleasant. The horse had shied at the lightning more than once and side-stepped far too many times, trying to rid himself of the added weight. He finally decided to dismount to make it easier on the weary animal. Trudging through the sticky mud and driving rain, head bent against the wind, he led the gelding the last mile or so. Never had a mile seemed so long.

William's best clothes were soaked and his tall black boots were brown with mud. He was so chilled even his teeth trembled. All he wanted to do was toss this man into a jail cell and lock him up for the night. Maybe for good.

Bear had wisely wounded the robber instead of killing him, and the man would need medical care. But first, William needed to see what this man knew about where the robbers hid the state's gold.

After tying the horse in front of the blockhouse, he yanked the still knocked out fellow off and then drug him inside his office. He dropped the dripping wet man on the wooden floor. Leaving the prisoner tied securely, he went upstairs to wake his deputy. William provided the young man with quarters in the blockhouse as part of his salary.

William hurried downstairs and found the robber moaning. He was sure this one deserved to suffer, but he would get him medical care as soon as he got the information he needed.

When Mitchell joined him, he briefly explained to the deputy what had happened. Then, grabbing the robber's feet and arms, they carried him to the next room and put him in one of the dirt-floor cells fitted with bars and padlocks. After untying the ropes, he locked the jail securely, and returned to the office.

"I could sure use a fire and some coffee deputy," William requested. "Hopefully it will also wake this bloke up and we'll get him to talking."

As the rain continued to drum against the roof and the thunder rumbled overhead, he removed his soaking tricorne and hung it on an antler hat rack by the door. Then he took a moment to pour the rainwater from his muddy boots and set them aside to dry out. He hung his wet coat on the back of a chair, dried his face off, and reloaded his pistol with dry powder.

While William changed into a spare shirt he kept in his office drawer, the deputy scraped flint against a firesteel to light some kindling and soon had a small fire going in the office's undersized hearth. Before long, the strong smell of the coffee brewing did help to wake the robber.

"Where am I?" the man asked in a voice so weak William barely heard it.

William grabbed the handbill off his desk and, followed by Mitchell, strode into the room that held the cells. "I'm Sheriff Wyllie and you're in my jail," he answered.

He could see the prisoner through the bars. He looked pale, cold, and obviously in pain. "We know who you are—the fourth robber of the state's treasury." William held up the handbill so the thief could see the drawing depicting the four men. "And many other pilferings have been attributed to you and your three dead cohorts."

"One of them was my younger brother," the man hissed, his fervent anger rapidly bringing him to life.

"All three were killed while committing an armed robbery. We don't abide stealing in Boonesborough."

"Go to hell."

"What's your name?" Deputy Mitchell asked.

"You can go to hell too," the man shot back.

"All right, we'll just call you Mister Thief," William said. "I have a 'T' brand hanging right over there that has in the past been used to brand the hands of thieves." William had never used the brand himself, but didn't want this man to know that. "Perhaps Judge Webb will order branding as part of your punishment, Mister Thief."

"I want a doctor. Get this lead out of my shoulder," Mister Thief demanded. "And get me some dry clothes. I'm freezing." The man's teeth were rattling.

The robber's tone was belligerent and William was in no mood for either defiance or demands. "There are four classes of punishment Judge Webb imposes—fines, public shame, physical chastisement such as whipping, and death. I have a feeling you have all four in your future," William said.

"That coffee sure smells good," Mitchell said. "Would you like some sheriff?"

"Indeed, I would," William said.

For a few minutes, they both sipped the fragrant brew in front of Mister Thief. William leaned comfortably against the wall and he could see the man swallowing and licking his lips, craving the hot coffee.

"Can I have some of that?" the thief finally asked in a meek voice.

"Only cooperative prisoners get coffee," William said. It was bait that hid a hook. "But we have a barrel of stale water over there if you want a dipper full."

172

Mister Thief pinched his lips and glared at William. "My name is Jacob Miller."

"Is that your real name?" he asked.

"Yes."

"Thank you, Mister Miller." William said. "Deputy, please get the man a cup of coffee."

As the deputy retrieved a cup, William asked, "Where did you and the others hide the gold you stole from the state treasury?"

Miller just stared at William. "If I tell you that, what do I get?"

"First, a doctor. I'll send my deputy to wake the town physician now instead of waiting until morning. That way you won't bleed all night and it will be less likely to fester."

"And?" Miller asked, through narrowed eyes.

"And, I'll tell Judge Webb that you cooperated during questioning," he answered. "Perhaps that will cause the good judge to not send you straight to the gallows."

"Only *perhaps*?"

"Well, Judge Webb has a well-earned reputation for being an intolerant and impatient judge. I cannot guarantee what he has in store for you. But if I were in your boots, I'd sure try to win his favor."

Mitchell passed a cup of steaming coffee through the bars and the man took it with his uninjured arm.

William knew it wouldn't be long before the bleeding worsened if the lead weren't removed soon and the shoulder stitched up.

"Where's the gold?" William asked again.

"I might as well tell you. You'll find it anyway," Miller reluctantly answered. "It's in my saddle bag. I was going to take off for Tennessee after I robbed the four of you and took my revenge on that fellow who killed my brother."

No wonder the horse had such difficulty. The poor animal had been carrying the weight of two men and the gold. It had been raining so hard he never took the time to look inside the two saddle bags. The gold had been hidden in plain sight.

"Deputy, go outside and bring in the saddle bags hanging on that horse. Then take the weary animal to the stables and see that he's feed properly, watered, and sheltered from the storm. Give him a thorough wipe down too."

"You'll say a good word for me?" Miller implored, returning William's attention to the robber.

"I'll let the judge know you revealed where the gold was and anything else you're willing to tell me."

"And the doc?"

"As soon as he gets back from tending to your horse, I'll send my deputy to fetch the doctor."

William shut the outer door to the jail and eyed his still scrawny deputy as he drug in the weighty bags leaving a trail of water behind them on the wooden floorboards. "Thanks deputy, I'll take it from here. Please tend to the robber's poor horse as quickly as you can and then fetch the doc."

After Mitchell left, William inspected the well-soaked leather saddle bags sitting in the middle of his office floor.

He opened one bag. The thief had told the truth. The shining gold coins glittered in the dim light of William's oil lamp. The heavy bags held a mixture of gold eagles, half eagles, and quarter eagles. William knew the coins in the dazzling assortment were eleven twelfths pure gold, the same 22 karats level as English crown gold.

Governor Garrard would be well pleased. He needed a safe place to store the gold. He used his knife to pry up one of the floor boards under his desk and tucked the weighty bags inside.

He retrieved writing materials so he could make an accurate list for the judge and went back to question Miller. "Now, I want you to tell me what other robberies you four committed and where," William demanded.

Once he had the list, he would send messages via the postal rider to each of the towns' sheriffs and determine if any murders had been committed during the robberies. He wouldn't be surprised to find out that the four committed numerous slayings.

If this were the case, he had a feeling Miller would wind up hanging despite his cooperation.

With his quill and another cup of coffee in hand, he sat at a rickety pine table against the wall in the narrow jail room and Miller began relating a lengthy list of crimes. It was going to be a long night and he wouldn't be going back to Whispering Hills anytime soon.

Bear and Artis would just have to wait to get married.

He hoped his brother would not be too distraught.

Chapter 25

Kelly sat across the table and Bear waited for her to begin. She seemed to be choosing her words carefully. For several minutes he listened to her relate what had happened when she arrived at the cabin. A man named Steller had been waiting here for Artis, holding a pistol on her father. The name lingered around the edges of his mind as he continued listening to Kelly. Then he remembered where he had heard the name before—from Artis. His father taught him to forgive his enemy, but remember the bastard's name. So he'd made a point to remember the name of the man who had caused Artis so much grief. "Wait, did ye say the man's name was Steller?"

"Yes, I did."

"He's the devil that slit her mother's throat!" It was no wonder Artis drug herself out to the smokehouse. She must have been terrified.

"Murdered her mother?" Kelly asked, her eyes widening.

Plainly, Kelly had not overhead the conversation he'd had with Artis in the back of the wagon on their way to town for the delegates' meeting.

"Aye. And the devil drove Artis and her village from Scotland. He burned many other Highland towns to the ground to make room for sheep farmin'."

"That doesn't surprise me. The man is beyond cruel. If he'd found

176

Artis, he would have taken her with him, despite her severe wound."

The questions mounted in Bear's mind. "Why? Why did he come all this way for her and how did he find her? And why would he want to take her with him?"

Kelly turned her pensive face away from him.

He reached out and put a hand on her forearm. "Tell me lass."

"Oh, Bear. I don't want to be the one to tell you."

"Tell me what?" He tried to stay calm, but he was losing his patience. The veins in his neck throbbed and strained against his skin. Why was she being so perplexing?

Kelly rubbed her lips with her fingers as if to hold in her words. Then she took a deep breath and shot the words out. "Steller says she is his wife."

Her words thrust through him like a knife to the heart. He felt as if his breath were cut off. He withdrew his hand from her arm. It started shaking. He was glad he was sitting down because he might have fallen down, so great was his shock. Could it be true? The question hammered painfully on his heart. He'd known Artis only a few days and had no way of knowing if everything she'd told him were true. Was it the worst sort of naiveté, even madness, to believe everything she'd said was true? All the tenderness he sensed coming from her, was it genuine? Had he unwisely rushed into marrying her? Did he give his heart to a married woman?

His entire body knotted, his muscles twisting and tightening, as he sat there considering Steller's outrageous claim. He ignored the mocking voice inside his mind that repeated *'she's his wife,'* over and over. Another more forceful voice answered *'nay, she's my wife'* again and again.

He gazed over at Artis, lying on the bed, fighting for her very life. She looked so pale and helpless. His mind replayed everything she'd told him over the last few days. In his mind, he heard every word of the pledge she made to him. Her vow felt as true as God's word. He tasted the sweetness of her kisses again. He felt her warmth against his chest. He touched their clan crest. It all meant something. Everything.

And, somehow, with complete clarity, he knew he could trust her.

He pushed back from the table and stood. He would give no credence to anything Steller said. The man was the vilest sort of human—capable of anything. Lying would come naturally and easily to him. It was nothing more than a despicable lie.

"Nay, I do na believe the loathsome man. He's lyin'," Bear said fiercely. "I trust her. I trust her heart. She said she loved me and only me and I believe her."

Kelly's eyes widened. "Oh Bear, I know you're right. Artis would never have married a man like that. I haven't known her long, but I trust her too."

"So do I," McGuffin agreed. "But I don't trust Steller. Bear, the man nearly killed Nicole trying to force Kelly to reveal where Artis was. What kind of man could kill a child?"

"The kind that dies by my hand," Bear said harshly. "*Na sir 's na seachan an cath.* Neither seek nor shun the fight. Steller came here seeking Artis to hurt her again. I'll na give him the chance."

"No, you can't follow him! He said he'd come back and kill Nicole and Papa if anyone came after him," Kelly insisted.

"What else did the whoreson say?" he asked.

Kelly seemed reluctant to say anything, so McGuffin spoke up. "He said he would come back for Artis. And maybe Kelly too."

He could hear the worry in McGuffin's voice. Steller's vile threats clearly terrified both of them.

"Did he beat ye?" he asked McGuffin.

"We fought. I refused to tell him where Artis was. That was while all of you were at the ball—before Kelly brought Artis back in the wagon."

He turned to Kelly. "Did he hurt ye?"

She answered in a rush of words. "Yes. He slapped me harshly and nearly strangled me when he couldn't find Artis. He thought I'd hidden her somewhere."

"How did Artis hide?" he asked.

Kelly explained, telling him how she provoked Steller into a shouting match, hoping it would wake Artis and give her time to hide. And that it must have worked, because when Steller went outside, Artis was gone.

"So, she was so fearful of Steller, she forced herself from the wagon and even after losin' all that blood, managed to drag herself to hide?" he asked.

"She did. She was exceedingly brave. I found her on the smokehouse floor clutching the mountain lion's skin against her heart."

Bear had to swallow the raw emotions that welled up inside of him. His love for Artis grew even stronger. He had not been able to protect her from the robber's bullet, but by God, he would protect her from this Steller or die trying.

"I'm goin' after him," he told them.

Kelly's face filled with alarm. "No, please, you can't. He'll find a way to kill Nicole. And maybe Papa too. His warning was deadly serious."

"At least wait for William," McGuffin pleaded. "Kelly's right. The man is profoundly dangerous."

"I canna. Steller's trail will grow cold. And William may be tied up with that robber for a while. I wounded the thief so William will have to see to his medical care and question him about the stolen gold."

"Then I'll go with you," McGuffin offered.

"Nay, this is somethin' I must do for Artis. I need ye to tend to her and protect our family. He glanced over at the spot by the door where Kelly normally kept her weapons. "Where are yer weapons?"

"Steller stole them, along with the pistol you handed me in the wagon to reload," Kelly answered. "He took my lead and powder too."

"Anythin' else?"

"Food, water, and blankets," she answered.

"That means he's plannin' to hide away for a while," Bear said. "What did he look like?"

"He a big man, and tall, but not as big as you," McGuffin said. "Dark hair, severe features, and evil eyes."

"He's riding a magnificent black stallion," Kelly added.

"Mister McGuffin, in the interest of time, I'd appreciate it if ye'd feed and water Camel. I'm goin' to your cabin to change into my spare buckskins and get my weapons. I'll bring your rifle and lead back too. Keep the rifle loaded and the door barred to everyone but William. You never know what kind of tricks Steller might pull."

"I'll take care of them," McGuffin said.

"Kelly, if ye have any food left and a spare blanket, I'd appreciate it. While I'm gone, please do all ye can for Artis, includin' prayin'. And do na worry about Steller coming back to hurt yer daughter or father."

"How can you be so sure he won't?" Her voice shook with anxiety.

"Dead men can't shoot."

He moved over to the bed and stood by Artis. Lightly he fingered a loose tendril of hair on her cheek. Then he bent and delicately kissed her lips. "Get well, my love, *my* wife. Do na worry. He'll never hurt ye again. I swear that on the MacKay clan name."

Chapter 26

C aked mud covered Camel's hooves and wet dirt hung on the horse's coat up to his hocks as Bear had made his way north through the dense dripping forest. The storm had blown through allowing some star and moonlight to penetrate the darkness and he had taken advantage of his keen night vision.

The first night, the ground was still largely a quagmire, and made following Steller difficult. It was like trying to track someone through thick brown gravy. With owls hooting and wolves howling, he'd tenaciously pursued the man through the dark.

He'd managed to spot a few signs of Steller's general movement—tall grass with heavy mud clinging to it in a straight line, a hoof print now and then, and an occasional broken twig or branch. And the next morning, he'd found where the man had camped.

But the rest of that day, yielded no sign of Steller's direction.

Bear had to relentlessly fight his lack of sleep and his eyes grew tired from focusing so intensely on the ground, searching for any clue that would tell him where Steller went. Hour after hour, as the sun first climbed and then descended in the sky, he combed the tree-covered hills, still damp from the heavy rain. Normally he loved the woods, and would have reveled in the wild blazing color of the fall leaves. But not now—not with his mind focused steadfastly on finding Steller.

The next day also yielded nothing. Somewhere, he had taken the wrong way. It made him pissing mad. But it also made him even more determined to find the man. He'd promised Artis. And Kelly and her father. God how he hoped they were all still safe.

He wished Sam were here with him. His oldest brother could track a butterfly flying over solid rock. Sam called Bear's tracking skills excellent too, honed during his many years as a hunter. But somewhere Steller had managed to elude him.

He worried that the man had doubled back. But William would be there by now and wouldn't leave until Bear returned. He also thought it unlikely that Steller would go back so soon. He figured the man would hide about three days ride away from Whispering Hills. That way he could come back for Artis in about a week when she would be well enough to ride. He might even wait as long as two weeks. But there was no way to tell what the devil planned.

"Another day. This better be the day I find him," Bear swore as he woke. He'd slept with his hatchet clutched in his hand. Camel would alert him if anything or anyone came near, so he'd allowed himself to sleep for a few hours. But his sleep was troubled and restless. He'd dreamt of Artis. He kept trying to wake her, but she wouldn't wake. No matter what he did, no matter how he pleaded. He shook his head trying to rid himself of the disturbing dream that left him feeling uneasy.

He stood and stuck the hatchet in his belt. He scratched his itchy face, covered now with three days of whiskers and dirt.

His frustration had multiplied with every hour of unproductive searching, but this morning it swelled enough to cause his jaw to ache and his stomach to feel like it carried a rock. He decided not to even eat and saddled Camel. There wasn't much left to eat anyway and he wasn't about to take the time to hunt or fish for something.

He chewed on his lip instead. His constant worry for Artis was nearly beyond endurance. And after the unnerving dream, his fears grew stronger than ever. He could not go much longer without going back to check on her. He resolved to give the search the rest of the day and if he hadn't found Steller, he would head back to Whispering Hills tonight.

He'd prayed fervently for Artis every morning and every night. He struggled to trust God to heal her, but he couldn't stop the incessant concern that gripped his heart like a tightened fist.

Before taking off, he rode to a higher hilltop close by and, sitting atop Camel, studied the hills around him. Where to next? Due north, the terrain turned nearly vertical. So, Steller had to have gone either west or east. But which? To the west, he could see the hills gradually descending, which would make the land boggy and difficult to traverse after such a severe rain. To the east, the hills gradually climbed which would allow a rider to reach higher and drier ground.

It was time to make a 'By Guess and By God' decision that relied upon experience, intuition, and faith.

Bear headed east. "I know yer out here somewhere, ye slippery bastard."

As he had in the past when fatigue crept into him, Bear imposed an iron control on himself. Through the morning, he forced himself to stay extremely focused, scrutinizing everything. He watched for any signs of the turf, brush, or trees being disturbed.

He would also look up regularly to be sure he stayed on a due east course. It was then he spotted it—a thin thread of light gray smoke, almost invisible against the cloudy sky.

His heart leapt. Could it be Steller? It had to be.

As he headed in the direction of the rising smoke, he prepared himself mentally to be the warrior he was. The difference between an ordinary man and a warrior was the difference between a puffy white cloud and a thunderstorm.

And a warrior gave his enemy only two choices—surrender or die.

But Bear didn't know if he could give Steller that choice. The man deserved to die for murdering Artis' mother. He hated Steller and knew Artis did to. Rightfully so. He could just picture the aftermath of Steller's destruction of her village and her life—fire, smoke, the wails of children and their distraught mothers, her half-scorched uncle dying in her arms, and most tragic of all—her beloved mother's body burning within the walls of her childhood home.

How many tears did Steller force Artis to shed? How hard did her heart break when she'd boarded that ship? And Steller's actions caused her to become a slave for seven long years. He'd figured it up—it was two-thousand, five-hundred, and fifty-five days. Days of her life taken from her forever.

The misery Steller inflicted on Artis and many others was beyond imagining.

He'd been able to repress his anger when she first told him about Steller—choosing instead to focus on the future and encouraging Artis to do the same.

But now that Steller had invaded their world, hurt Kelly and her father, threatened Artis, and even claimed that he was married to her, he allowed his rage to flare within him. How dare the man lie about Artis? The devil would live to regret his lies.

But not for much longer.

His eyes burned and his body tensed as he studied the exact location of the smoke, wanting to pinpoint the spot in his mind in case Steller put the fire out.

Pinpoint where Steller would die.

He checked the powder in his rifle. He could aim the weapon extremely accurately, making the lead's flight deadly at over two-hundred yards. But he did not like the idea of just shooting a man. He preferred to fight him face to face.

He'd lost one of his pistols during the storm. Steller had stolen his second pistol as well as Kelly's, and probably also had at least one he owned himself. He would have to engage the killer in close combat. He'd sharpened his long knife the night before to an edge that could peel a grape. He'd also honed the blade that hung from a pouch on his neck. His smaller bladed *sgian dubh* remained tucked into the top of his tall moccasins. And he had his hatchet—his weapon of choice.

When he'd ridden closer, he stopped a safe distance away and tied Camel. He didn't want Camel to alert the man to his presence. He used the cover of trees and brush to make his way forward, step by step.

He could smell smoke now. The normally welcome fragrance of a cook fire put his senses on high alert.

His enemy was near.

Chapter 27

I s he back?" Artis asked. Her voice was still weak.

"No, not yet," Kelly answered once again. "He'll be here soon."

Kelly hoped Bear would return soon. Artis' fever was rising and she hadn't been able to even sit up in bed for three days. Yesterday, she'd eaten for the first time, taking a few bites of bread soaked in sweetened milk. That was the only sign of improvement though. Artis had lost so much blood, it would take quite a while to regain her strength.

"Here you must drink more of this." She lifted Artis' head and held the pewter cup to her lips. "Willow bark broth will relieve your pain."

William had stayed with them while her father went to town for laudanum—a mixture of opium and brandy. But the doctor only had enough opium to make enough for the first day. He told McGuffin that after the laudanum was gone, Kelly should brew a tea made from the bark of a willow tree to ease the pain and that it was also beneficial for reducing fever.

Her father had spent a good part of that day searching for a willow tree and finally found one. When he brought a plentiful supply of the bark back, he told both her and William where it was located in case they ever needed it again. Lord forbid.

"My pain has lessened," Artis whispered. "But I'm so hot."

Kelly touched Artis' cheek. The skin was warm beneath her fingertips. She lowered the cover down to Artis' waist and put a cool cloth to her forehead. Then using her fingers she brushed the damp hair away from Artis' clammy neck.

"Better?"

"Aye."

"Do you think you could eat a little something?" Kelly asked.

"Nay," she said, closing her eyes again.

"How is she?" William asked as he strode in.

Kelly stood and went to speak with William who was hanging his lead pouch and powder horn by the door.

"Her discomfort has eased, and she's talking more, but her fever is rising. Oh William, I'm afraid her wound is festering. You or Papa must go to town and get the doctor," she said softly.

"I'll send your father. I'm not leaving here until we know Steller is either dead or in my jail." He walked over to Nicole and gazed down at his sleeping daughter.

As soon as he'd came back from town, she had told William everything Steller had done, including threatening to kill Nicole. William had gotten so mad he wanted to go after the man himself. He'd agreed with Kelly that Steller was lying about being married to Artis. He had questioned Kelly and her father thoroughly and in the end, much to Kelly's relief, decided to stay there to guard all of them in case Steller came back.

"I doubt Bear will allow Steller to live long enough to reach your jail," Kelly declared.

"If I knew where Bear was, I'd go after him," William said. "I hope I made the right decision staying here with you. If something happens to Bear, I'd never forgive myself for not going to help him." He raked a hand through his blonde hair.

Kelly could tell William was extremely worried this morning. The last couple of days, he'd managed to stay busy around the cabin with chores, trying to keep his mind off Bear and Steller. But it had now been three days and they were all growing more concerned and ill at ease.

Kelly knew William would need to get back to his duties soon. The doctor had removed the bullet from the prisoner's shoulder before William left for home. Aside from his constant complaining, William said the robber was all right and could just sit in his jail until William was ready to deal with him. William had asked her father to let the deputy know that he would have to remain at Whispering Hills until Steller was captured.

"I need your father to check on my prisoner too. Even though he told me where the gold was—largely because I would have found it there anyway—I'm going to suggest that Judge Webb punish him to the fullest extent possible. I still can't believe the bastard shot Artis and none of us realized it. Bear must have been devastated."

"Is he back?" Artis asked, turning her head their way.

"She keeps asking the same question," Kelly whispered.

"Just keep telling her he will be soon. I'll go tell your father to get the doctor."

"Tell him to hurry," Kelly said as William slipped out the door. She thought a lot of the good doctor. Doc McDowell completed his medical training in Scotland. He'd told her once that Edinburgh was a mecca for medical students from all over the world. But he also accepted many Indian and African healing methods and believed the plants of nature provided remedies for nearly every human sickness. He practiced medicine in Danville two weeks a month and two weeks in Boonesborough. Kelly prayed the doctor was still in Boonesborough. He would know what to do.

She went back to Artis and took the cloth from her forehead. "Bear will be here soon, I'm sure." She dipped the cloth in fresh water, wrung it out, and put it back on Artis' forehead. "You have a bit of a fever, but this cool cloth will make you feel better."

"Kelly," Artis said, gripping Kelly's hand. "Steller may have killed Bear." Tears welled up in Artis' eyes and slid down the side of her face and into her hair.

"You mustn't think like that. I know Bear. He's a fierce warrior. Steller doesn't stand a chance against him."

"And I know Steller. He's vicious and capable of the worst kind of atrocities. Kelly, he killed my dear sweet mother," she said, her voice breaking.

"I know Artis. Bear told me. And I am so sorry. But please try not to think about that now. You must save your strength so you will be feeling better when Bear gets back."

Tears still flowed from Artis eyes. She covered her face with her hands, as though she were hiding her sadness. Then Artis' shoulders quaked as her weeping grew harder.

Kelly just sat next to her on the bed, letting Artis weep. Sometimes it was better to let all the sorrow out. Artis was clearly still grieving for all her losses.

Artis' hands clenched into fists and she pounded the bed on each side of her. "I brought that evil man to ye. He could have killed ye and yer wee daughter. And he may kill Bear. Please forgive me." She turned pleading eyes toward Kelly.

"There's nothing to forgive, dear one," Kelly said. "You didn't bring him here. His own hatred did."

"I know why he hates me. It's because I would na marry him. I spurned him. That's why he killed my mother." She buried her tear-stained face in the crux of her bent arm.

"And you are worried that he will kill Bear too?"

Artis pulled her arm down and gazed up at Kelly, her expression one of deep wretchedness. "Aye."

Kelly could see a war of emotions—grief, anger, and worry—raging within Artis. Her face was blotchy and red with both rage and fever. She had to get Artis to calm down.

"Here blow your nose." Kelly gave her a cloth. "Do you remember Philippians 4:8?"

Artis nodded that she did, but didn't say anything.

"...whatever is lovely...think about such things," Kelly quoted.

Artis blew her nose, and after she took a few deep breaths, she seemed less agitated.

"Good, now I want you to drink some more of this broth and then sleep." She held the cup up to Artis' parched lips once again and after two swallows, she laid her head down. "I've sent for the doctor. He'll know what to do about your fever."

"Bear, Bear, please come back to me!" Artis bit her lip and squeezed her eyes, as though she were trying to hold in her emotions.

"He will. I promise," Kelly said.

"How can ye promise?"

"Because I know the Wyllie brothers. Someday, I'll tell you how they rescued me and later how they saved the people of Boonesborough from some dreadfully bad men. They're brave unyielding men, well used to fighting for their family. He'll fight for you Artis."

"With a strong hand," Artis said, wistfully. "Our clan's motto."

"I saw Bear proudly wearing your clan badge at the ball. Did you give it to him?"

"Aye, I did. And he gave me a luckenbooth—the symbol of love and union between two people. Where is it?" Her eyes widened in panic.

"Be easy, it's right here." Kelly retrieved the beautiful brooch from a side table and handed it to Artis.

She clutched it against her palm, and laid that fist upon her heart as she closed her still wet lashes and fell asleep once again.

Chapter 28

S teller threw another log on his cook fire. He wasn't too worried about one of those farmers deciding to chase after him. He'd seen the fear in Kelly's eyes. She'd make sure they'd stay close to home to protect her. Just in case, though, he used dry wood because it burnt with little or no smoke. And after his long trek through the woods, they'd never find him here.

He'd shot the rabbits earlier and had them cooking over the fire for the last hour or so. His stomach growled and his mouth watered. The sizzling meat was almost done.

He wanted to cook himself a good meal because today he would start back toward Artis. He couldn't wait to literally get his hands on her. He'd spent the three days getting here imagining ways to have his way with her. The thoughts fed his unrequited need for vengeance.

First, he would take her forcefully, shoving his rod into her, over and over, until her privy parts bled. He'd show her what kind of man he was— what she'd been missing all this time.

Then he would bugger her soul to hell.

He tugged one of the rabbits from above the fire and left the other to cook a little longer. He blew on the meat too cool it.

He'd almost enjoyed his three days in the Kentucky woods. At first, the silence had been a little unsettling. So were the occasional howls of wolves and the shrill yapping of coyotes. But now, as he leaned against a big oak tree and pulled strips of the hot meat from the rabbit, he found the forest peaceful and calming to his soul.

Sometimes he wondered if he still had a soul. If he did, he was sure it was long ago condemned. Maybe someday he'd give up his wicked ways and start a new life. But not yet. He still had things he had to do that some would consider sinful or depraved. Gratifying his need for vengeance was all he had left of his life.

He licked one of his greasy fingers and then glanced up when he heard something off in the distance in front of him—a log cracking perhaps. It was probably just a forest animal. But he'd better check just to be sure. He tossed the meat aside onto his camp plate and quickly wiped most of the grease on his breeches.

He stood and reached for the long rifle he'd taken from Kelly, which was leaning next to him against a tree, but it slipped from his still oily hand and fell to the ground. He bent to pick it up.

"Stay down," he heard a deep voice growl, from right behind him. "Move away from that rifle, but don't straighten up."

Startled, he started to reach for the rifle.

"If ye move that hand another inch, yer a dead man. Move away from that rifle. Now!"

Steller shuffled a few feet to his right.

"Now toss yer pistols—all of them—behind ye."

He threw a flintlock behind him.

"The rest of them now! And be quick about it," the voice demanded.

He flung one more.

"I said the rest, I will na ask ye again," the man warned.

He pitched the other two and could hear the man picking them up and sticking all four in a belt.

"Ye can stand erect now, but keep yer hands in the air. And turn so I can see yer slimy face."

Steller turned slowly. Before him stood one of the biggest men he had ever seen—a heavily-armed hulk of a man. Not only did he have the pistols, he had a long rifle, at least two knives he could see, and a wicked looking hatchet.

Bloody hell! Where had this man come from? And why? The man's speech sounded as though he were from the Highlands too.

"My Highlander friend, ye are welcome to share my meal. Ye do na have to rob me," he tried.

"I am na yer friend and I am na a robber."

"Well then, may I have yer name?"

"No."

The man just kept staring at him with narrowed flinty eyes. The face was a mask of carefully controlled rage, his ire revealed only by the muscle that clenched along his firm jaw. He held his head high and his massive shoulders back. He kept his stance wide and wore tall moccasins. No wonder he hadn't heard this man sneak up on him. Moccasins were much quieter than boots.

Growing nervous, Steller swallowed, even though the man wasn't holding one of the pistols in his hand. "As ye can see, I'm just a weary traveler, passin' through Kentucky."

"What is yer name weary traveler?" the man asked mockingly.

"It's Patrick Steller," he answered hastily, and then at once regretted giving the man his real name.

"Yer a long way from any of the main roads in Kentucky. Did ye get lost, Mister Steller?"

"Aye. But I think I'm headed in the right direction now." He tried to keep his tone light and friendly.

"Tis a fine animal ye have there. Where did ye get him? And what is the horse's breedin'.'"

So that's what this man was after. His horse. He was nothing more than a common horse thief. He couldn't let this man take his horse and leave him stranded out here in the middle of bloody nowhere.

"He is a fine stallion. I bought him in Virginia," he answered smoothly. He ignored the question about breeding. "But he can be a wee bit high headed, as most stallions are inclined to be. He still needs a lot of training to make him level headed. He's pitched me more than once," he lied.

"Tell me more about ye, Mister Steller."

"Well, I am a respected lawyer in Virginia," he lied. "But I am movin' my practice to Kentucky—Louisville perhaps."

"What is your legal opinion of habeas corpus?"

Steller had no idea what habeas corpus meant. "Och…ye must be hungry. Can I interest ye in some of my tasty rabbit?" He gestured toward the meat still sizzling on the fire.

Bear was enjoying his verbal torture of the man. He wanted to confirm what he knew in his heart—that this man was a deceiver. That his black heart spewed lies as easily as his lungs released a breath.

As a brother of William, he'd learned quite a lot over the years about the law, including that a writ of habeas corpus demands that a prisoner be taken before a court to determine whether the custodian has lawful authority to detain the prisoner. It had been common legal practice for hundreds of years.

"Ye did not answer my question about the meanin' of habeas corpus. Tell me. Now!"

Steller stiffened and just stared at him, looking annoyed.

"And ye could not tell me the horse's breeding," Bear added in the same cool tone.

Infuriated now, the man's lips tightened and his dark eyes heated.

Growing impatient, Bear took a step toward Steller. "Now ye've proved what I already believed. Yer a bloody liar. And a thief. And a murderer. Why did ye lie about being married to Artis?"

Shock registered on Steller's face. Then mockery tainted his stare. "You have na idea what Artis' past is. I do. I was there. How do ye know she's *not* married to me?"

He squinted his eyes and gave Steller a penetrating glare. "Tell me the truth if ye do na wish to die this day."

"I…" Steller stammered. His features contorted with hatred. The man's overly bright eyes clawed at him with talons of anger as he yanked a long knife from his belt.

Bear withdrew his hatchet. "The truth!"

They stared at each other across a palatable cloud of contemptuous hostility.

Then a distant movement in the timber beyond Steller caught Bear's eye. A black blur, no two black blurs were moving toward them through the forest shadows. While Bear snuck up from the west, they'd been stalking the campsite from the east.

Steller came at him at a charge, yelling with fury, and wielding the knife with wild rage.

Bear easily side-stepped and then pivoted a few feet away. He did not want to use his hatchet on Steller. Not yet anyway.

He would need it for the bears.

Chapter 29

The forest vibrated like thunder as the enormous black bears barreled toward them, their fear-provoking jaws agape.

The smell of the roasting rabbits must have drawn them.

Steller turned around at the ominous sound. "Bloody hell."

Bear stuck the hatchet in his belt again.

Steller's stallion squealed in panic, reared, tore his bridle off the tree branch, and ran off.

"Shoot them!" Steller screamed.

Bear already had the larger male in the sights of his long rifle, but the animal, running faster than a horse, unexpectedly plunged in Bear's direction and the shot missed.

"Ye damn fool!" Steller swore. "Ye missed."

The bears were closing the gap between them with astonishing speed.

Bear threw down the rifle, giving Steller a black look. He didn't have time for fools or time to reload. He glanced over at the rifle Steller had knocked to the ground. He didn't have time to reach it. "Are the pistols loaded?" he shouted.

"Yes! Give me one!"

For a split second, Bear considered it, but his distrust for Steller was so great he decided against it. He grabbed two pistols and aimed for the head of the closer smaller bear.

He realized the tiny balls of lead would do little to stop the massive bears. The female looked to be the size of two men put together. The gigantic male, lagging a few yards behind the female, was even bigger. But if he could manage to shoot at least one of the fearsome beasts in the head, that would improve their chances.

Perhaps because Bear was the larger man, the male headed straight toward him. He could see intelligence and determination in the beast's brown eyes. Steam puffed out of his drooling mouth. Rippling muscles foretold astounding strength.

He put determination into his own eyes, letting the brute know he was in for a fight. For this battle, Bear would have to call on his own savage inner fire.

When the bears were within range, he fired, then immediately fired the second set of pistols at the larger of the two bears.

But the black bears merely ran through the murky smoke of the flintlocks, as though only a bee had bitten them. Bear threw down the pistols.

Steller brandished his knife uselessly at the approaching female as she honed in on him. Terror swathed the man's face. He wouldn't be surprised to see Steller run. If he did, he would be a dead man. He might be anyway.

Bear drew his hatchet with his right hand and his long knife with his left. The muscles of his forearms hardened beneath his sleeves. He stood ready for battle, his knees slightly bent, and his stance wide. Fiery blood coursed through his veins.

He'd faced death at the jaw of a black bear once before, and had the scars to prove it, but he'd managed to live through the attack by keeping his wits and his weapons sharp. As a bear hunter for many towns in New Hampshire, hired by farmers who wanted to protect their livestock and children, he'd killed and skinned numerous bears before. But he completed those kills from a distance. Now, he would have to use his knowledge of bear anatomy to strike the bear where it would be most vulnerable.

In the next moment, absolute chaos erupted as both bears pounced and the men fought with howling biting balls of fur. Steller was soon screaming. But Bear couldn't look. He had his own bear to fend off.

He lashed out wildly with both weapons and used his arms to protect his face. He also kept his body bent, trying to keep the vicious claws away from his organs. If the bear got to his heart or other vital body parts, he would be a dead man. After slashing the bear several times, and receiving several cuts on his arms, he succeeded in getting the male to back off long enough for him to take a much needed breath or two.

"Ye didn't expect such a fight, did ye?" Bear sneered through clenched teeth.

He clutched both weapons tightly, his heart pounding harder than he could ever remember, as the bear bellowed and growled. Then, grunting, it circled around him, came at his right side, and threw one powerful swipe to his shoulder with an immense paw.

Bear used his hatchet and every bit of strength in his arm to block the blow. His arm felt as if it might break so great was the force of the wallop, but with his other hand, he sunk his long knife into the bear's side. He had to leave the knife where he planted it when the monster twisted away.

He pulled the knife sheathed in the Indian pouch hanging from his neck. Regrettably, it was much smaller, but he squeezed both the knife and the hatchet tightly in his hands.

A ferocious roar deafened him. The angered bear leapt at him and clawed at the side of Bear's torso, ripping his buckskin shirt and his flesh. It tried to bite his side too, but he pivoted just out of the reach of the jaw's razor sharp teeth. As he spun, he raised his arm in a sweeping arch and slammed his hatchet toward the bear's back. The wood handle held in his hand reverberated violently, all the way to his shoulder, as the cutting edge sunk deep into the bear's back and stayed there.

Bear stepped away and, holding only the small knife, stood ready for another attack. Behind him, he heard Steller scream again.

In pain and bleeding, the male tried to slap the hatchet off his back but was unable to reach it. Incensed, he rose on his hind legs, howled, snarled, and locked maddened eyes directly on Bear.

He looked like some sort of angered mythical god of the forest, draped in a shining black robe. Bear half expected a lightning bolt to fly from his colossal paws so great was the bear's aura of power.

The forest god roared. Once more, the woods filled with a reverberating thunder that echoed off the trees.

The bellow sounded more like a gravelly devil than a god.

Bear would not let the animal bully him. He took a deep breath, filled his lungs, and teeth bared, let out his own booming roar.

The enormous animal would not be intimidated either. Blood pouring onto the ground from both wounds, it lurched straight for him. Bear was tempted to run, but knew that would likely be a fatal mistake. Even wounded, the bear still had the power to kill him. Instead, he stood his ground until the fiend reached him and, in a split second, it slapped the pouch knife out of Bear's hand with one paw, and with the other paw knocked him several feet backwards. He felt a puncture to his scalp when the tip of a claw connected to his head.

Bear's back slammed into the earth and air flew from his already heaving lungs. Time slowed as he laid there trying to breathe, awaiting the bear, expecting the monstrous creature to maul him to pieces. He was seconds away from death.

He had only one weapon left. Only one slim chance at a life with Artis.

He had to do this for her.

He bent his knee and reached into his moccasin for his *sgian dubh*.

The enraged monster dove and straddled Bear's body, lowering his head. Bear was literally facing death. The bear's pink nostrils flared as it prepared to bite Bear's face off. To taste his blood. To end his life.

Bear could feel the hot stinking breath of the brute gust against his neck. It smelled like the rotting meat of its last kill.

'With a strong hand.' Gripping the weapon with both hands, he plunged the blade between the killer's eyes with all the strength he had left.

Only then, did the beast grow still and start to crumple.

Bear swiftly rolled and ducked to his right between the bear's arm and shoulder to keep the heavy animal from falling on top of him.

Still on his knees, he peered over at Steller.

The disemboweled man was being drug away by the other bear. Even though he'd also been nearly scalped, Steller wasn't dead yet.

His terror-filled eyes were open.

Bear lost his breath at the horror.

The female bear stopped and turned her mouth sideways. The creature's big teeth started chipping away at Steller's skull. He heard teeth crushing bone and saw pieces of flesh falling to the ground.

Steller's eyes were still open but all the life in them was gone.

Bear quickly yanked his hatchet and knife out of the male and then stood. Staying bent, he stealthily stepped to where Kelly's Kentucky long rifle still laid on the ground. He didn't want to draw the female's attention. He leaned down slowly to pick up the weapon and prayed it was still loaded. He could not take the time to check. He needed to kill the second bear before she came after him. He leaned his left shoulder against a tree to steady himself and slowly raised the powerful weapon to his shoulder. He carefully lined up the sights on the feasting bear.

He fired, killing the second bear with a shot to the head.

The bear crumpled, covering Steller's soulless body.

Chapter 30

Doc McDowell followed Mister McGuffin into the cabin.

"Thank you for coming so speedily," Kelly said.

"It's good to get away from my apothecary now and then, and breathe some fresh air. Your father very nearly missed me. I was packing to leave for two weeks when he arrived."

"God must have known we needed you," Kelly said.

"Now, tell me about this woman," the doctor said walking over to the bed.

Her father filled the doctor in on what he had done to get the lead out of Artis and Kelly described what she had done to care for her.

"Well it sounds like you have both done all that you could. It's helpful that you used the willow tree bark. The natives call it a 'plant of virtue' for a reason."

"What else can be done?" Kelly asked.

"I'm sorry to say that about half of people who have a surgery such as this die."

"No! You can't let her die. She was just married by pledge to Daniel MacKay the same evening she was shot. And William would have married them that very night had it not been for the man who tried to rob us on our way home."

"I know, I was at the ball," McDowell said. "She was quite stunning."

"I'm sorry. I forgot," Kelly admitted. "This whole mess has me quite frazzled."

"There were a lot of people there. By the way, where is Bear?" McDowell asked.

"Pursuing a murderer," William answered.

"The one that shot her?"

"No, he's after the one that killed Artis' mother in Scotland. A man named Steller followed Artis here. The man that shot Artis is the one in my jail that you removed the bullet from." William explained how and why the robber managed to shoot Artis.

"Oh, that nasty fellow. I should have known. Well, let's get to work on Artis."

McDowell pulled the bed coverings back and bent his graying head to examine Artis' wound.

Artis continued to sleep, but she moaned often and kept moving her head back and forth against the pillow.

The doctor nodded his head a couple of times. "The good news is that there are no red streaks shooting out from the puncture site. That would be an extremely bad sign." McDowell glanced over at her father. "You did a skillful job. And your stitching is fine work. These do not look like the stitches of an amateur. Are you a surgeon?"

McGuffin took a deep breath and let it out. "I was."

Kelly gasped and put a hand to her mouth. She thought her father had always been a trapper. She gave him an incredulous stare, but he said nothing further and his posture stiffened.

Then McDowell touched Artis' forehead with his fingers. "Her fever is not high, and that's another sign to my liking. The heat from a low fever will fight against festering."

"Thank God," Kelly said.

McDowell studied Artis' face for another moment. They could all see that she was distressed. She started to whimper and continued to move her head about. "Her unsettled sleep concerns me. Is she troubled about something?"

"Yes—she's terrified of the man Bear is tracking. She's afraid he'll come back and hurt all of us," McGuffin answered.

"And she's worried about Bear. She knows he's gone after a devil," Kelly added.

"She'll heal quicker if she's calmer. She's clearly agitated. The sooner Bear gets back and reassures her that he's all right, the better," McDowell said. "When do you expect him?"

"This is the third day since he left," William answered. "In truth, I'm concerned about him myself."

"I'm sure you want to try to find Bear," McDowell said, "but it would not be wise now to leave your family alone."

"You're right, I'd rather not leave with that killer lose. But Mister McGuffin is quite capable of defending them," William said, looking over at her father, "but I have no way of knowing where Bear is. I'll give him one more day and if he doesn't show up, I'll start hunting for him."

Kelly sincerely hoped Bear would return. She hated the thought of William going after that vicious killer.

"I'd recommend something to help her sleep and this medicinal salve. I brought some from my apothecary. Both are made from roots, bark, and other materials." Doc McDowell reached into his bag and removed a brown and a blue jar. "Put a drop or two of this in a tea twice a day for two days and after that only at night. She'll sleep soundly," he said holding up the blue jar. Then he reached for the brown jar. "This salve will help speed the healing. Apply it three times a day." He applied some himself as Kelly watched over his shoulder.

"Is there anything else you can do?" she asked.

"Well, I would not recommend bloodletting. She's lost too much blood already to breathe a vein," he answered. "You said her pain has lessened so we don't need to give her any more laudanum. I believe we are better off just letting her sleep and heal. Give her light meals until her appetite comes back. She should come around in a couple more days. She's young and strong."

Kelly let out the breath she'd been holding. "I've been so worried."

When the doctor stood, she smoothed the covers back over Artis.

"You need to be sure you're getting rest yourself," he admonished with kind eyes. "How's your little girl?"

"As you can see, she's growing like a spring weed," Kelly said, pointing to her daughter. Nicole sat pounding a wooden mixing spoon on the floorboards on the other side of the cabin where Kelly prepared meals.

MacDowell went over to Nicole and picked her up and much to the child's delight sat her on the table. "I'll take a quick look at her while I'm here."

Kelly, William, and McGuffin all watched the doctor examine the girl.

"She looks healthy and happy," he pronounced.

"Aapp peee," Nicole tried to say, and smiled up at the doctor.

Kelly let out another sigh of relief.

MacDowell, still holding Nicole's hand, said, "She is one of the prettiest little girls I've ever seen. But it's no wonder with you two as her parents," he said, glancing over at Kelly and William.

"Thank you doctor. And thank you for all your help," William said and paid him.

The doctor handed Nicole to Kelly and said to her father, "Mister

McGuffin, in a couple of weeks, I'll be back in Boonesborough. Come by my office again and I'll treat you to a coffee."

Her father merely nodded at the doctor.

McDowell turned to William. "When I get to town, I'll check on your prisoner before I go back to the apothecary for my things and leave town. Do you have a message for your deputy?"

"Tell him I said to stay alert and to not trust that bloody robber with even a handkerchief," William said. "I'm awaiting word from the other settlements on what murders he or his cohorts may have committed during their robberies. When Judge Webb gets back into town, he'll take care of the man's punishment."

"I'll tell him. And I'll pray for your brother's safe return and that the man he is tracking receives his just punishment as well."

Chapter 31

B ear just stood, breathing hard as he surveyed the destruction and carnage around him. Two majestic bears and one heinous man lay dead among the scattered remains of what was Steller's campsite.

The hellish battle even disturbed the cook fire. Fingers of flame snaked out in several directions. The breeze and abundant fall leaves scattered on the forest floor quickly fed the flames causing them to multiply and gain strength in seconds.

He used his hatchet and feet to toss and kick dirt on the largest fire and then shifted to the next and the next. Fortunately, the soil was still damp from the heavy rain and effectively smothered the fires. Soon there was more gray choking smoke than flames. By the time he finished, he was weary and his wounds throbbed, but he was pleased he'd been able to stop a fire that could have easily spread into the woods.

He found a spot to stand where the smoke wasn't blowing and scrutinized the campsite once again. The female bear's body hid most of Steller's ravaged remains. Unfortunately, he would have to see him again when he buried the man.

The first order of business was to reload the rifles and pistols and put all the weapons back on his person again. He set about accomplishing that task as quickly as he could. When he finished, he found Steller's canteen lying on the ground near where the cook fire had been. Fortunately, it wasn't crushed. He drank greedily and then poured some water on a rag and wiped the blood that had dripped from his head onto his face. After that, he went to retrieve his horse.

The walk to where Camel was tied gave him time to settle his raw nerves and plan what he would do next. He needed to accomplish his tasks quickly and then get the hell away before the scent of blood drew more hungry animals like wolves.

He found Steller's fine black stallion grazing near Camel. That didn't surprise him much. Horses are herd animals and seek out other horses, especially when they are scared.

"Whoa now, whoa," he said as he eased toward the jittery animal. "The bears are dead now, ye need na be afraid. What a handsome fellow ye are," he whispered into the horse's twitchy ear. "I do na blame ye one bit for runnin'. But tis time to go back now." At the sound of Bear's soothing voice, the stallion calmed and did not object when Bear picked up the reins that were dragging the ground. He led the steed toward Camel. Bear mounted and he headed back to the campsite with the big horse in tow.

When he returned, he left both mounts a short distance away from the campsite, near a patch of grass growing in a low area where the horses could graze for a little while. Camel wouldn't run off and he thought the stallion would stay close to the gelding.

He trudged back and started digging a grave for Steller with his hatchet. His right shoulder was painfully sore from the vicious blow he'd blocked, but he ignored it and got the grave dug. When he hauled Steller out from under the bear, revulsion welled up inside of him and threatened to make him gag. But his revulsion for the man Steller had become during his life was even greater. He considered saying a few words over his grave, but couldn't find even one thing to say. He couldn't even ask God to rest his soul. What the good Lord did with this man was up to Him. But he suspected Steller's soul, if he had one, would never rest peacefully.

He was about to toss dirt over the man when he decided he needed to search Steller's pockets. He completed the gruesome task quickly, finding only a few coins. In another pocket, he found a document releasing Steller from an indenture in Wilmington, North Carolina. So, he'd been banished from Scotland and impoverished too. Steller clearly did not profit from his cruelty and pilfering. He was sure Artis would find that news comforting. She'd be even more comforted to learn her tormentor was dead.

As he hurriedly tossed dirt and then rocks over the body, Steller's motivation for coming after Artis became clear—revenge. The same thing that had compelled Miller to come after him. Their lives wasted, all both men had left was revenge.

When he finished, he set about skinning the bears. Their shiny black pelts would make a beautiful warm covering for the bed he would share with Artis.

For what must have been the hundredth time since he left, he prayed again she would grow well while he was gone. He wanted to start their life together so he could make her happy. After everything she'd been through, she deserved some tranquility in her life—and a great deal of happiness.

He procured a tooth from each bear for a necklace. He'd given his last bear-tooth necklace to a native chief as a peace offering and wanted to start another. Maybe, he'd even give the one that killed Steller to Artis, if she'd have it. Nay, she'd not want a reminder of the man. And he couldn't blame her one bit.

It was time to go. It took him three days to get here, but without having to search for tracks, he could easily make it back in half that time. He couldn't wait to be on his way and marched toward the horses, glad to be alive.

I'm coming Artis.

જ

"Kelly," Artis called. "Kelly."

"I'm up here Artis, in the loft. I'll be down in a second. Just let me get dressed," Kelly hollered. "Her voice sounds stronger William."

"Indeed."

Artis heard what Kelly said. She did feel stronger and not as sore. Her fever was gone too. In fact, she felt so good, she wanted to get up for a moment.

When Kelly descended the stairs, Artis smiled at her. "Thank ye for comin' again to my rescue. I believe I need to use the chamber pot."

"That's wonderful news!"

Artis let out a small giggle. "That's the first time anyone's called it that."

"Well it means you're getting better, of course," Kelly said. "William stay up there for a few minutes."

Kelly helped her gingerly complete the chore and when they'd finished and washed, Artis got back in bed but managed to sit up. "I have to ask. Is Bear back yet?"

"I wish he was," Kelly said, rubbing the sleep out of her eyes. "William said he was going out to look for Bear later today. I'm concerned for Bear, but I also fret about William going after that killer, and I worry for us if the man decides to return."

Just the thought of Steller returning made Artis' heart sink and her insides quiver. She'd remembered his promise to kill her. That was why just the sound of his voice, when she'd heard it from the wagon, was so disturbing it caused fear, stark and vivid, to tear at her insides. She'd been so terrified, she hid like a wounded animal. If she'd been her normal self, she would never have done that. She would have confronted him. But she wasn't. She'd been so weak she was near death. All she could think of was getting away.

Images of what Steller might do to her new family now flashed through her mind. Her mouth grew dry as she struggled to keep her fragile control. "May I have somethin' to drink? My mouth feels like I have a ball of cotton in it."

"Of course. Do you want water, coffee, or tea?"

"Aye. All three."

"Oh, you are feeling better! I'm so pleased you are recovering," Kelly said, bending to scrape a piece of flint against a firesteel to light kindling in the hearth.

"It will be awhile before I'll be ready to wear a corset or dance a jig again, but I think I'll be able to walk a wee bit later today. Kelly, I'm so worried about Bear I can hardly think of anythin' else."

"Don't worry. He'll be back." She blew on the small flames to give them life.

"But ye just said you were concerned for him."

"I am. But I also believe in him. Don't you?"

"Oh, aye, more than anyone else I've ever known."

She watched as Kelly added a few more twigs and when they caught fire, a few logs. Before long, the hearth glowed with a cheerful cook fire.

"Then, what do you say we spend the day getting you prettified for his return?"

"Oh Kelly, that would be so wonderful. I smell bad even to myself. I must smell dreadful to ye. And my hair itches."

"I can't promise to get you looking as grand as we did the night of the ball, but I can at least get you clean and smelling good with some of my wildflower-scented soap. And we'll get your hair washed and braided."

The thought of being clean again, lifted Artis' spirits. "I have a fresh shift in my bag too. Is it still up in the loft?"

"No, it's here beside the bed. I'll get it out for you later. William, ye can come down now. And I need a lot of water from the cistern please."

William retrieved several buckets of water and Kelly heated them.

When he sat the last one down, she told Artis about the first time he'd gotten water for her. "He slipped at the creek bank, swollen from a storm, and wound up covered head to toe in mud," Kelly said, snickering.

"And I was forced to ask Kelly to help me wash it all off," William added, laughing with her, and giving Kelly a roguish wink.

"Hush, you'll wake Nicole. Off with you now. You'll have to eat breakfast at my father's cabin. Artis needs to eat something light so we'll have just a simple custard or pudding. Here, take this loaf of bread, sliced ham, and these eggs. Papa will know what to do with them, even if you don't," she said, snickering.

Artis chuckled just a bit at their recollections. She couldn't let out a full laugh just yet. Her wound and her worry for Bear would not allow it.

She couldn't wait until she and Bear could share a story or tease each other as Kelly as William did. She smiled as she remembered how good it had felt to laugh with Bear. She desperately wanted to feel that way again.

Laughter is the sugar in happiness.

And with Bear, her life would be sweet.

Chapter 32

Every muscle in Bear's body ached by the time he stopped and tied the horses up late last night. The moon was high in the sky and made it easy to find his way, and he'd wanted to keep pushing himself toward Whispering Hills. He was so close. But he had badly needed rest. And food. Even though it was late, he had built a fire and warmed the last of the dried meat and corncakes Kelly sent with him. They were hard and stale, but better than his growling empty stomach.

With his hatchet clutched tightly in his hand, he'd fallen asleep, afraid he would dream about the monstrous bear.

But his thoughts had turned to Artis and he'd slept well, dreaming of kissing her, endlessly.

This morning, he awoke to a brilliant and stunning dawn, and felt refreshed and eager to be on his way. He ate the one apple he had left and saddled Camel. The cool fall air held a note of crispness and it reminded him that he would need to make building their cabin a priority. He might even make it grand enough to be called a house, funds permitting.

Within two hours, he crossed the creek that signaled he was close. He squeezed his legs to Camel's sides and urged the horse to a gallop. As he splashed through the water, it dawned on him that he needed a bath—badly. He smelled foul and still bore bear and his own blood on him. He was sure he smelled like smoke too from putting out the fire. Although he was anxious to reach Artis, he didn't want to be repulsive to her when he arrived.

He tugged up on Camel's reins and walked the horses to a spot where they could drink and rest.

He pulled out the wedge of lye soap he always kept in his saddle bag, stepped into the knee-high water, and started scrubbing his clothing. His buckskin shirt was ripped open along one side and torn in several places on each sleeve. And his black leather breeches revealed the pale skin of his legs in a few places. The stains might not come out, but at least he would get his clothing dirt-free. The tough buckskin and sturdy leather had helped to protect his flesh from the bear's claws. If he'd worn a linen shirt and wool breeches, his injuries would have been far worse.

When he finished, he took everything off and washed his entire body vigorously, except for the side with the gashes from the bear's claw. That side he washed with a feather light touch, wincing when the lye soap burned the deep scratch there and the cuts on his arms and hands. The strong soap would help to keep the cuts from festering.

The last thing he washed was his hair, taking great care around the puncture wound on his scalp. He scrubbed everywhere else vigorously, and made sure he got all the blood out of his hair. When he finished rinsing the soap out, he squeezed out as much water as he could.

It took quite a while, but at last, he felt clean. Actually, he felt a lot better too. The cool water seemed to benefit his wounds. His cuts were still stinging but they weren't as sore and tender to the touch. And he smelled a whole lot better too. He took a twig, chewed the end until it softened, and then used it to clean his teeth with the pumice he carried in his saddle bag. Too anxious to be on his way, he decided not to bother with shaving.

He started up again and his heart beat faster with each pound of the horses' hooves. He could think of nothing else but Artis. She had to be all right. She had to be getting better. She just had to.

When he caught sight of the cabin, joy exploded through him. He raced

Camel up to the porch, leapt from the saddle, and swiftly tied the two horses. He didn't bother to knock and threw the door open.

When he stepped in, a cry of relief broke from his mouth. "Artis!"

"Bear!" Her face lit up with an enormous and glorious smile. She remained in bed, but she was sitting up and alert. Kelly's blue shawl was draped around her shoulders. The color in her face had returned and her plaited hair hung in a long tidy braid down her front.

"My love, yer better!" He rushed to her side and knelt to one knee. He took her hand in his. The feel of it nearly made him weep.

"Aye, I am indeed."

"I've been so worried about ye."

"And we fretted over ye day and night. What took ye so long?"

"That is a very long story, that I will gladly tell ye later. But right now, I just want to look at you." He gazed into her eyes, sparkling now with her emotions. He did na think it possible, but his smile broadened even further.

"May I kiss ye Artis?"

"I was wonderin' when ye would get around to that!"

He stood and then lowered his lips to hers, kissing her with all the joy he felt to find her alive and well. He kissed her again with all the happiness she made him feel. And he kissed her once more with the love bursting from his heart.

Kelly cleared her throat. "You can't be wearing my patient out. Lord's sake, I just got her well."

But Kelly was smiling when she said it, so he dared to kiss Artis one more time.

He reluctantly released Artis' lips when William burst in behind them.

"You're back! I saw the horses tied outside." The warmth of William's voice was echoed in his big smile. His brother strode over and hugged him firmly, clearly relieved to see he'd returned.

Bear winced, but tried not to reveal his discomfort.

McGuffin came in right behind William. "Another hour and William would have left to go find you. He was worrying me to death."

"Yer lookin' recovered too Mister McGuffin," Bear said, noticing that Kelly's father appeared to be much better than the last time he saw him.

"I'm well enough. But you look like you've had a rough time of it. Don't keep us in suspense. Tell us what happened," McGuffin insisted. "Did you find that madman Steller?"

"Shall we sit? This may take a while," Bear suggested. He poured himself a cup of coffee, drug a chair over to the bed, and took a seat next to Artis.

It was then that Artis noticed his torn shirt and scratches. "Yer all cut up," she said, sounding alarmed. Her brow creased with worry.

Much to his vexation, everyone took a closer look at the claw marks and gashes on his side, arms, and scalp.

"That must have hurt," William said.

His brother had a tendency to state the obvious.

"What on earth did that?" Kelly asked. "Surely not Steller."

Bear's eyes met McGuffin's. The man's knowing look told Bear he knew what had attacked him.

He ran a palm over his stubble and sighed. "I'll tell all of ye in a minute. Just let me have a sip of this coffee first."

"Kelly please put some of the doctor's medicinal salve on his wounds," Artis said.

"Nay, I just cleaned them with lye soap," he protested. "I'd rather ye gave me some food, Kelly. I'm starving."

"Ye'll do as I say," Artis vowed, setting her chin in a stubborn line. "The doctor's salve helped my wound immensely and it will help yers as well. I will na have ye get ill from those wounds just when I finally got ye back!"

Bear grinned, glad to see that Artis' pluck had returned.

While Kelly doctored the deeper scratches on his side and arms, Bear winced a time or two as he related the details of his search and how he finally spotted Steller.

"Then what happened?" McGuffin asked.

Bear described the questions he asked Steller and the lies the man told. "I quite enjoyed catchin' him in his lies, particularly the question about habeas corpus."

"That was clever," William said. "I didn't realize you'd been paying attention all these years."

"Ye'd be surprised how closely I keep an eye on ye."

"Well, get on with it," McGuffin urged.

"I gave Steller a chance to tell the truth. But he didn't. Instead he drew his knife."

Bear glanced over at William. He could almost see his brother wondering whether he'd shot Steller in cold blood.

William was loyal to the letter of the law.

Bear was loyal only to justice.

Sometimes law and justice unite. Sometimes they are worlds apart.

It made him wonder what he would have done if Steller had not resisted. What if the bears had not shown up? He might never know. He frowned and took a sip of coffee.

He told them all of his own horrific battle with the male Bear, making it an elaborate and animated story—because, like all Scots, he loved telling stories.

As he expounded, Artis cried out in dismay twice and Kelly's eyes widened.

Then the time finally came to reveal how Steller met his demise. He did not offer any explicit details because of the women present, but he did not hide what happened. "And so, the ghastly man's grisly fate was decided by God," Bear concluded.

"Not by God," Kelly corrected, "Steller earned what he got all by himself."

"Let he that commits evil expect it," Bear said somberly.

Artis had remained stone-faced as he described what happened to Steller. When she finally spoke, her voice was shaking. "He's...dead?"

"Aye, dead and buried."

"Ye saw him die?" she asked.

"Aye, Artis, I wish I had na seen it, but I did. The man deserved to die, but it was a gruesome death, even for him."

"It's a wonder you weren't killed too," McGuffin said. "I've encountered black bears in the woods when I was a trapper. They can be ferocious. Lucky for me, none ever attacked."

"Bears have a keen sense of smell. I think they smelled the rabbits Steller was cookin' and they were particularly hungry," Bear said. "All the new settlers must be killin' off the game they would normally feed on. And speakin' of being hungry, could ye spare some food Kelly?"

"Is that Steller's horse tied outside?" William asked. "It's an exceptional stallion."

"Aye, he's a fine animal, but I suspect Steller stole him," Bear said.

Kelly sat a loaf of fresh bread and creamy butter in front of him. The hearty bread smelled wonderful. His mouth watered as he cut a huge slice, the crackling crust yielding to a spongy soft middle. He lavished butter all over it and took an enormous mouthful.

"We'll feed you a proper meal a little later Bear," Kelly assured him.

He swallowed the bite he was chewing. "That sounds grand."

"I canna believe Steller followed me here all the way from Scotland," Artis said grimly. "How did he find me?"

"I found a document on him releasin' him from an indenture in Wilmington. Perhaps because of the murder of yer mother, he was banished and forced into indenture too. That's why he was here in the colonies," Bear explained. "My guess is that he blamed ye for his banishment, since ye reported yer mum's murder to the Countess, and he spent seven years figurin' out how to make ye pay for it. I suspect he found the record of yer indenture by telling the same lie he told here—that he was tryin' to find his wife. They must have told him who bought yer indenture and what plantation ye were taken too."

"Then from Mister Roberts, he found out that I was given land near Boonesborough and came here." Artis' face suddenly looked panicked. "I pray he didn't murder Roberts or hurt his family. They were good to me." She tossed back the bed cover. "Help me out to the porch. I want to see that horse."

They all went outside. Leaning on Bear for support, she said, "That's Mister Roberts' prize stud. I used to take the stallion out for exercise and then groom him."

"Then I will write to Mister Roberts and tell him that his horse is here and that the man who stole him is dead," William said. "He can come and claim him here if he's willing to make the trip or send someone."

They went back inside and after they got Artis settled in bed again, Bear turned his attention back to her. "I am so relieved ye appear to be recoverin' well."

"Thanks to Kelly's nursin' abilities and her father's surgery skills," Artis said.

"Surgery skills?" he asked, looking at McGuffin and taking another big bite of bread.

Everyone else turned his or her eyes on McGuffin too.

"I guess my secret is out." He seemed reluctant to proceed. His mouth was tight and grim. "During the Revolution, I was a surgeon for Washington's army. Month after month, I treated every conceivable battle wound under the worst possible conditions. One day, like so many other days, they brought a badly wounded young man to me. His shattered leg needed to be removed. When I looked down at his dirty pain-hardened face to tell him, I recognized the only son of my brother—my nephew John." McGuffin swallowed his emotions and then continued. "I did the best I could for the boy, but it wasn't enough. He died later that day." McGuffin paused and stared down at the floor for a moment.

When McGuffin glanced up, the creases around his eyes had deepened. "I wrote the letter to my brother myself. My grief was so great, my tears smeared my words. That was the last surgery I performed. I took the boy's belongings back to his parents. When I told them what happened, they blamed me for his death. I couldn't fault them really. Maybe I could have done more for the boy. Only God knows."

Kelly stared blankly at her father with her mouth open.

"I decided I needed a new profession and a new environment. A new life really. I asked my longtime sweetheart, Kelly's mother, to marry me. No one was more surprised than I was when she said yes. I'd done a lot of trapping as a youth, so we moved to the base of the Shenandoah Mountains and I became a trapper. We ate the meat, and sold the skins and furs. When she grew old enough, Kelly learned how to help me clean and stretch them."

"Was the loss of the boy why you started drinking heavily?" William asked.

Although McGuffin was no longer imbibing, in the past he had drunk to excess and treated Kelly poorly after her mother died. But he came to his senses and gave up the bottle when they almost lost Kelly forever to an abductor.

"No, not really. I started drinking the same night Kelly's mother died. I had been away trapping. By the time I got back, she was too far gone. I realized that I could have saved her had I been there. She had a simple case

219

of wood poisoning. A large nasty cedar splinter had imbedded itself into her upper arm. I guess she got it chopping wood. Cedar can be highly poisonous. I could have operated and removed it, saving her from the toxins that took over her arm and then her body."

By now, tears were flowing down both McGuffin's and Kelly's faces. She wrapped her arms around her father's shoulders and cried with him, while Bear and the others sat quietly.

"Mister McGuffin," Artis said.

McGuffin and Kelly both looked over at Artis.

"I owe ye my life. I also owe ye the life Bear and I will have together. And we owe ye the lives of the children we shall bear. I thank ye for all of that, and bless the Almighty for sendin' such a fine man here to help me. Ye will always have my gratitude."

The smile in McGuffin's eyes and on Kelly's face warmed Bear's own grateful heart.

They spent the rest of the evening enjoying a celebratory dinner and toasting Bear's return and Artis' health with an excellent brandy. All except Mr. McGuffin who savored only Kelly's good coffee.

Artis soon tired and Bear knew he would have to tell her goodnight. He wished he could climb into that big bed with her and hold her, but knew it would not be proper, nor was she healed enough yet. If it killed him, he would wait until he was sure she was well.

He dragged a chair up next to her. "When ye've recovered completely, we'll have William marry us on yer land, under the stars, just like ye wanted."

"*Our* land," she said, giving him an exasperated look. "How many times will I have to tell ye?"

"Aye, *our* home."

"Kiss me goodnight, Bear."

And he did. *Sweet dreams, my love.*

Chapter 33

Within two weeks, Artis was up and about and feeling more like herself. Kelly wouldn't let her climb the stairs to the loft yet, and so she still slept downstairs, dreaming of the day when she would have her own bed. And, of the night when she would first share it with Bear.

The day after he'd returned, Bear went into Boonesborough to find a builder looking for work. He learned that a number of builders had moved to the settlement because they considered the fast-growing frontier as a land of opportunity. Bear had hired a housewright and craftsmen the very same day, bought some stakes, and on his way home, hammered them into the ground where the house would stand.

For the last two weeks, Bear and the builder worked tirelessly creating the building materials that would become their home. The craftsmen started by felling and stacking timber. Then they split some of the logs in half to make clapboards, using a froe and maul, Bear had explained. The larger logs were kept whole and would be used for the outer walls.

Every evening they would spend hours discussing their ideas and Bear would leave early the next morning to help the builder execute their plans. Artis soon learned a number of building terms and how the carpenters would make a window sash, join a mantle, dovetail corner joints, or frame a staircase. Bear said he had learned a lot helping McGuffin and the other men build Sam and Catherine's spacious new home.

The Governor had generously increased the reward when he learned the gold was recovered. William refused to accept any, saying he was just doing his job. So Bear was able to use the funds to pay the workers and buy supplies and manufactured articles such as square nails, glass, hardware, and bricks. He even bartered for some of the worker's services by hunting game for their families. Bear and McGuffin also contributed their labor to the project. Every evening, they would return, tired and famished. But a sense of urgency drove Bear to leave again before daylight. McGuffin would always follow a little later, bringing Bear the big breakfast that Kelly and Artis cooked for him.

Artis desperately wanted to see the progress they were making. Even more, she wanted to marry Bear. But he insisted that they wait until their home was finished and they would have a proper place to consummate their union. They were making rapid progress, he told her, and it would also give her time to heal completely. She decided that he was concerned about hurting her and wanted to be certain she was entirely healed before he took her to bed.

But she found the wait excruciating. Never in her life had she wanted something so much. Every time he smiled at her, his eyes contained a sensuous flame that warmed her to her core. And she often caught him staring at her with longing. When his beautiful blue-green eyes met hers, she felt her heart quiver. The prolonged anticipation was becoming unbearable. She decided that tonight she would at least get him alone for a while for a few of his soul reaching kisses.

That afternoon, Kelly helped to fix her hair in a lovely upsweep and then Artis changed into her simple green gown that Kelly mended for her. Despite Kelly's protests, she was determined to spend some time outside. She pinned on her luckenbooth and strapped the leather belt that held her dirk around her waist.

"You should also take your pistol with you," Kelly advised.

Artis agreed, and Kelly went upstairs to retrieve the weapon along with the shoulder bag that held her powder and lead. She had only fired the weapon once, when she'd shot the mountain lion, but she was confident that eventually she could learn to shoot as well as any man. When she had enough funds, she would buy a long rifle as well, like the one Kelly owned.

When she was ready, she let Kelly help her put on her boots so she wouldn't have to bend over, and then she stepped outside.

She glanced up at the cloudless sky, the color of a robin's egg and it reminded her of springtime skies in Scotland. She closed her eyes and let the sun bathe her face. It felt like a soft warm blanket laying lightly on her skin. She opened her eyes and strolled toward the creek at the bottom of the rise. The flowing water sparkled with a thousand diamonds, each glistening star floating downstream, urged on by the slight breeze.

By the stream, she found an enormous rock to rest upon. She leaned back on her palms and admired the tenacious ruby, coral, and honey-colored fall leaves still clinging to tree branches. Many of those same colors lay under the trees as well and she heard them rustle in the gentle wind. The hills beyond the creek, where she could hear the songs of hundreds of birds, beckoned to her. She longed to go for a long walk as she used to do along the loch near her home.

Before long, she would be able to start hiking around Whispering Hills. She would soon have her strong body back. She had been helping Kelly out as much as she could, watching and feeding Nicole, folding laundry, and other light household chores. And day by day, she could feel herself returning. Soon she would be able to help Kelly with her other duties as well—cooking; making butter and apple butter; sewing; creating soap, candles, and baskets; cleaning; and tending to the cow, chickens, and vegetable garden. Kelly never seemed to finish no matter how hard her friend worked.

But Artis couldn't wait to have her own home and family to care for.

"Are ye waitin' down here for a charmin' prince to show up?"

"Bear! What are ye doin' home so early?" She was thrilled and more than a bit surprised to see him.

223

He took a seat beside her. "Well, if yer feelin' up to it, I thought maybe I might carry ye to *our* land—you see I can learn. I want to show ye what we've accomplished so far. The carpenters ran out of wood planks and they all left for the day. But I have another load of timber being delivered tomorrow."

"Oh Bear, that would be so wonderful. I felt well enough today that I just had to get outside for a while. And the doctor said it would be good for me to walk around a bit. I would truly love to go with you."

"Well then, my love, let's go!" He took her hand and led her back to where he had tied Camel. He stuck his head inside the cabin and told Kelly where he was taking her. Then smiling broadly, her charming prince put his big hands under her arms and gently lifted her up, setting her just in front of his saddle. Then he mounted and eased her into his lap. He gave her a quick kiss on her cheek and they were off.

Bear could almost feel Artis' heart beat against him, so great was her excitement. As they approached their land, she was wide-eyed and breathless with anticipation.

When he turned Camel onto the land, his own pulse beat faster and his senses heightened. He'd dreamed of doing this so many times. At last, their home had taken shape enough that she would be able to grasp what it would look like when it was finished. With a wide grin he said, "There it is my love."

"Take me there," she said, clapping her hands together. She leaned forward in the saddle trying to see it better.

"Are ye sure, yer up to this?" he questioned.

"Go, go!" she said, impatiently waving her hands.

"Perhaps we should just admire it from here," he said, teasing her.

"Bear, do ye want me to jump down and run up there?"

"Ye would na dare."

"Aye, I would!"

He laughed and nudged Camel's sides with his legs. He soon had them both standing in front of their home, nestled at the top of the rise among several magnificent hardwood trees. He picked her up and carried her over the threshold. It was just a framed threshold, leading to more framing, but it was the entry to where they would spend their lives together.

He sat her down but didn't release her, keeping her back pressed against him.

She gazed around her, looking everywhere, and then took in a deep breath. "The new timber smells so wonderful."

"Aye, it does," he said, "and so do ye." Her beautiful hair was piled charmingly on her head, like a crown made of copper and gold. So he nibbled little kisses down her exposed neck, breathing in her tantalizing scent. He forced himself to stop or he would soon be unable to.

He walked her through the generously sized rooms, explaining what each area was.

She started shaking with excitement when they reached their bedroom.

"Truly? This is it?" she asked.

"Aye, unless ye want it somewhere else."

Longing showed vividly in her smoldering eyes. "Nay. I just want it."

He did not miss her meaning. He wanted it to.

"I vow our first night here will be worth waitin' for," he promised.

Her eyes gleamed with an inner light and an expectant glint lit her face. "That's a vow I can believe."

And it was a vow he meant to keep.

"Shall we continue to tour our castle my prince?" she asked.

"We will have three hearths. One here in the bedroom," he said as he led her out. "One in the parlor, and one in your cookin' area. I've already hired a skilled mason."

"Ye canna imagine how happy this makes me, Bear."

"Oh, I can imagine that just fine. I feel like I'm in a wonderful dream, livin' in heaven and a beautiful angel loves me. But it's na a dream."

"I do love ye Bear."

He put his hand behind her waist and gently tugged her to him. Then he kissed her in their home for the very first time.

Chapter 34

A month later on an evening in late November, Artis leaned into Bear's chest, breathing in his clean scent. He wore a new dark green jacket and a black shirt with laces at the neck. With his dark-red auburn hair, shining and slicked back, and just a hint of a copper-flaked beard, she thought him the most handsome man she'd ever seen.

His family, no *their* family, had joined them and they had all just finished sharing a pre-wedding feast inside her new home. William and Kelly truly felt like a brother and sister to her now. And she adored Kelly's lovable child and Mister McGuffin too. They were the new family her uncle had told her to go find.

She remembered her uncle fondly and rested her fingers against the Clan MacKay badge he'd given her, now pinned on Bear's chest.

The evening was cool but comfortable and she wore her tartan shawl, pinned together with her luckenbooth, on the arms of the wedding dress Kelly insisted she have made. After several fittings, the gold gown with tiny pink flowers stitched into the bodice, seemed to hug her figure perfectly. Everyone must have noticed bear's wide-eyed admiration when he first set eyes on her as she walked out in it. He'd choked on the celebratory whiskey he and William were sharing as they waited for the ladies to come outside. He'd scanned her head to toe and beamed his approval.

William patted Bear on the back and told him to settle down, he'd soon be married.

As the sun slipped away, casting everyone in a warm gilded light, the family stood in front of Bear and her for a *Livery of Seisin* ceremony in the front yard of their newly completed house. Afterwards, William would perform their wedding ceremony and Artis' excitement grew with every passing moment.

She picked up her dirk that she'd sat by the front door earlier and cut a twig off a nearby tree. Next, she bent down, careful not to soil her gown, and cut a piece of turf out of the ground. She carefully stuck the twig into the center of the soil, picked the clump up with both hands, stood, and looked at Bear. Holding both up to him, she said, "This land I now share with you as symbolized by this turf and twig I give to thee."

Bear solemnly took the turf and twig in his outstretched hands. "This land I now share with thee as signified by this deed." Bear stooped to the small hole she'd left and put the turf back into the ground. He carefully patted the grass and soil into place and then stood, giving her a soft loving gaze.

"The *Livery of Seisin* ceremony is where the word 'deed' comes from," William explained. "We are witnesses to the *deed* of transferring land by turf and twig. It was a common practice, especially in remote areas, before we had land commissioners and written records of registered deeds."

Artis wanted Bear to fully believe that the land was his as well as hers. She could tell by the broad smile that now lit his face that the ceremony meant a lot to him.

And it meant a great deal to her as well. They had both lost their family land in Scotland, but now their family could put down roots here in Kentucky. She was sure those roots would run deep and honor Scotland— onto generations—for it was often avowed that a Scot is a Scot, even unto a hundred generations.

❧

Bear helped Mister McGuffin build a campfire to provide light and warmth next to an area that Bear had readied the day before for dancing.

William took a seat on a tree stump and played a mixture of lively and romantic music on his violin. Kelly danced in circles holding a smiling Nicole in her arms. And afterwards, Kelly handed Nicole to Bear. He'd gladly held the child while Mister McGuffin joyfully danced with his daughter. Soon, the other invited guests began to arrive; Judge Webb, Doctor McDowell, Lucky McGintey, the general store owner Daniel Breedhead, Commissioner Simmons, Colonel Byrd, and their wives, and they joined in the dancing too. Deputy Mitchell stayed in town to guard the prisoner.

The guests all brought gifts for their new home, but wanting to repay Bear for defending his store, Breedhead brought a delicate brass and crystal oil lamp that Artis thought would look pleasing in the center of their new dining table.

They'd only had a chance to sparsely fill the home with furniture, but Bear told Artis they would acquire the rest of what they needed in the coming months. He'd laughed when Artis said the home was so large, she thought it might take years.

Judge Webb opened the fine bottle of brandy he brought and shared it with Bear and William. After toasting to Artis, he said, "I regret that I must hold the robber's trial tomorrow morning. I must be in Lexington the day after tomorrow. William, you and I can start the trial bright and early at 8:00."

William groaned, but then quickly nodded his agreement.

"But Bear, there's no need for you to get to the courtroom until 8:30 or 9:00. It should be a swift trial and hanging with all the evidence against the robber."

"Indeed," William agreed. "Several locations responded to my letters of inquiry and confirmed what I suspected—that the four robbers committed numerous murders during their raids of the other settlements."

"I'm glad Artis wasn't among them," Webb said.

"She very nearly was," William said.

Bear took a deep breath. He couldn't believe how close he came to losing her. He suddenly needed to find her and excused himself from the conversation. When he located Artis, he locked his hands against her spine and drew her close. Without speaking, he rested his head on hers, just wanting to hold her like this forever.

While the others continued to celebrate and inspect the new candlelit home—one of the finest in the entire Boonesborough area—Artis took Bear's arm and they strolled a short distance away.

The soft poignant notes of the violin drifted through the thick trees surrounding them. "Bear, the beauty of our home and our land exceeds everythin' I could have hoped for. I could never have imagined this when I stepped onto that ship and left Scotland," Artis said.

"Nor I, love," Bear agreed.

"But here we are and we're about to be married."

He reached for her hand. "My heart married ye the very first time I beheld your face."

"And my heart dreamed of ye when I was but a young daydreamin' lass walkin' the Highland hills."

"Speakin' of the Highlands, what do ye say we call our new home Highland?" he asked.

"That's perfect!" she declared. "May we always feel at home at Highland."

"Are ye ready to be married my love?" he asked.

"First I must tell ye somethin'." Her courage floundered, but she forced herself to continue. "It grieves me to reveal this to ye, but I feel that I must before we say our final vows."

"I will na have ye grievin' on yer weddin' day, so whatever it is, save it for tomorrow."

"Nay, this is somethin' I must tell ye now," she pressed. "I should have told ye before now. But I have done my best to forget it ever happened. And, I confess, I thought that perhaps I would never have to tell ye. "

His gaze searched her eyes. "All right love."

"But while Kelly was helpin' me get ready, she told me that ye would know."

"I do na understand what ye are tryin' to say."

"Bear, when I was on board the ship on the way to the colonies, the Captain began lookin' at me in a way that was too familiar. He kept doin' that and I kept tryin' to avoid him. I had na family or close friends to confide in. After about two weeks, he caught me and forced me into his cabin. I fought him with all that I had, but he was a large burly man and he threw me onto his bed. He gagged me and had his way. It was my first time and I bled on his sheet. Afterwards, he told me he would have me thrown overboard if I dared to tell anyone. So, to my shame, I kept quiet about it and stayed in my quarters for the remainder of the journey."

"Oh my dear Artis, what a bloody bastard. I wish I could get my hands around his neck right now," Bear swore.

"I know that a woman who is na longer pure is not as desirable to a man, but I hope ye can find it in yer heart to overlook that I have been soiled by another man."

"Nay! Na man could ever soil ye. Yer soul is sinless and untainted. Yer heart is pure and virtuous. Yer body is beautiful and innocent." He drew her against him and his mouth grazed her earlobe. "I love ye," he whispered into her ear. Then he kissed her. His lips felt warm and tender against hers.

Tears of joy slipped down her checks as her smile broadened. He had not let her down. He accepted her as she was. Her relief was so great her heart felt light and ecstatic. "Now, I can marry ye."

He gently wiped the tears from her face with his big hand. "Let us both think no more about the past—let us think only on our future. Especially tonight."

"Aye."

They strolled, arm in arm, back to the others.

Artis glanced up at the stars popping out, one by one, with each step she took. If she lived to be a hundred, she swore to herself that she would try to never look back again. She would always try to look forward.

And, she would waste no more time looking down at her feet. During the day, she would let the light of the sun shine upon her upturned face. And at night, she would gaze at the stars that light the streets of heaven.

She would also look up to Bear—not just because of his size—but because he was a good man. He'd just proven that to her once again. She gave him a smile of thanks.

"Are you ready to become husband and wife?" William asked as they reached him.

"Aye!" they both said at once.

Bear had spent weeks dreaming of the moment Artis would become his wife. And now the time was nigh. He was marrying an angel and he knew it for a certainty. She was a wee bit of heaven he could hold in his arms. Created just for him. He wasn't sure what he had done to deserve such a blessing, but he thanked God for it.

She looked like an angel too. An angel who was a particular favorite of heaven, for on his last visit, the doctor had pronounced her fully healed with no permanent damage. With every day that passed since her injury, she'd grown stronger and seemed healthier than ever. And now, she radiated such grace and beauty she nearly glowed.

And if he wasn't mistaken, based on the way her beautiful gown showed off her figure, she was able to wear a corset again too. The corset made the soft curves of her bosom peek out from the top of her gown and made him yearn to run his fingers across them. In truth, his fingers ached to caress her entire body. A quiver surged through his veins at just the thought.

He'd fully recovered too from all his scrapes and scratches from the horrendous battle with the bear. And all the work on their house had left him feeling brawn and hearty.

He gazed at Artis and, completely enthralled, he had to fight the urge to go kiss her before the ceremony even started. There would be plenty of time for kissing, and a whole lot more later, so he forced himself to behave.

He caught the eye of Lucky McGintey. His friend's face held a look of amusement. Lucky winked at him as though he knew exactly what was going through his head.

Bear shrugged his shoulders and gave Lucky a sheepish smile. There was no sense denying it.

Kelly handed Artis a bouquet of fall wildflowers that she and Nicole had picked together and tied with a ribbon that matched Artis' gown. Artis patted Nicole on the head and thanked her.

William said he'd written a ceremony just for them and Bear was anxious to hear it. A tremor of excitement gripped his heart as his brother began.

"Put your right foot forward to symbolize that you will willingly walk together in life and come to the aid of the other when needed," William instructed.

Bear put his right foot forward, and smiling, she did the same.

"Now, join your right hands to signify that tonight you gladly merge your lives together into one with all your heart, mind, and soul," William instructed. "And that when your vows are spoken, your hearts will beat only for each other."

Bear took Artis right hand in his and smiled down at her. His heart felt like it truly was merging with hers. His mind could think of naught but her and making her happy. And tonight, his soul would forever be joined with hers.

"Please repeat after me," William said.

"I, Daniel McKee, now take you Artis MacKay to be my wife. In the presence of God and before these witnesses, I promise to be a loving, faithful, and loyal husband to you," William said.

Bear repeated what William said, but preceded the words with, "Because I believe God has brought us together…" He also added at the end, "And I now change my surname from MacKee to MacKay, as that is the traditional spellin' of our noble clan's name. I vow that we will both remember our Highland heritage and teach our children to be proud of the Scots blood than runs in their veins."

Artis gave a genuine exclamation of delight.

Repeating after William, Artis said, "I, Artis MacKay, now take you Daniel Bear MacKay, to be my husband. In the presence of God and before these witnesses I promise to be a lovin', faithful and loyal wife to you, for as long as we both shall live." She winked at him. "And maybe a wee bit longer."

William pronounced them married, and there under the brilliance of the stars, they became one.

Crushing her to him, Bear kissed his angel.

Chapter 35

With his arm around her shoulders, Bear and Artis stood on their front porch waving goodbye as all their guests left. The wedding merriment lasted far too long as far as Bear was concerned and he was glad to see them all leave. He couldn't wait to begin their private celebration.

They stood there, arm and arm, on the porch for a moment, gazing heavenward. But even the majestic beauty of the heavens could not keep his eyes off Artis. "Ye made a stunningly beautiful bride my angel."

"Thank ye, my braw husband. Thank ye for helping me truly find freedom. For helping me to see the beauty in life. And in the future. And in love."

"And speaking of love…I'll go put that fire out and meet ye…"

"…in our bedroom," she finished, touching his cheek with her finger.

With a mysterious smile, Artis turned and went inside.

Bear suspected she had no idea how seductive she was.

He nearly jumped off the porch and raced toward the fire. He poured a bucket of dirt over the flames and waited until he was sure the fire was out.

He grabbed an opened bottle of wine from the beverages table and the two crystal wine glasses they'd received as a gift, and he went inside, blew out all the candles, and locked up.

Taking long strides, he headed for their new bedroom. He was glad he'd finished stretching, preparing, and washing the two bear hides well. When they'd dried, he'd carefully sewn them together with rawhide strips and mended the cuts. Before the wedding ceremony, he'd snuck into their bedroom and covered their bed with the beautiful fur blanket. He was looking forward seeing her pale body against the dark furs.

He nearly dropped the wine and fine glasses when he entered, for that was exactly what he beheld—Artis lay stretched out on the bear hide blanket in her sleeveless shift, a flimsy soft fabric he could see through. It revealed every curve of her erotic young body—her full breasts, her narrow waist, her shapely hips, and long pretty legs. Desire made a burning ache grow within him.

He could not stop staring at her. She was the very image of beauty and love. The dim candlelight made the gold in her long unbound hair glimmer. Her soft pink lips seemed to beg for a kiss. Her long throat looked warm and alluring. For a moment, he felt as if he were dreaming.

As he continued to enjoy just looking her, her sparkling intelligent eyes watched him eagerly. Yet, her eyes also spoke of her innocence and inexperience. She'd suffered the ugliness of a man taking her, but never enjoyed the beauty of a man loving her.

Tonight she would learn how different the two were.

He sat the wine glasses down and poured them both a half glass. He handed the glass to Artis and, without taking her eyes from him, she took a sip. He could see a drop resting on her lower lip and he instantly wanted to lick it off. But she removed it, running her tongue across her lip.

The simple act made desire surge through his veins.

He suddenly felt hot. He took a long sip of the wine, letting it cool his heated throat and began removing his clothing. First, he laid his clan badge next to the luckenbooth in a small pewter plate he'd put in the center of their bedroom table for just that purpose. They would rest next to each other, just as he and Artis would.

With Artis' watching him intently, he hastily removed the rest of his clothing until he stood before her in only his long black shirt.

"Please take that off too," she asked, her voice trembling.

"Would ye like me to snuff out the fire and candle?" he asked. "I do not want the sight of me to scare ye."

"I do na scare easily."

"If ye insist wife," he said, and tugged the shirt over his head.

Artis gasped and then swallowed. If he wasn't mistaken, her faced paled a bit. She shot him a look of utter bewilderment. Awkwardly, she cleared her throat. "Oh my."

Her reaction amused him.

He eased onto the black fur and reached for her, wrapping an arm around her middle. The intoxicating sweetness of her scent made his breath quicken. And the feel of her in his arms was something he'd dreamed of again and again. But he wanted to feel all of her.

"Would ye mind doing the same for me?" he asked, lifting her shift up her thigh, and arching a brow at her.

She reached down, pulled the shift the rest of the way up, and tossed it to the foot of the bed. She gazed back at him, a smoldering flame dancing seductively in her eyes.

He could not believe how beautiful and alluring she was. She was the epitome of feminine desirability. He nestled her against him again, and gave her a slow drugging kiss. When his lips finally left hers, he asked, "Are ye ready to truly become my wife?"

"Sir, I am already yer wife. I am ready to become yer lover."

Bear chuckled. As usual, she spoke the truth. He was ready to become her lover too.

With tingling fingertips, he began an exploration of her body. He intended to make a thorough study, taking his time to savor his discoveries and to prepare her for what was to come.

First, he ran a hand slowly down her back. When he reached her bottom, he let his hand learn its soft luscious curves. Then he traced a path upwards again. On her side, he felt her terrible scar, the skin rough and disfigured, beneath his fingertips.

Instantly, she tensed and squirmed beneath him, trying to move his hand away from the spot.

He lowered his head and gently brushed his lips against the scar, kissing her until she stilled. "The scar will only remind me how precious you are to me," he whispered.

She said his name and the sound of it from her lips made him feel contentment and peace.

With each new area he touched, she further revealed her innocence, crying out with wonder when she experienced her body's sensitivity for the first time. Each time she did so, his heart surged with excitement. He loved awakening her sensuality and bringing her pleasure.

And he was only just beginning. Before he was through, a tidal wave of passion would wash through her.

He sensed her confidence growing. Tentatively, she began to explore his body as well and it made his senses spin. Her innocent timid touches sent bolts of lightning sizzling through him, heating him from within. She ran her fingertips across his chest and down his arms making him quiver involuntarily.

Shyly, she peeked up to look at his face. "Am I doing it right?"

"Oh aye. It's so right, I may swoon from pleasure right here in our bed," he said.

Emboldened, her touch became less innocent and she let her fingers drift down his abdomen. Her fingers burned his tingling skin. His heart seemed to rush to every spot she touched and he let out a groan of pleasure.

He had to regain control or this would be over too soon. He took her in his arms, leaned over her, and focused on kissing her as he'd never kissed her before—letting his love flow from his lips to her soul. As he deepened the kiss even more, her eager response pleased him. Instead of cooling his passion, her fervent kisses aroused him even more. His impatience grew explosively.

Her lips felt like warm velvet. They tasted like the finest wine. The love that flowed from them reached all the way to his heart.

He trailed his lips down her chin and long neck then he explored her soft shoulders. He could almost feel the heat growing within her as he showered her flesh with kisses. He planted a fervent kiss in the hollow of her glorious bosom while he rubbed her midriff enjoying the feel of the indention between her hips.

She drew his lips to hers once more. Their kisses seemed to melt together in a dreamy intimate joining until she finally took a breath and whimpered softly into his ear.

"I love ye, Bear" she said, peering into his face. "I never dreamed I could feel like this."

"And I love ye my dear Artis—my Highland lover."

He kissed her again, fervently. His body ached with need. He was desperate to join with her. A wave of pure passion rose within him like the hottest fire.

When she raised her leg over his hip, as if to welcome him into her body, he could wait no longer.

Aye, he would be her lover.

Chapter 36

Despite exhaustion and spent passion luring them both to sleep, he'd woken her in the wee hours of the night needing more of her. She'd squirmed beneath him at once and he'd tucked her naked body against him. Their bodies in exquisite harmony, their coupling had seemed otherworldly—more like a deep pleasurable dream— where nothing existed but their love. And afterwards, contentment and peace lured them both back to sleep once again.

When dawn streamed light into their bedroom, she'd woken him with a cup of steaming coffee and a kiss that clearly said she wanted more of his love. He'd wasted no time rousing a melting sweetness within her as he enjoyed the morning light rippling across her creamy white breasts.

Each time they joined, it was different and precious. He wondered if it would always be so. He vowed to do his part to ensure that it was.

But now, Bear was late. He'd lingered in their bed longer than he should have. About halfway to Boonesborough, he urged Camel to a faster gallop. The gelding's long strides made him feel as if he were flying, but even at that pace, it would take him another ten minutes or so to reach the courtroom.

He decided to spend the time thinking about his idea. He needed a way to make a substantial living to provide a comfortable life for Artis and their future family. Boonesborough badly needed an inn. So he would build the town a beautiful one and Artis could hire a staff to run it. Between building Stephen and Sam's houses and their own home, he'd learned a great deal about construction. He could take out a loan to help finance whatever his savings didn't cover or borrow the funds from Sam and Catherine. He even had a name in mind—Boone's Tavern and Inn.

And with the proceeds from the inn, he'd invest in a lumber mill to supply building materials for the growing town. Maybe even other settlements in Kentucky eventually.

Perhaps he would also start breeding horses for profit. William had written Roberts and explained what happened to Artis and of Steller's just demise. And he wrote that Artis recognized the horse as one that belonged to the plantation owner. Roberts had responded saying that he was relieved that Artis was all right and that he'd already replaced his stud horse. He instructed William to give the stallion to Artis. Roberts said she was a fine horsewoman and deserved a first-rate horse.

The splendid stallion could become their stud. While he was in town, he planned to purchase the fifty acres adjacent to their home as a surprise for Artis. He would use the lush fertile property, which had an abundance of thick grass, for their horse pastures.

He had so many plans for their future that he wanted to discuss with Artis. She possessed a keen mind and he was anxious to get her opinions on his ideas. Kentucky was ripe with opportunity and he was sure she'd have ideas too. All they needed was the time to carry their ideas out.

A few minutes later, he spotted William racing Smoke toward him.

"What the hell?" he said aloud. William should be at the trial by now.

"Go back!" William yelled.

He didn't understand what William was trying to say. "What is it?" he shouted back.

William made his horse run even faster and he did the same. Soon the two pulled up on their reins and held their winded horses side by side. "The prisoner killed my deputy and escaped sometime around dawn!"

"Good God, bless the lad's soul," Bear said.

William clenched his jaw and swallowed.

No wonder his brother appeared so upset. "I'm sorry William. Deputy Mitchell was a fine young man."

"We need to go back to your house, now," William urged.

"But why..." Then Bear realized what his brother was so worried about. "Ye think Miller is still after revenge?"

"Yes, I figured he was coming after you. If Miller doesn't find you there, he might do something to Artis. He's desperate and has nothing to lose. He knows we would have hung him today."

"But how would he know where to find me?"

"Criminals have a way of finding out what they need. People in town wouldn't know who he was. All he would have to do is ask around to find out where you lived. Let's go!"

"Artis," he said, alarm filling him. Bear turned Camel and the two sped toward his home.

Stark fear gripped his heart. If anything happened to Artis...

It was her first morning in her new home. After Bear left, she wanted to lay in the drowsy warmth of their bed, just thinking. But she would not start her time as a wife being lazy and idle. She had much to do. She washed and dressed quickly and then braided her hair. She decided to start by making a list of the things they would need to buy—dishes, pans, utensils, towels, and a hundred other little things. Then she would have breakfast and go over the list.

But Artis' heart was so full, near bursting with love, all she could do for a few minutes was roam from room to room admiring her house. She still couldn't believe she lived here. In Scotland, it would be considered a stately manor house. And, even better, she lived here with Bear! He'd been so good to her last night. He made her feel things she didn't even know existed. Feelings and sensations that left her reeling.

As she wandered around, she continued to reflect on her wedding night. He taught her the very nature and meaning of making love. Her pulse quickened just remembering everything he did to her. She already longed for his touch and the security of his big arms. And she never dreamed yielding to the searing need he created could be so pleasurable.

She'd tried to show him pleasure as well, and he seemed delighted with her attentions, but she recognized she still had a lot to understand. Learning what pleased his magnificent body would be nothing but a joy. His muscled chest and arms were so impressive and arousing to touch. His massive shoulders had always nicely filled the clothes he wore. But to see them bare, nearly took her breath away. And when he'd stood before her completely unclothed, looking so powerful and virile, it did take her breath away.

When Bear had left for town, she felt an extraordinary void inside her. It was as if a part of her had suddenly disappeared. She hoped the trial would not take all day and he could come home soon. She decided to prepare a nice meal for lunch in case he was able to get home in time.

Home—their home. The wonder of it all still astonished her.

She heard a noise at the back door. It sounded like someone walking in. Bear could not be back so soon. She became instantly alert, fully aware of her surroundings. Her dirk. She raced for the bedroom, grabbed it, and stuck it in her boot. She snatched up her pistol. Damn, she'd forgotten to load it. Bear told her to keep it loaded and close before he left, and she had promised him that she would. But caught up in her musings, she'd forgotten.

She quickly began loading it but stopped when she heard something behind her.

She turned around and shrieked. A dreadful looking man stood before her. He had the appearance of someone who had just come from the dead.

A bowed back made him stand hunched. One arm hung limply. His skin was pasty white, his face bony, his beard grungy. His soiled clothes smelled sour with the pungent odor of sweat and filth. His large eyes leered menacingly at her.

And his pistol pointed directly at her.

She backed up a step, then two, and took a deep breath trying to control her thundering heart. "Who are ye and what are ye doin' in my home?" she demanded.

"So you're MacKay's wife. Put that pistol back on the table and I'll tell you."

Reluctantly, she complied.

"I'm the brother of the man your husband murdered. Shot him in cold blood in the general store. Later he shot me too, in this shoulder." He pointed to the spot. "Now I have a bum arm."

"At least yer alive."

"A lot of good that will do me. They took all my gold. I was a rich man. Now I'm a pauper thanks to them."

Her mind raced. It was the robber. The one who shot her! That's why he looked so pale. He'd spent more than a month indoors in William's dark jail.

"Yer brother was committin' a robbery, and threatened violence," she declared. "And ye attacked us and nearly killed me tryin' to get yer revenge. I am just now recovered from the dreadful wound ye inflicted on me."

"Then I will have to do a better job of it this time and ensure you don't recover," he sneered through yellowed teeth.

The thought of being shot again made Artis shudder. She had to get this man to leave her alone—one way or another.

"Ye should leave. My husband will be back shortly. He just went to borrow a tool from his brother's nearby cabin. If he finds ye here in our bedroom, he will kill ye."

"You're a lying bitch. I've been hiding behind your house. I saw him leave for Boonesborough. I was hoping you would come outside and start your chores, but you didn't. So I decided to come in and get you. I'll get my revenge now."

Artis' heart sank and her knees threatened to buckle. She felt a shiver of panic whip through her. "Please, just leave. If they find ye, they will take ye back and hang ye."

"I know that," he shouted. "And if I just run, that sheriff will chase me all the way to Canada for killing his deputy."

Artis gasped. The poor deputy. "How could ye have killed him? He was so young." She began to shake as she realized the grave danger she was in. He wasn't just a robber, he was a murderer.

Somehow, she had to survive this. She willed herself to stand tall and clenched her fists to keep them from shaking.

"Killing him was the only way to escape hanging. When he brought me some water, I reached through the bars and strangled him. He had the keys to the jail on him." The man's voice held no hint of regret, but he sounded tense and his expression darkened. He went to the window and peeked out but kept the pistol trained on her.

While his eyes were turned, she reached a hand toward the table that held the clan badge and luckenbooth brooch. Slowly she slipped the badge into her pocket.

"Let's get going, no one's out there," he said.

She cringed when she realized he meant to take her. A tight knot formed in her stomach and her heartbeat grew more rapid. What did he intend to do with her? Why was he taking her? Where were they going?

Bear, I need ye.

"Move," he shouted, pointing to the door with his weapon.

She grabbed her shawl, walked out, and proceeded toward the front door.

"No, we'll go out the back. My horse is tied down there." He shoved her toward the rear of the house. "Get your horse saddled and do it quickly."

As they passed the food left from the wedding feast, he grabbed a biscuit and a hunk of ham and cheese. With a mouthful of food, he said, "Hurry."

Artis picked up her pace and rushed down to where Beautiful stood in her pen. Her mare greeted her with a whinny. As she saddled the horse, she was glad Bear had already fed Beautiful when he fed Camel.

William had taken Steller's stallion to the fort for safe keeping. She was thankful he did or this despicable man would have undoubtedly stolen him.

She heard the man chewing vigorously behind her and then burping. The disgusting sounds made her nauseous. She tied her shawl in front of her, yanking the knot tight with her growing anger.

She couldn't believe her first wonderful morning in her new home had changed so quickly. Biting her lip, she peered in the direction of the road. But there was no sign of Bear or anyone else. Should she try to run? If so, she should wait until she was horseback. Then she could make a mad dash for Whispering Hills. No, that would not be smart. She didn't want to bring this trouble on Kelly or her father. She could try racing toward Boonesborough, but he would probably just shoot her in the back. That thought horrified her. She would just have to wait until she had a chance to slip away.

Or kill him.

She finished saddling and wondered if Bear would even be able to find their tracks. Dozens of construction workers' horses, wagons, and equipment had already torn up and trampled the grasses and shrubs behind their house. The workers and their horses muddled the ground in both directions.

246

"Mount up," he ordered. "And remember, you already learned what the lead from my weapon feels like. So don't even turn around unless I tell you to. Actually, this is the young deputy's weapon, but I'm sure your back would not know the difference." He chuckled at his own attempt at humor.

It made her mad. "Ye will never get away with this," she seethed, making her voice harsh and her anger evident.

"Maybe. Maybe not. But I will get even."

Artis followed the robber's directions. Actually, she told herself, he was a cruel murderer and she would be well advised to remember that. They wove through the dense trees and brush going in a southwesterly direction. He was clearly staying away from the main roads, but where were they going?

"What's yer name?" she asked him, leaning only her head back so that he could hear her. If William ever mentioned it, she couldn't remember what it was.

"Jacob Miller," he answered.

"Mister Miller, where are we goin'? I insist that ye tell me."

"You will learn soon enough Missus. Just keep going the same direction. And make haste."

Within but a few minutes at a gallop, they came across a swiftly moving creek. It must be the one that fed the stream that ran alongside their new home—Highland. She treasured the name Bear had suggested and longed with all her heart to be back there.

"Lead your horse into the middle of the water and then turn upstream," he said.

She did as he asked, but soon tried to exit up the creek bank, knowing that the longer they stayed in the water, the harder it would be for Bear to track her.

He growled, "Stay in the center until I tell you otherwise."

In several places, the water grew deeper, reaching to her boots, but

Beautiful navigated the waters bravely. Then the water rose to just below her knees and the current grew stronger. Her horse, wanting to get on land again, tried to swim to the bank. She had to keep urging her mare to stay in the middle of the creek. Pushing against the current, the horses were growing tired. She was as well. Fortunately, the depth of the water rapidly lessened and Beautiful's breathing eased.

But the longer they stayed in the water, the more difficult it became. The two horses struggled to keep pushing their hooves through the mud and their bodies through the water—shallow in places, deep in others.

Miller doggedly stayed right behind her, his weapon trained on her. Her exposed back started to tremble. Soon it felt like the shadow of death followed her.

Her mind began to quake with anxiety. The thought of another painful bullet wound filled her with terror. It became a constant struggle not to let fear overwhelm her.

Her heart, so recently overflowing with happiness, grew heavy with despair. She didn't want to die. She had so much to live for. Bear most of all!

Chapter 37

"Artis! Artis!" Bear yelled as they stormed through the front door. But he only heard the echo of his desperate cries in their still nearly empty house.

William ran from room to room and Bear raced to the bedroom. He could smell Artis' scent the second he entered.

But she wasn't there.

His heart was already breaking. What had happened to her? Crestfallen, he was about to leave when his eye caught sight of their table. Her brooch remained on the pewter plate but his clan pin was missing. She must have taken it. The thief would have stolen the more valuable luckenbooth with its beautiful stones. Why? Was she trying to send him a message? Or did she want to take a part of him with her?

He heard William searching the upstairs rooms.

"She's not up here," William called down. "Perhaps she's just outdoors or went for a ride on Beautiful," he suggested as he quickly descended the wooden staircase.

But they both knew better. They raced out the back door. "Careful, let's check for tracks," Bear said, holding William back with his arm. He studied the ground trying to remember if Artis had walked behind their house as yet. He didn't think she had. He'd asked her to stay away until the workers cleared all the construction debris and smoothed out the ground. She'd barely had time to see the inside of the house before their wedding.

But her boot print was clearly visible in the moist earth. The grass had not yet had time to grow back after all the construction.

"Look, there's her boot and a fresh print of a man walkin' behind her," Bear said, pointing to the spots. He was dismayed to find that his hand was trembling. "Damn it! He was here. William, he's taken her." His voice broke with huskiness.

"Miller didn't kill her. As far as we know, she's alive. But he likely had a gun pointed on her back since he was following her," William theorized.

Bear fought to control his growing anxiety. And anger. He couldn't help Artis if he lost control of his emotions.

The two sets of tracks led to the new stable and they found Beautiful missing as well. Bear stepped into the mare's pen and studied her hoof prints. He wanted to memorize their size and shape to distinguish them from the many others in their yard. Like a dog following a scent he kept his face near the ground, sometimes going in circles, until he found where the horse's prints led. Then he began following them on foot. "Get our horses," he called back to William. "And fill our canteens."

"All right and I'll write a quick note and leave it under a rock by your front door. If I don't make it back home tonight, Kelly will grow worried and send her father out to look for me. He'll likely come here first."

Bear kept studying the ground on foot until he found the prints of another horse, which had stood tied in the same place for some time. Beautiful's prints continued going in a southwesterly direction, but this time another horse followed. It had to be Miller's mount.

At least she was alive. But for how long? Would Miller kill her because he killed the man's brother? If only he'd known that killing the store's robbers would lead to this.

Oh God, please, please, do na let anythin' happen to her.

Bear continued on foot even after William caught up to him. Nearly blinded with worry and fury, he needed to stay close to the ground to be sure he didn't miss anything.

Shortly, the tracks disappeared into a brisk creek. But which direction did they go? Upstream or down? Or did they cross?

"They wouldn't have gone in the direction of Boonesborough," William suggested.

"Agreed." He mounted, but went to the other side of the bank. He wanted to be sure they didn't cross here. He searched up and down the creek bank and found nothing.

"He stayed in the water to conceal his trail," Bear finally said. "Let's go!"

With every step of the horses, Bear's worry grew. He had to keep making himself focus on the creek bank to his left as he looked for signs that the two had exited the water. William watched the right bank.

They followed the creek's course for about an hour until it forked. "We have a fifty-fifty chance of choosing the right direction to go," William said. "Or do you want to split up and we each take a different direction?"

William's question caused a tumult in Bear's brain. His thoughts raced. "It's near impossible for one person to watch both banks for signs of exit. It can be done, but only at a snail's pace and we need to hurry. The consequences of making the wrong choice could be disastrous."

"Perhaps she left some sign," William suggested.

Bear agreed. He began searching at once and William did the same at the beginning of the right fork. After several long minutes and about to give up, he spotted it. The smallest twig hung broken on a low-hanging cypress tree branch jutting out over the left fork. "Here," he said, pointing to the spot.

"You're sure?" William asked.

"Aye, it's too high for an animal to have done it and it has not been broken long. The wood is still moist within the twig. And look, there's another one," he said, pointing.

"Let's go get them," William said.

They rode side by side through the varying depths of the creek, continuing to keep a careful watch for any signs of exiting to the bank, until the waterway branched again—one branch flowing from the northwest and the one on the left streaming from the southwest. They halted, and Bear studied both sides of the deeper stream.

"It worked once, maybe she did it again," William said.

They both started examining all the foliage on either side. But nearly fifteen minutes later, they had found nothing. Bear's mind clouded with uneasiness. Should they split up? They had a better chance of rescuing Artis with both of them to help. But if they chose the wrong direction, the delay could be costly and they might not rescue her at all. And they had to hurry. He needed to decide quickly.

"What lies to the north?" he asked William.

"A small settlement or two not far from here. Then a few native villages further north."

"And to the south and west?"

"Nothing to the west that I know of," William answered. "To the south there are a few settlements, but they are some distance away."

Bear took the left branch and William followed. The murderer would want to avoid anyone spotting him, so that direction was the logical choice.

As they passed each turn in the stream, Bear's anxiety grew. He continually expected to find her around the next bend. When he didn't, his uncertainty grew and made him doubt his decision to take the left fork. If they were wrong, it could mean Artis' life. "Do ye think we took the right way?" he asked after several miles of no sign of her.

"There's no way to know for sure, but yes I do," William said, continuing to keep his eyes focused on the opposite bank. "We'll find them. And when we do, you keep Artis safe and let me take care of Miller. I have a necktie social I want to invite him too."

Bear heard the anger beneath William's carefully controlled voice, as his brother used the common term for a hanging. The young deputy's death had hit him hard.

"Does anyone else know Miller killed Mitchell and escaped?"

"I'm sure they know by now. When I found my deputy lying there, his body was already growing cold. That whoreson strangled the boy. Choked the life right out of him. I knew I had to warn you and Artis since Miller already tried to exact revenge on you once before. So I just jumped back on Smoke and raced off. In hindsight, I should have told someone. But I'm sure, when none of us showed up for court, Judge Webb figured out that something was wrong and headed for the jail. He's probably organizing a posse from the militia right now. But they will never find us unless he locates a tracker as skilled as you. You could follow a wood tick on solid rock."

"Followin' one through water is a wee bit harder. Unless we figure out where they exited the water, we'll never find their tracks." That possibility made his entire body tighten. He twisted the reins in his hands. All his nervousness slipped back to grip his gut.

For some time, Bear continued to study the creek bank diligently. Several times they thought they had found something, but every time it turned out to be an animal leaving the creek after watering. Each time, his disappointment grew.

He stirred uneasily in the saddle and asked, "Why do ye think he took her? If it was just revenge, he would have killed her back at our house."

"He needed a hostage in case we caught up to him," William said. "He thinks we won't shoot him if he has a gun on her."

The explanation seemed plausible, but set off even more alarms in Bear's head. "So when we do catch up to the bastard, he'll likely try to exchange her for his freedom. How can we trust the fiend?"

253

"We can't. He's not a man of scruples, but he'll bargain with us, expecting us to honor our word. He'll want our promise that we won't pursue him. He'll likely say he'll take her with him for a distance and force us to stay back. Then, if he keeps his word, which is doubtful, he'll release her."

Bear did not see any good scenarios in the situation, but he did see several possibilities for bad outcomes. "I do na like this one wee bit," he spat. His temper flared again.

"I agree. There's much at stake."

Bear's fears mounted, stronger than ever. Something nagged at the back of his mind. "Whatever Miller's plan is, we'll have to be smarter than he is," he said.

"First we have to find her."

We're comin' Artis. I swear it!

Chapter 38

Was Miller going to shoot her here in the creek? Would that be his revenge on Bear? Even if the shot didn't kill her, she might drown in the water, unable to pull herself to land. Would her body lie rotting in the water until Bear found her?

She needed to dispel thoughts of dying—just thinking of it tore at her insides and built fearful images in her mind. The dark thoughts made her more afraid of herself than of him. She had to get a grip on her emotions or she would lose her ability to fight when the time came.

And fight she would!

The only way she was going to survive this was to replace her fear with strength and cunning. She would not allow any more dire thoughts into her head. She needed to keep her heart cold and still—erect a wall of defense against him. She took a few deep breaths, trying to release the tight knot clutching her lungs and throat. She tried to relax her shoulders, so tight with tension it felt like her muscles had turned to layers of rock. She reached into her pocket and let her fingertips caress the precious clan badge. She squeezed her eyes shut and pictured it on Bear's broad chest.

When she opened her eyes, she made herself focus on the beauty around her for a few minutes—the warm fall colors on the trees that lined the bank; the sound of a cardinal tweeting nearby; the rays of light that streamed through the tree branches and lit the leaf-lined forest floor.

It would be paradise if not for the man who rode behind her.

Think, Artis, think. Use your wits, she told herself. You have your dirk. Actually two weapons. The clan badge had a sturdy pin that would serve too. Miller's stay in jail clearly weakened the man. He has one bad shoulder and arm. He didn't appear to be particularly intelligent or clever. And the horse he was riding, likely stolen from the fort's stables, did not look as stout or as young as Beautiful. She was obviously better mounted and judging from the graceless way he sat his horse, she would bet she was a better rider than Miller.

But she needed to remember that Miller was motivated by revenge. She understood herself just how powerful that motivation can be. If circumstances had permitted, she would have sought vengeance against Steller for murdering her mother. In fact, in the past, she fantasized about doing just that, many times, especially on her voyage across the ocean. Like Miller, she would have risked everything to be able to make Steller pay for what he did.

It would likely be useless to try to persuade him to release her, but she had to try. "Mister Miller, if I could convince my husband and his brother not to follow ye, would ye let me go?"

"No."

"Ye could go somewhere far away from Kentucky and start a new honest life. God will forgive yer sins, even murder, if ye repent and sin na more."

"I don't believe in God," he said flatly.

His voice was totally emotionless and it chilled her.

Miller kept their pace hurried and they continued to trudge through the center of the creek for what must have been an hour. She couldn't judge the time from the sun's position because gray and pepper-colored clouds now packed the dull sky. Soon the watercourse forked and he told her to take the left fork. Within a mile or so, the water grew deeper, becoming a full-fledged stream, running bank full. The horses soon had to swim. Then it branched for a second time. Again, they took the left fork.

Rain began to fall, and it showered just long enough to dampen everything and then it quit as quickly as it had started. Artis' wet boots and soggy clothing, and the cool November day, made her shiver. It made her glad she'd grabbed her shawl as she'd left her bedroom. She wondered whether being cold would be the only thing she would have to endure today. She would give almost anything to be back safely in her home again.

Finally, the terrain climbed upward and the stream became only a trickling brook scampering through rocks and pebbles. Along the shoreline, layer upon layer of limestone joined together to create a stalwart barrier to the tall woods beyond.

"You and your horse can water here, but just for a minute," Miller instructed. "And relieve yourself if you have a need."

She dismounted and threw Beautiful's reins across the saddle and let her mare water. Artis knew Miller would keep watching her, but she ignored her mortification and forced herself to stoop down behind a waist-high boulder. When she finished, she washed her hands and face and then hastily gulped down some water. While she drank, she heard him relieve himself on the opposite bank. She took that time to look back, hopeful she would see Bear and William coming up the creek. But only disappointment filled her.

"No sense looking for your man, just yet."

There was something odd in his tone that bothered her. Why did he say, 'just yet'? But she ignored his taunt and leveled a stern look in his direction. "He's a Scot. He'll not only track me here, he'll use his hatchet to relieve ye of yer head." She plunged on carelessly. "And if ye touch me even once, he'll likely relieve ye of yer manhood too!"

Triumph flooded through her when he winced at her words.

"Mount up," he commanded.

She took a few more sips of water and then a deep breath and tried to calm herself.

She wanted to leave a piece of her gown or something for Bear to find, but Miller was watching her every move.

They remounted and turned away from the stream weaving their way between the larger boulders and limestone lining the riverbank. Artis noticed that the ground was still pebble and rock covered where she exited the stream. Even if Bear made the right choices where the creek and stream had branched, he wouldn't be able to tell where they crossed the bank. Miller had found a place completely devoid of vegetation. The horses could not trample anything down or leave a track on the thick layer of stones and gravel.

That meant she was now on her own. Her life was in her own hands. As good a tracker as Bear was, he would never be able to track her here. But if Miller wanted to extract his revenge by killing her, why didn't he just do the evil deed? Why take her so far away? Unless…unless his real target was Bear. But if that were the case, why was he making it so hard for Bear to follow? Perhaps Miller wasn't. Was *he* leaving clues? If so, Miller was definitely cleverer than she had given him credit for being.

She was suddenly anxious to escape. She chanced a glance behind her. He still held the gun aimed at her back. Part of her wanted to make a run for it. If he missed, Beautiful could easily outrun his horse. But if he didn't, she would not only lose her life, she would lose her future with Bear. That would be worse. Much worse.

Be patient. The right time will come.

"Keep going," he said, scowling at her.

Artis squeezed Beautiful's sides and urged her mare to a trot. Soon they were once again weaving through heavy woods and dodging low-hanging boughs and limbs. She wondered again, where they were going. She realized she would have to recall how to get back when she finally managed to get away. She made a point to study the landscape, marking landmarks in her mind. She had an excellent memory and thought she could remember her way back if she concentrated on memorizing the markers.

"Pick up the pace," he demanded.

If Miller wanted her to pick up the pace, she would oblige him. Deliberately, she took Beautiful as fast as she dared—riding hard, twisting, and curling her way through the trees with the skill of a natural horseman. Burdette had been right about the horse's training. Beautiful reined well and the mare skillfully made the sharp cuts and snaking zigzags.

"Slow down," he yelled.

Artis smirked to herself as she brought her mount to a slower pace. She tossed her head back and eyed him with cold insolence. Then she stroked and patted the mare's neck, thanking Beautiful for performing so splendidly.

They continued on for miles in silence, the only sounds coming from the horses' hooves and leathers.

"Turn south," he yelled without warning.

She flinched at the sudden sound of his voice. She tugged Beautiful to a stop. "I thought we were goin' south," she said, deliberately sounding confused.

"No, we were headed west," he said, "go that way." He pointed to his left. "Move."

Actually, Artis was fairly certain which direction they had traveled since leaving the stream, but she wanted to be sure. That knowledge could be important later when she made her way back to Highland.

A few minutes later, Miller directed her into a steep ravine. They made their way through the gulch until she spotted an opening in the side of the canyon wall. A cave.

The thought of being trapped in a cave with this man made her extraordinarily uncomfortable. She hated dark cramped spaces— especially caves. Her dismay grew when he dismounted and tied his weary horse nearby. But she remembered her resolve to stay strong and summoned her courage once again.

"Get inside," he ordered.

She dismounted, tied Beautiful, and stared at Miller. She narrowed her eyes and met his icy gaze straight on. "We have to take care of the horses first. Your geldin' is about to drop. They need to be unsaddled and allowed to water and graze."

"They can rest just fine standing right there for now."

She tossed her braid behind her back in defiance and placed her hands on her hips in a not so subtle challenge. She was tired from a lack of sleep last night and the long ride, cold, hungry, and thirsty. She was in no mood to be cooperative.

He met her gaze without flinching. "Get inside," he said again, pointing the way with the pistol.

"Nay, I will not! It would na be proper."

Miller scoffed at her response. "To hell with proper," he roared, "get inside now or I'll properly skin you."

She stiffened and marched up a steep incline, over rocks and grass toward the darkness of the cave opening just as rain started to fall in earnest.

Chapter 39

A rtis stood at the cave entrance unable to make her feet move.

"Get in there," Miller commanded, pushing at her back.

"I can't."

"You will unless you want to die right here and become food for the wolves tonight."

Artis let out a breath and took another deeper one. Old fears, large and looming, shadowed her mind. As a child, she'd found a cavern in the hills around her home. And, like all children full of curiosity, she just had to explore it. But she lost her way and spent hours trying to find her way out of the dark labyrinth, crying the entire time. When she finally did locate the exit, she swore she would never enter a cave again.

"Please, do na make me go in there," she pleaded. She reached into her pocket and made a tight fist around the clan badge, hoping it would give her strength.

"What are you afraid of? Ghosts?"

She would rather face ghosts than the cave. "Can I just wait out here? I promise on my dear mother's soul I will na run away."

Miller must have reached the end of his patience because he shoved her inside. Then he pushed her again, hard, and she stumbled and fell scraping her hands on the rough rocks.

She peered around, her eyes wide and her heart thundering within her breast. For a few moments, she sat crouched, paralyzed with fear, and couldn't move. The cave's shadowy walls and black tunnel seemed to hide horrors that fed her panic. She forced herself to breathe deeply and clutched her gown's skirt with her hands to keep from shaking. Then she remembered the clan badge and held it tight in her closed fist against her heart.

Gradually, her terror lessened and she furtively studied the cave and her situation.

Miller seemed to ignore her as he moved about and settled several things.

The cave looked as though someone had previously occupied it. There were several pallets for beds, an overturned bucket, a coffee pot, some other gear, and signs of a previous cook fire.

She eyed him apprehensively. "Why did ye bring me here, Mister Miller?"

"You're my bait. I didn't really want to kill you. I want to murder the man who killed my brother. I wasn't going to risk getting shot by him again, so while in jail, I concocted a plan—I'd lure him to our cave. I deliberately broke a branch or two to let them know what fork to take. At the other fork, I knew they would head toward the more isolated area, because they would think I would. And when we stopped to drink and then left the creek bed, I made it look like a piece of my shirt tore off on the boulder by the path we took."

"But if ye wanted them to find us, why make it so hard to follow us by goin' through the water?

"I could tell that sheriff and your man are smart fellows. I didn't want to make it too obvious that I was setting up an ambush. I want them to ride right into my trap unawares and unsuspecting."

Yes, Miller was definitely far more cunning than she'd given him credit for being. He was as conniving as a weasel.

He showed her where he'd torn off a piece of his shirt. "That and my fire should ensure that I lured that man of yours into my trap. From here, inside the cave and from this vantage point, I can shoot him with my long rifle from a fair distance as they approach. He'll never know what hit him. And if that sheriff comes along, I got a piece of hot lead waiting for him too." Miller's mouth twitched with amusement.

"Ye have a rifle here?" she asked warily.

"No, I got *four* long rifles, and plenty of powder and lead too. Miller went further into the cave, reached up to a hidden spot just above his head, and pulled down a long package covered in oiled cloth. He sat it down and unwrapped it. "One of these belonged to my brother. The other two were our partners. We kept an extra set of weapons here. We used this cave as a hideout in between our gold gatherings and other robberies."

For the first time since he took her, Miller put his pistol back in its sheath on his belt. As Artis watched, he proceeded to load all four long rifles. Would one of those balls kill Bear? Or William? The thought made her want to scream.

When Miller finished, he leaned all of them against the wall by the cave entrance. "I'll probably only need two of these. I'm an excellent shot," he bragged.

Good God. From the cave's elevated vantage point, Bear and William would be as vulnerable as two deer in the forest if they didn't know Miller waited in the cave and was heavily armed. She would have to find a way to warn them.

Or kill Miller. Could she do it?

"I think I'll to use my brother's rifle to kill your man. I think he would have liked that."

Yes, she could kill him, she decided. She would have to.

Bear's heart leapt when he spotted what appeared to be a piece of fabric stuck on the sharp edge of a crevice in the limestone along the riverbank.

He urged Camel to the spot and jumped off. Grabbing it, he examined the cloth. It was part of a man's faded blue shirt. It did not look weathered so it could not have been there long. "I found somethin'! I think they left through this openin' in the boulders," he called over to William.

"What did you find?" his brother asked, riding up on Smoke.

He showed William the cloth and then handed him Camel's reins.

"I'm goin' to proceed on foot until I pick up their trail again on the other side of these boulders. Follow, but na too close in case I miss a track and need to double back."

It took him but a few minutes to find the tracks again. The two horse's had left clear prints in the damp leaves. He remounted and wove Camel through the thick woods as swiftly as he could without losing the trail.

They were getting close. He could sense it. Maybe it was his heart sensing her heart. He just knew somehow that she wasn't far away.

Then the worst possible thing happened. It started to rain.

"We've got to hurry," he yelled to William. "We need to find them before this rain washes away their tracks."

Bear urged Camel to trot faster but continued to study the ground whirling past him. The rapid pace combined with looking down constantly became dizzying, but he forced himself to continue.

The rain steadily increased and soon became a deluge. He heart felt like it was drowning.

His chest tightened with dread. Right before his eyes, the tracks melted into the ground, disappearing forever.

"No!" he shouted into the storm.

&

Miller used his flint and firesteel to start kindling to flaming. Then he added wood from a pile stacked next to the cave wall. When he had a fire going, he made coffee.

It didn't surprise her that he built a fire. Miller wanted Bear and William to find them. He'd set his trap and was just waiting to spring it.

Artis bit her lip, trying to quell her old fears about caves and her new distress for Bear and William. She needed to act soon. They might not be far behind.

When the coffee finished brewing, Miller poured himself a cup and to her surprise offered one to her as well. Chilled and thirsty, she took a sip. It was so bad it could quality as coffin varnish—the expression the locals used for bad coffee.

Miller made his way to the cave opening and hunched down. He sat there calmly drinking his coffee, waiting, watching.

For Bear. For her husband.

For William. Kelly's husband.

And little Nicole's father.

She had to do something!

She sat the cup down, walked over, and stood behind him. "Mister Miller, ye can na shoot them in cold blood. At least be a man and stand up to them. Fight them face to face." Perhaps if she appealed to his male pride, she could get him to abandon his plan to ambush Bear and William.

"I'll let the lead from these here rifles stand up to them. Far more effective."

"Please, what can I say to make ye change yer mind?"

"Not a thing. Not a damn thing."

She would make one last effort. "Ye do na want to go to hell do ye?"

"I imagine the devil, if there is one, is holding a hot seat for me there already. Nothing I do matters to anyone anymore."

It mattered to her. She knelt and reached down for her dirk. She had to do this. For Bear. For their unborn children. For Kelly and Nicole. She raised the blade, her hand quivering.

She let out the tiniest cry just as she plunged the blade toward his back.

It was enough to warn him. He spun away just in time, pushed her aside, and fell on his knees.

She collapsed on her back, still clutching her dirk.

Miller scampered to his feet and drew his pistol.

She jumped up, whirled around, and sprang forward.

As he took aim, she ran into the cave's darkness.

Chapter 40

Bear's stomach clenched at the echoing sound. He turned toward William. "Did ye hear that?"

"Yes!" William hollered back.

Bear took Camel to an all-out run toward the sound of the gunshot. It came from a ravine. *Oh God, had Artis been shot again?* The thought made his heart race and feel like it would explode with fear.

William's horse thundered behind him and then drew up alongside Camel. The rain stopped abruptly but they had to avoid several treacherous spots where water had pooled, hiding what lay beneath.

"There," William called and pointed to the canyon wall.

The slightest trail of smoke and a dim light could be seen coming from within what looked like a cave.

"Watch out," Bear shouted. "A rifle is pointin' our way."

Both men grabbed their rifles, jumped from their horses, and crouched behind a massive boulder, just as a bullet struck the same rock. With an experienced warrior's eye, Bear assessed their surroundings and the situation.

"It must be Miller," William said. "Where did he get a rifle?"

Bear didn't wait to answer the question. He was already moving forward, wanting to get closer before the man reloaded. But without delay, another lead ball followed the first. The shot missed him by a hair's breadth and made his heart race even harder as he crouched behind a brush covered limestone rise.

This time William dashed toward Bear and another shot nearly hit him.

"Damn. How many loaded rifles does that man have?" William swore.

"At least three too many," Bear answered, his muscles still quivering from William's near brush with death. "It's time we gave him a taste of his own medicine."

Like William, Bear kept his rifle under an oiled cloth on his horse, but that was no guarantee it would work after the downpour. Hoping his powder was still dry, he lined up his sights. But he could not get a fix on Miller. "I can na see him, he must be reloadin'."

"Shoot anyway, then leave your rifle. I'll fire mine, while you move further forward," William said. "Then I'll reload and fire both rifles when you're ready to charge into the cave."

"Okay, but I have to get closer first."

Bear targeted the spot where he'd seen the smoke from the flintlock and fired. Leaving his rifle, he dashed forward while William shot his own rifle.

Bear raced right up to the base of the canyon wall. *I'm coming Artis.*

Another shot rained limestone down around William.

Bear put fresh powder in both his flintlock pistols. He inched forward, hugging the canyon wall with his body. If Miller leaned out and fired, Bear knew he would make a big target. He'd have to move with lightning speed to avoid being shot.

He motioned for William to shoot again. When his brother fired, Bear raced up to a large rock outcrop situated just outside of the cave entrance. It was just big enough to hide him. He pulled both pistols. He glanced down at William and waited for his brother to reload both rifles. William nodded when he finished.

Bear readied himself. He gave William the signal to fire. A split second after first one rifle shot and then another exploded into the cave's mouth, Bear rushed in.

Instantaneously, Miller raised his own pistol but Bear fired first. He heard the distinct thump of both shots as they ripped through Miller's chest.

The murderer was dead. Was Artis alive?

Frantically, his eyes searched the cave. Where was she? When he didn't see her, worry filled him so completely he had difficulty breathing. He turned back to the opening and motioned William to come up. "Hurry," he yelled.

William arrived a moment later. "Artis?"

"She's na here," he said, wanting to weep. "Did he kill her?"

"Bear, calm yourself. We followed two tracks here. Her horse is tied outside. Maybe she ran to hide when the firing started."

He prayed William was right. "Artis!" he yelled.

"I'll make a couple of torches out of these logs and the bedding," William said.

"Make haste. I'll keep callin' her name."

While William quickly assembled the torches, Bear hiked into the darkness yelling her name into the cave, over and over. Every time he did so, his heart cracked a little more. Soon it would shatter.

William caught up to him, they each took a torch, and with Bear bending over slightly, they made their way into the darkness. The cave was damp and smelled of ancient decay.

Bear kept calling Artis' name, again and again. Each time, the only response was the echo of his own voice. His hope dwindled and the ache in the back of his throat grew into a bigger lump. He swallowed his despair once more. She had to be in here. There had been no sign of her outside the cave. But was she lying dead somewhere in the darkness ahead?

Then he heard her scream. Screaming at the top of her lungs. She sounded desperate.

"Help!"

It was her voice. It was Artis. He rushed toward the sound so fast his torch nearly went out. William trailed right behind.

"Artis!"

"Look, there's her dirk," William said.

"Here. I'm here. Help me. Help me," she shrieked.

In a few seconds, they found her hanging from the edge of an abyss so deep they could not see the bottom of the void. His heart almost stopped.

He dropped the torch and grabbed her arms, wrapping his hands securely around each. In another second, he had her in his own arms and they were both crying, but she was nearly hysterical. Her face looked frenzied and panic-stricken. Her eyes were over-bright. She continued to sob and wail.

"Let's get her out of here," he called to William, who was retrieving the torch Bear dropped and her dirk.

"Aye, aye, out, out" she cried.

She clung to him desperately, grabbing fistfuls of his clothing, as they made their way back.

"Yer all right Artis. We'll get ye out of here."

"Miller, he, he…" she pointed a shaking hand toward the cave opening.

"He's dead Artis," Bear said, "he canna hurt any of us now."

She closed her eyes and big tears fell from beneath her long lashes.

"Take my torch," he told William.

Bear swept Artis up into his arms and he carried her until they reached the fire at the cave entrance.

"I'll take Miller's body down to the bottom of the ravine and take care of the four horses," William said. "It's too late to go back tonight. Maybe I can find us a rabbit or two before full dark for dinner."

Bear nodded his agreement and William grabbed Miller's legs and drug the bleeding body away.

Bear knelt to sit them down on the nearest pallet.

"Nay! Take me outside," Artis insisted.

"Aye lass, but foul weather threatens again."

When they reached the cool rain-soaked air, Artis closed her eyes and took a deep breath.

Being outside seemed to calm her but it took several tries and the nearby booms of thunder to convince her to return to the dry cave and the warmth of the fire. When he promised to keep holding her in his lap, she finally consented and he took her back inside. Sensing that she might be afraid of the cave's darkness, this time they sat on the pallet closest to the entrance.

He removed his wet coat and shirt and laid them out to dry. Then he pulled her into his lap. Hugging her closely against his bare chest, he leaned his head against hers and stroked her hair continuously until her breathing finally calmed.

Slowly, his own heart settled down and the tension in his body eased. His wife was where she belonged, in his arms, his love sheltering her against his heart.

Chapter 41

Bear watched as William gazed forlornly over at Deputy Mitchell's empty desk. They were in William's office awaiting the judge's arrival and then the three would attend the deputy's funeral together, along with many others from the fort and town.

His brother's palatable sorrow filled the room. Once they had recovered Artis, William had allowed his grief to surface. The trip back from the cave took far less time since they hadn't had to look for tracks or navigate the creek waters. But William spent the time in silence, growing more and more despondent the closer they got to Highland. William had left for Whispering Hills immediately, knowing that Kelly would be worried sick about him.

This morning was the first chance he and William had to talk.

"Do ye know what yer going to say at the funeral?" Bear asked.

"No! Nothing will come into my head except regret—regret that I left him alone to guard that bastard. My head is too full of remorse to think of anything else."

"He was doing his job," Bear said, "and he was good at it. Until the devil's own trickery hoodwinked him."

"But I picked him for the job," William replied, his face grim and tormented.

"Nay, remember, he was the deputy when we arrived in Boonesborough."

"I could have found another deputy—someone more experienced. But I didn't have the heart to tell him he was too young," William said, shaking his head. "I thought I could train him and let him grow into the job."

"Aye. And Mitchell thought he'd already grown into a manhood. But even though ye knew he had not quite reached it, ye gave the boy a chance to become a man. He may well have grown into a lawman as strong and as wise as ye," Bear said, "but that was not his destiny." Bear knew his words would mean little. William needed more time to ease the pain.

"What am I going to say to his family?" William asked, his voice cracking with misery.

"That ye were proud of yer deputy. That he lost his life protectin' Boonesborough. And its citizens and ye will never forget him."

Judge Webb threw the door open. "Let's get this over with."

His abrupt entrance and words didn't surprise either Bear or William.

Judge Webb turned to Bear. "I wish you hadn't shot the son-of-a-bitch. I was looking forward to hanging him."

"I was tryin' na to get shot myself," Bear said.

"Actually, I'm glad you killed him Bear. He took the life of a fine young man," Judge Webb said.

Bear heard William let out a deep sigh. He perceived the stab of guilt that wounded his brother nearly as much as a real knife wound.

Judge Webb went over and placed a hand on William's shoulder. "William Wyllie, you are a man of the law. Men of the law often die in the line of duty. Sometimes they die too young. As long as we are fighting hardened criminals who follow the devil and not the good Lord, some of those who uphold the law will continue to die. The sooner you accept that the better."

The judge's adamant statement made Bear recognize again that his brother's duties put William's life at risk every single day. He prayed God would send a robust guardian angel to watch over his brother.

William studied the judge's eyes, as though he were seeking absolution.

"Do not blame yourself, sheriff. Blame the man who did it," the judge said adamantly.

"Aye," Bear said, "the judge is exactly right."

The tension in William's face eased just a bit. "I want to find a positive way to honor Mitchell. A way for the entire town to pay tribute to him."

"A way to honor fallen heroes of the law?" Judge Webb asked.

"Exactly. But maybe not just fallen heroes. Maybe a symbol of all those who dedicate their lives to protect the weak, the defenseless, and those in danger. An emblem worn by those who fight for the general welfare of all."

"The English knights posted in Scotland wore their coat of arms on an oval badge or sometimes on a patch on their left arm, signifyin' their sworn duty to protect. How about a badge?" Bear suggested.

"Yes!" William agreed. "That would be the ideal way for us to pay our respects. We could award it posthumously to Mitchell's family."

"Why not make it an even more significant tribute by having all those who enforce the law in Kentucky wear the badge, including you. It could become a permanent symbol that is respected and honored and would identify sheriffs and their deputies to all our citizens," Judge Webb added.

"It should be worn over the heart," Bear proposed. "As a reminder of their vow to protect."

"Let's make the first one from one of the gold pieces Miller and his friends stole. I'll have the Governor give me one," Webb proposed decisively. The judge grabbed a piece of paper and William's quill and stuck the tip in his ink bottle. He drew a five-pointed star and in the center carefully printed the word 'Deputy'.

"Two points of the star point down," William noticed. "That should symbolize the safety of the town resting on the shoulders of the badge wearer."

"And the two pointing left and right could symbolize that their duty spans east to west and west to east," Webb said.

"Aye, and the one at the top—pointin' up—should signify lookin' to God for protection, wisdom, and strength," Bear finished.

William tapped his finger on the paper. "I can't wait to have the gunsmith design this. In the meantime, we'll give this drawing to Mitchell's mother and father. I'll add a commendation at the bottom expressing Boonesborough gratitude for their son's service."

Bear could hear the relief in his brother's voice—William could now give Mitchell's parents a badge of honor as a memorial. However, the small smile on his brother's cheeks could not conceal the anguish of his heart. But, together they had come up with a way to ease the pain of the boy's murder for both William and his family.

While William and the judge wrote the commendation, Bear stepped outside to smoke his pipe. The sun had finally decided to make an appearance and shoo away all the clouds in the sky. He hoped Artis would make time to get out and enjoy the sunshine. It wouldn't be long before the days grew shorter and the temperature lessened.

That morning, he had insisted that she skip the funeral, saying she needed time to recover from the trip back to their home and her ordeal. He wanted her to take it easy for a couple of days.

What could he do to make it easier for her to relax? Then it hit him— a tub. As soon as the funeral was over, he would go straight to the cooper's and order one made. In recent weeks, he visited the cooper's shop several times to order items needed for their new home—pails, a churn, and barrels. The cooper used white oak staves split from the dense center of the tree. He and his helpers heated the slats to make them pliant, bent them into shape and then bound the staves with iron. On several occasions, he watched them work, admiring their skill as they cut grooves in the lips to

275

fit the staves snugly. Artis might have to sit on a towel to ensure she didn't get splinters in her adorable bottom, but he was certain she would enjoy bathing regularly.

He would also relish seeing her unclothed body resting in a tub and he always reveled in the scent of her freshly washed skin. He grinned broadly, pleased with himself for coming up with the perfect gift for both of them. He decided he would pay extra to have it built right away and delivered sometime tomorrow afternoon.

His thoughts filtered back to the day he'd first met Artis. It was the same day as her arrival in Boonesborough and his return. So many events transpired to bring them to the point where they both stood over the carcass of a mountain lion, looking into each other's eyes for the first time. An old Scottish proverb says no man can plan his own destiny, but he had no doubt they were destined to meet despite the obstacles thrown in her path. Nay, perhaps it was because of the adversities she'd overcome.

She had lost her home, her family, her country, and seven years of her life. She could have wallowed in unhappiness and self-pity. Lord knows, she had a right to feel both. But instead, her hard work and determination resulted in a generous grant of land and coin that would allow her to start a new life.

She showed her amazing courage when she'd joined a group of strangers to travel to a wilderness, where she also knew no one. All to finally have a home again. Then a gunshot nearly stole her new life from her. Despite her wound, she found the will and strength to hide from her old cold-blooded enemy. If she hadn't, she surely would have died. Then the severity of the wound made her have to fight for life once again.

Afterwards, when she'd recovered, and finally had a home and love, Miller stole Artis away, using her as bait to lure him. He was glad Miller was dead, not just for the callous murder of Deputy Mitchell, but for Artis. He would have done anything to rescue her. Once again, he thought with fearful clarity, he could have lost her.

But he didn't. It wasn't luck. He didn't believe in luck. With God's help, they had both survived the onslaught of two killers.

Love, an unbeatable ally in the battle for life, always triumphs.

Camel and Smoke both snorted, interrupting his musings. Evidently, they had both grown tired of standing tied to the rail. Soon though, the horses would take them to bury a young man.

Bear remembered his own youth. The loss of his parents, leaving him completely alone in the world, had burned one truth onto his young mind—family was important. They can be taken from us so easily. He guessed that was why he was so protective of his adopted family—Sam, Catherine and Little John; Stephen, Jane, their lively daughters Martha and Polly, and young son Samuel; and William, Kelly, little Nicole, and Mr. McGuffin.

But now, with Artis, he had his own family. And the joy they found in lovemaking would undoubtedly make that family grow larger very soon. He couldn't wait to have a wee bairn of his own. He didn't care if it was a son or daughter. He hoped he had a half dozen of each.

And at their home, Highland, he would tell them all wonderful stories of the rugged mountains, rolling glens, abundant streams and the deep sea Lochs of the true Highlands of Scotland.

And he would tell them of their mother's bravery.

William and Judge Webb walked out. It was time.

Chapter 42

Artis strolled toward their bed. As she passed their bedroom table, she glanced down at her precious luckenbooth and the clan badge. They now rested again, side by side, where they belonged. Just as she and Bear belonged side by side.

She smiled at Bear as she climbed into their bed after a long bath soaking in warm rose scented water. Bear worked with the cooper to design the tub, complete with a place to rest her back while bathing. After her baths, all she would have to do is toss the used bath water out the window onto the rose garden she planned to put outside their bedroom window. And the hearth right there in their bedroom was be a convenient place to heat the water. It only took one or two potfulls of boiling water to heat the rest of the room temperature bathwater.

After the coopers delivered the tub to their home earlier that afternoon, they'd helped Bear place it in the wash area he built next to their bedroom to give her a quiet and private place to relax. She was ecstatic and would be forever grateful.

She'd washed her hair earlier in the day and brushed it until it gleamed. Now, her locks hung loose down her back and shoulders the way Bear liked it. She didn't bother to wear anything. Bear would just make her take it off anyway.

He'd given her a couple of days to recover from the ordeal, but tonight, she was ready for him to make love to her.

"It's about time ye joined me," Bear half-heartedly complained. "I was afraid ye'd gone missin' again." His smile was wide, his teeth white against his tanned face and shadow of a beard.

"Do na joke about that," she admonished, frowning at him. "I never want to think about goin' missin' again."

He raised up on an elbow. "Me either. It was a horrible time of it for ye," he said, "and I'm sorry I made light of it." His handsome face looked contrite.

"Yer forgiven," she said, "but in a minute ye will have to make it up to me somehow."

"I believe I can find a way. I'm exceptionally creative ye know," he said with a roguish grin.

She did know. Some of the ways he'd shown his love for her had surprised her and made her realize just how naïve she had been of what happened in the marriage bed. And she wanted to experience all of them again.

But first, they needed to talk about something that had been bothering her ever since they returned home.

She already told him why she hated caves and about how she braved racing blindly into the darkness, despite her terror, to avoid being shot. She shuddered as she remembered running in utter darkness. It had felt as if she had jumped off a high cliff. Then her left boot caught the edge of a rock outcropping causing her to stumble abruptly. She fell, her feet flailing beneath her. Frantic, she had latched onto the rock wall with all her might, desperately clinging to the edge. Her fingernails biting into the earth and rock, her feet scrambled for leverage finding only tiny footholds. She heard loose rock and dirt sliding below her and hitting the cave floor long seconds later. Below her, there was nothing but sheer blackness.

If Bear had been even a minute later, she would be dead now.

But she had not yet told him that before she ran she had tried to kill the man. She sat up and turned to face him. "I need to tell ye somethin'."

He lifted his head and leaned it back against his bent arm.

"Bear, I tried three times to persuade Miller not to ambush ye, but he seemed determined to kill ye and William too. So, I decided I had to do somethin'. I'd hid my dirk in my boot before we left."

Bear nodded approvingly.

"I tried to stab Miller in the back when he was watchin' for ye. I was terrified and my hands were shakin', nonetheless I was determined to do it. But when I raised the blade, he heard me make a little squeal and he shoved me backwards. I scrambled up and ran into the cave, despite my terror. He shot at me. That was the first shot ye heard."

"And thank the Lord it missed and that I heard it," he said. "With the torrential rain erasin' yer trail, I would never have found the cave."

"I guess it was all meant to happen the way it did, but I'm disappointed in myself that I wasn't able to defend ye."

"Nay, do na think harshly of yourself. Killin' a man is never an easy thing to do, even for seasoned warriors. If yer help is ever really needed, I'm confident ye would find the courage."

"Do ye think so, truly?"

"Aye, Artis MacKay, ye would find yer *Manu Forti*, yer strong hand."

"I do hope so because here in the wilderness I intend to be strong—to defend my family when needed. Without hesitatin' like I did in the cave with Miller."

"Artis, why did ye take the clan badge along?"

"I knew I would carry a part of ye with me if I had it. It made me feel safer just bein' able to reach into my pocket and clutch it. I just imagined I was holdin' on to you."

"And ye were lass."

"I know, Bear. I was holdin' on to yer heart. Holdin' on tight enough for ye to find me."

"All things happen for a reason for them that love the good Lord. Let it be and think na more about it," he said, drawing her up against his chest. "What say ye? Are ye ready to start workin' on that family ye want or do we need to talk some more?"

She giggled. "Let's talk a wee bit longer," she teased.

He moaned loudly and leaned his broad shoulders back against his pillow. The light of the hearth fire glimmered over his dark copper hair and bronzed skin. He looked so appealing she could hardly keep her hands off him, but she was enjoying making him wait.

"How many wee bairns do ye want? A few or a lot?" she asked, and nestled herself against him, enjoying his warmth against her bare skin. Breathing in his scent, she caught whiffs of leather, sweet tobacco, horse, and hearth fires.

"A lot—at least a dozen. And maybe a wee bit more," he answered happily. Studying her eyes, he ran his fingertip across her lower lip and then down her jaw to the hollow at the base of her neck.

She marveled at the amazing power of just his fingertip to awaken desire within her.

"Then we had better get to work, my Highland lover," she said, gazing into the blue-green loch of his eyes. She would never see her beloved Highland Loch Naver again, but even its stunning beauty could not compare to what she saw in her husband's eyes. She would never grow tired of seeing the love Bear shared every time he gazed at her.

He stroked her back and shivers of delight followed his gentle touch. He rested a hand in the swell of her hips and moved his fingers in small circles, his touch light and teasing. Then he grabbed her bottom, filling his hand, and tugged her closer. When his hand roved intimately over her breast and then cupped her bosom, she moaned aloud with pleasure.

As her body responded to his tantalizing seduction, touch by touch,

281

kiss by kiss, she ached to caress him as well.

His form exuded a virile masculine power that was entirely captivating, enticing, and tempting. Using both her fingers and her lips, she traced her own paths over his bare body. Each path became more enchanting than the last. Each part of him, precious and treasured. And loved.

Her fingertips could feel the strength beneath his firm chest and arm muscles and it caused her to gasp with sweet pleasure. Just touching him made desire surge through her. She ran her fingers across the soft flesh of his back and let her nails slide softly across his skin.

He groaned with pleasure and then palmed her cheeks between his hands. "You are puttin' a magical spell on me, wife," he breathed. "I am utterly at your mercy." He pushed away stray tendrils from her moist face and wove his hands through her hair.

She nuzzled her head in the hollow of his neck and let him cuddle her. She felt so loved, so treasured. And when his palm gently held her belly, where she might someday carry their child, she wanted to weep with joy.

As if he sensed what she was thinking, he kissed her, movingly, tenderly, letting the kiss be more about love than passion. "I love ye," he said, "and I vow if we make a babe this night, I will love our child with all my heart too."

"I love ye," she said, as tears of joy filled her eyes. She found the thought of him begetting a child in her womb extraordinarily arousing and incomparable to anything else. It was as if their love took on a higher purpose and had even more meaning.

He kissed her again, hungrily and forcefully, this time making it more about passion.

She sensed a possessiveness, an earnestness, in his kiss that she hadn't felt before. As though the whole experience of chasing after her, not knowing her fate, made his love deeper and all the more intense.

In response, she felt a primal awakening rise from deep within her. Intense desire spread out from the core of her body and radiated up and down her entire length making even her fingers and toes tighten with need. She kissed him with a hunger made desperate by their forced separation and brush with death.

He released her lips and Artis drew in deep breaths of air to feed her rapidly beating heart. She returned the kiss with her own urgency, letting him feel her own desperate need. She craved his reassurance, yet again, that they were both safe at Highland—in their home, their bed, and beneath their warm furs.

She was so grateful to him and thankful for her new life. And for the safety she would always have in the haven of his arms.

She wanted him to hold her and never let go. Because in his arms she'd found happiness. The happiness her uncle, so long ago, sent her to find. But she'd found more than happiness—she'd found contentment, bliss, and ecstasy—in a wilderness paradise.

He seemed to recognize her compelling need and gathered her protectively against his warm body.

Instinctively, her own body ached toward his, needing him, wanting him, and craving his love.

His hands held her tighter and they molded—heart to heart as one—into the safe sanctuary of forever love.

And a wee bit longer.

We hope you enjoyed reading

American Wilderness Series Romances *Book Four*
FRONTIER HIGHLANDER VOW OF LOVE
The story of Bear and Artis

Other Titles by Dorothy Wiley
Book One
WILDERNESS TRAIL OF LOVE
The story of Stephen and Jane

Book Two
NEW FRONTIER OF LOVE
The story of Sam and Catherine

Book Three
WHISPERING HILLS OF LOVE
The story of William and Kelly

Coming soon…
Book Five

Please tell your friends…
Thank you for reading my novel. If you enjoyed reading this book, I would be honored if you would share your thoughts with your friends. Regardless of whether you are reading print or electronic versions, if you particularly liked the experience of reading Bear and Artis' story, I'd be extremely grateful if you posted a review on http://www.Amazon.com. Just enter my name *or* the title FRONTIER HIGHLANDER VOW OF LOVE in Amazon's search box and it will take you to the correct page. Then just scroll down on the page where you can write a customer review.
Please visit www.dorothywiley.com for the release date for new books. Thanks for your support.

All the best, **Dorothy**

About the Author

Compassionately written, richly authentic, powerfully dramatic, Dorothy Wiley's books will make you weep, laugh, cringe in fear, fall in love, and remember. Wiley's American Wilderness Series Romances are epic love stories of the frontier. Her Amazon best-selling and award-winning novels are set in 1797 Kentucky and are heart-wrenching, unforgettable, fast-paced action adventures. Wiley skillfully breaches the walls of time, bringing readers to a young America, where romance and danger are as powerful as the wilderness. Spellbound by horrific events and villains, action readers fear for her valiant characters. And charmed by the beauty of Wiley's love stories, romance lovers cheer for her endearing heroes and heroines. Like Wiley's compelling heroes, who from the outset make it clear they will not fail despite the adversities they face, this author is likewise destined for success. Her books continue to earn five-star reviews from readers and recognition in literary contests.

WILDERNESS TRAIL OF LOVE

• Historical Novel Society (HNS) Editor's Choice and long listed for the prestigious 2015 HNS Indie Award

• Readers' Favorite Five-Star Award 2015

• Finalist in the CFRWA Touch of Magic Contest 2014

NEW FRONTIER OF LOVE

• Amazon's Breakthrough Novel Award Quarter-Finalist 2014

WHISPERING HILLS OF LOVE

• Prize Writer Finalist – Romance 2015

Wiley received a Bachelor of Journalism degree, with Honors, from The University of Texas. After a distinguished 35-year corporate career in marketing and public relations, she is living her dream—writing historical romances about the heroic settlers of the Ameican wilderness. Follow Dorothy Wiley on Amazon www.amazon.com/author/dorothywiley. To see trailers for each of her books, enter Dorothy Wiley in YouTube's search box. She would enjoy connecting with you through her website www.dorothywiley.com or:

Facebook: Dora May Wiley   **Goodreads.com**: Dorothy Wiley

Twitter: @WileyDorothy   **Pinterest**: Dorothy M. Wiley

Acknowledgments

Although the characters and account of the Highland clearances described in the Prologue in this book are fictionalized and not a real version of events, sadly, in reality these clearances did happen. Bliadhna nan Caorach, 'The Year of the Sheep,' actually occurred in 1792. Many violent and merciless clearances took place and the MacKays suffered severely in the Strathnaver clearances between 1815 and 1818. Artis' story could have been real and, like her, many expelled Scots fled to the colonies in search of a better life. I have to admire their unwavering courage and I am so grateful for the many contributions they made to our country.

I should also mention that Black bear attacks, as described in this book are rare, but they do occur. Black bears have killed more than 60 people across North America since 1990. Many of these attacks were extremely aggressive and predatory.

As I did in the first three books of my American Wilderness series, I would also like to thank America's daring and brave first-wave pioneers, many of whom, like my own ancestors, were Scots. Their hard fought struggles for a place in the vast wilderness gave us the majestic country we enjoy today. Their stories must be remembered! If you agree, or would like to comment on the books, please send me a note through the "Contact" tab on my website.

I would also like to thank my patient husband (also my muse) and my dear talented sister for their help in polishing this manuscript. Thanks for your continued faith in me. And my thanks to my fellow author and friend Deborah Gafford, a wonderful writer, for her suggestions and support.

Also, my thanks to my designer Erin Dameron-Hill, at http://edhgraphics.blogspot.com, who created stunning covers for all four of my books. And, I'd like to recognize models Jimmy Thomas and Jax Turyna who romantically portray Bear and Artis for this cover.

The source of the Clan MacKay crest badge on the cover is: http://commons.wikimedia.org/wiki/User:Celtus. For more information on Clan MacKay visit: clanmackayusa.org or mackaycountry.com.

46803733R00165

Made in the USA
Charleston, SC
25 September 2015